Rachel Pollack

The Tarot of Perfection

*To Zoe Matoff,
the Founder and Director*

MAGIC
REALIST
PRESS

2008

Rachel Pollack reserves the moral right to be identified as the author of this work.
© Copyright 2008 Rachel Pollack

Illustrated by Alex Ukolov, Baba Studio
Cover design by Alex Ukolov
© Copyright 2008 Alex Ukolov

Magic Realist Press
Baba Studio
Břetislavova 12
Malá Strana
Prague 11800
Czech Republic
www.magic-realist.com
www.baba-baba.com

Printed and bound in Prague by TRICO, Czech Republic.

All rights are reserved. No part of this book may be reprinted or reproduced or used in any way, including by any digital, electronic, mechanical or other means, including photocopying or other forms of recording or reproduction, or in any database, information storage or retrieval system, without prior permission in writing from the publishers.

British Library Cataloguing in Publication Data.
A catalogue record for this publication is available from the British Library.

ISBN10: 1-905572-09-3
ISBN13: 978-1-905572-09-0

Rachel Pollack

The Tarot of Perfection

List of Stories

Introduction-Tarot and Stories 6

The Tarot of Perfection 10

The Pickpocket's Destiny 38

The Girl Who Went to the Rich Neighborhood 52

The Fool, the Stick and the Princess 64

The Souls in the Trees 75

Carolina in the Morning 95

Simon Wisdom 114

Master Matyas 177

Acknowledgements

I am very grateful for the help and encouragement of Karen Mahony and Alex Ukolov, the brilliant creators of Magic Realist Press. I also want to thank the Rhinebeck Writers, Carla, Jillen, and Linda, for their attentive ears, their ability to look inside the story, and their helpful suggestions. Thanks also go to all those who listened to or read parts of these stories in progress, especially Frankie Green, Mary K. Greer, Christie Ley, and Claire North. Bart Lidofsky and others on the internet group TarotL offered interesting ideas to my question of what might constitute a "tarot of perfection." Anne Ogborn told me the Sufi story that inspired "The Pickpocket's Destiny." I am grateful as well to Steve and Dave, and everyone else at the Starr Library, where so much of this book was written. And finally, my thanks go to Wonder and Lucy, the best dog and cat in the world.

"The Girl Who Went To The Rich Neighborhood" originally appeared in *Beyond Lands of Never*, ed. Maxim Jakubowski, Unwin, London, 1984. "The Fool, the Stick, and the Princess" originally appeared in *Fantasy and Science Fiction*, No. 567, October/November, 1998.

Introduction—Tarot and Stories

"A machine for constructing stories." This is how the great Italian writer Italo Calvino described the Tarot deck in the afterword to his fairy tale novel *The Castle of Crossed Destinies*. In Calvino's story a group of people find themselves trapped in an enchanted castle where they are all struck mute, with only an ancient Tarot deck to communicate with each other. One by one the people at the table take up the deck and turn over a series of cards. The narrator then interprets them as characters and actions in a story, from a tale of a thief to visions of Hamlet and Oedipus.

Calvino wrote that over a period of years he became obsessed with the Tarot, that machine of stories, so that *The Castle* became a kind of exorcism, a way to free himself from a spell. We might think of Samuel Taylor Coleridge's "Ancient Mariner," compelled to tell his story over and over to any unfortunate wedding guest who strays too close to his bony hand. Or maybe all those fairy tales of cursed women and men who must remain silent for seven years, no matter what is done to them.

To paraphrase Calvino, I would describe the Tarot as an engine of pattern-making. Even one card may suggest events, characters, possibilities. What does it mean to see a man hanging upside down by one foot, his posture relaxed, his face serene and beautiful? If we put down two, three, or more cards we may find it almost impossible *not* to see some kind of story in them.

There are reasons why we call the interpretation of Tarot cards a "reading." We see the cards, and the person's life through them, as a story. The different kinds of readings that people do, from simple fortune-telling to more complex levels of self-knowledge or spiritual awareness, are like the levels in stories, from plot-heavy adventures or romances, to psychological novels, to myths and mystical tales. With Tarot we attempt to help people understand themselves, and what life holds for them by creating a story of their lives.

One of the great figures in Tarot history is the 18th century cartomancer Etteila (his original name, Aliette, spelled backwards). Etteila created the first full system of divinatory meanings, he drew his own deck, he first incorporated Egyptian imagery into the cards, and was the first person to suggest separate interpretations for when the cards appear reversed. With all this we tend to overlook another of his innovations, one that has had possibly the greatest impact on the uses of Tarot. Etteila was the first person to draw more than one card for a reading. In effect, he began the use of the cards to tell complex stories about people's lives.

Before Etteila, fortune-telling with Tarot was done as a kind of sortilege, or choosing of lots. Whatever the person's question the cartomancer would take one card and that would be the answer, similar to the way many people still do the Runes. Etteila showed us how we could lay out several cards and look at the relationships between them as well as their individual meanings. By enlarging the *story* he enlarged the reading.

I have been using Tarot cards to make up stories almost as long as I have used them to look at people's lives. I used to think this was an innovation of mine, for I had not seen it elsewhere. When I demonstrated the method by making up a story for an international conference on the theme of Merlin, writer and Tarot creator Caitlín Matthews was so taken with it that she first tried it herself, then suggested we edit an anthology together. We invited a group of writers to make up stories with the cards, resulting in the book *Tarot Tales* (Arrow Books, 1989).

Recently, however, I made an amazing discovery. Making up poetry with the cards is older, at least by the evidence available, than using them for fortune-telling. According to Paul Huson in his book *Mystical Origin of the Tarot*, in 1527 a poet named Teofilo Folengo, writing under the pseudonym Merlini Cocai (Merlin!) wrote a sequence of five sonnets incorporating the names and imagery of the twenty-two trumps, or "Major Arcana" cards. The poem was a hit; it launched a craze for what was called *Tarocchi Appropriati* (Appropriated Tarots). Someone would select a group of trumps and hand them to someone else, who then would be expected to write verses about someone based on the pictures.

There are many ways to use the cards to create stories, and in a moment I will give a spread I developed for writers. For myself I tend to prefer a very open approach, similar to that of *Tarocchi Appropriati*.

I will mix the cards and choose a small number at random, then turn them over to see what plot or characters they suggest. Most often I will ignore the cards usual meanings and qualities and instead let the pictures work on me as if I have never seen them before and know nothing about them (this alone is an interesting exercise to try) The story "The Souls In The Trees" began with a handful of cards from a deck called The Golden Tarots of the Renaissance, whose medieval images include a picture of a headless woman, and another of a group of women looking cruelly at a young man suffering on his knees. The story developed far beyond these original images and the moments they suggested. At various times I drew more cards to help at transitions or difficult moments.

Other tales began with various inspirations but then the cards (various decks were used, such as *The Tarot of Prague*, and of course *The Fairytale Tarot*) helped to elaborate where the story might go. The idea for the final story, "Master Matyas," originally came to me after looking at an inscription on an antique fountain pen. Possibly because of such a tenuous beginning, or maybe because I wanted it to bring together the themes and images of the previous stories, it was very difficult to write. I found myself turning to the cards several times, not to develop new ideas, but almost the opposite, to simplify an over-burdened plot. Just as we might ask in a reading "What is the person's core truth in this situation?" so we can choose cards to look at the essential qualities of a story or character.

Most of the stories in this book have something to do with Tarot or some other form of divination. Some have a Tarot reader character, such as the mysterious Dr. Apollo in "The Souls In The Trees." Others are a little less obvious. "The Fool, the Stick, and the Princess" began as a story I would tell in classes to illustrate the qualities of the Fool, for isn't that very word used to describe the hero of countless fairy tales?

In some stories the Tarot itself might be described as a character, such as the title story, "The Tarot of Perfection." The "perfect" Tarot returns in the final two stories, saving a boy from a monster in one, and a magician from his own self-destruction in another. The Tarot has often seemed to me like a living being. The cards themselves are just cardboard and colored ink, but a kind of spirit inhabits them. It gave me pleasure to weave them into the stories.

For some years now, I have taught creative writing for the Master of Fine Arts degree out of Goddard College in Vermont. As part of my work with students I have developed a workshop called Tarot For Writers. Here is a spread from that workshop. More than one card can be pulled for each question.

1. Who is my character?
2. What situation does he or she face?
3. What is the outer motivation?
4. What is hidden?
5. What opposes her or him?
6. What helps?
7. What is at risk?

Of course, stories are not primarily for writing, they're for reading. Enjoyment of the tale is its own reward, but sometimes we want to understand something about how a particular story has affected us. Here is a spread for looking at a favorite story from childhood.

1. What gift did this story give me when younger?
2. What about it stayed with me?
3. What lesson can I find in it?
4. What secret truth does it carry?

The Tarot of Perfection

Once upon a long long time there lived a great scholar, a man whose knowledge could fill the storehouses of angels, a sage known to all the world as Joachim the Brilliant. People said of him that wherever he walked the heavenly powers trailed behind, in hopes they could learn from the words he muttered under his breath.

In those days the great thinkers used to construct detailed "palaces of memory" in their minds, with imaginary room after room dedicated to large or small pieces of information, such as the effects of phases of the moon on each of the bodily humors, or the names and ranks of all the demons and spirits who live in the forests. Unlike the others, however, who struggled to keep a clear vision of a single structure, Joachim constructed seven such mental palaces, for the seven "palaces" of the planetary spheres. Each of Joachim's mental palace had its own colors and properties, from the Sun's palace of fiery light, to the Moon's crystal reflection, to Saturn's palace of darkness and ice.

As a child, when Joachim became excited with new ideas light would pour from his mouth, causing superstitious neighbors to worry that an angel had escaped from heaven and taken refuge in the boy's body. And even though the light hid inside him as he got a bit older he still became famous for his dazzling thought. Shortly after Joachim's seventh birthday a monk brought him and his family to a great university in the capital city. He'd never seen anything like it, colleges and libraries all of stone and glass and polished wood salvaged from an earlier age of the world. The scholars, dry old men with scraggly beards, who dressed in silk robes stained with chemicals and ink, had summoned twenty children from across the land, all locally famous as prodigies.

They brought the children to a large room with a stone floor, and set before them ancient books with cracked covers, whose pages contained faded ink and intricate drawings, and even more intricate notes and references. They told the children that the books were a gift, to use as they pleased. While all the others ran to grab the books Joachim just stood there, staring at the walls, the ceiling, smelling the parchment, the leather. Finally he took for himself a book no one else had wanted, for it was very old and very thick. Carefully he carried it from the table to a corner of the room and sat down to read.

When all the children had begun to leaf through the pages a peddler dressed in multi-colored rags came into the hall with a large pushcart stacked high with shiny books in luminous colors. "New books for old!" he called out. "Trade in your dull unreadables for the sharpest smartest latest works, so fresh the parchment still smells of the sheep who gave their lives for knowledge. *New* knowledge. New books for old!"

The children all ran up, Joachim included, and eagerly looked at the thrilling words, the vivid pictures. Just as quickly they all ran back to their places, where they scooped up the old works and carried them to the cart to trade them in for the modern wonders. Joachim too lugged the heavy old volume up to the peddler, who was smiling and applauding the children's wise choices. Just as he was about to hand over the blackened leather book with diagrams of the human body in all its layers, he stopped. Slowly he looked from the tiny letters of *The Book of Secret Anatomy* to the cheerful face of *Everyone's Book of Joys and Wonders*. With a nervous reluctance he said "Thank you, sir. Your offer is very generous, but I hope you will not be insulted if keep the one I have. I'm sure your book is very nice and could teach me a great deal, but I haven't really learned this one properly." He walked back and sat down heavily at his place.

The peddler, who was in fact Grand Guardian of the Keys— the official title for the master of this oldest of colleges—clapped his hands and announced that the test had ended. All the children but Joachim were sent home with their new books, so shiny and useless, while Joachim was taken to the library, and placed on a polished oak chair so high it would be three years before his feet could touch the floor. They called him Joachim the Bright, and for many years that was his name, until he became fully grown, and his mind shone so wondrously that "Bright" became a dull understatement, so that the scholars who came to see him from all over the world named him Joachim the Brilliant.

One night, just after his eighteenth birthday, when a trio of scholars from Isfahan, Babylon, and Damascus had presented him with a magnificent model of the planetary spheres, each one formed from a different precious metal or stone, Joachim found himself unable to sleep. As he lay in bed it seemed to him he heard a strange and marvelous voice from somewhere on the far side of the college. He got up, put a coat on over his night shirt, and tried to follow it. As he crossed the courtyard everything seemed oddly dark and quiet. The great stone towers, usually lit with the lamps of students at their desks, abuzz with deep discussion, now stood dark and stolid.

The sound grew very faint, but Joachim listened closely and wound a path to it. He found himself before a bricked up opening that might have been a narrow doorway. Strange, he thought, that he'd never noticed it. Someone had painted crude spells across the bricks, to repel anyone who tried to remove them. They were full of mistakes, a syllable misspelled, a curlicue turned the wrong way, an extra repetition of a demonic name. Besides, Joachim knew at least six verbal counter-spells; to amuse himself he spoke one that contained an interesting turn of phrase.

A narrow section of brick crumbled into brown and yellow dust. Coughing from the foul air Joachim slid through into a long hallway. He spoke a spell for light, and something like a giant firefly danced in front of him to lead the way.

The sound was stronger now, lyrical and intricate, unlike anything he had ever heard, like nothing less than the humming of an angel. Finally he came to the end of the corridor and there he found something he had read about many times but had never expected to see—an oracular head. The head appeared that of a beautiful, and perhaps dissolute, young man, with golden curls (twisted and matted from millennia of dust), eyes closed with long lashes so perfect they looked like delicate swirls of ink, and full lips a warm red despite the coating of dirt. The head stood on an ebony pole inlaid with spirals of gold, at a height a foot or so taller than Joachim.

The singing (or humming) stopped, for indeed the head had been the cause of it, and now it closed its mouth and opened its eyes. Joachim could see the tiny puffs of dust released from the eyelids. "Small little human," it said, in a voice high and musical, "do you think me the remains of some arrogant young prince who dared too much and paid the price?"

"No," Joachim said.

As if Joachim had not spoken, the head declared "I am a high prince of the Kallistochoi!"

Joachim said quietly, "Yes. I know." For he had studied and pondered the Kallistochoi over many years. A tribe of angels who had refused to take sides in the heavenly wars, the Kallistochoi had come to Earth (indeed, some scholars insisted that they had *created* the Earth, as a haven of escape). For many cycles of the Great Year they roamed the Earth's gardens and sailed its oceans, delighting in the bodies they had fashioned for themselves. But then the Host Triumphant discovered them.

The Kallistochoi could no longer escape battle. They fought with courage and ingenuity, but finally fell. As punishment their bodies were shredded but their heads remained, forced to watch as their beloved Earth passed to the brutish hands of men. And still worse—the Regent of Heaven declared that if any human should discover them he might command the heads to reveal great secrets of Above and Below.

As if it could read Joachim's thoughts, the head said, "Just because you have found me does not mean you can compel me. I answer only to the Kallisti language." And with a slight sneer, "Can you speak Kallisti?"

Joachim the Brilliant in fact did know the language. He knew all seven dialects of it. "Wretched head of the once mighty and beautiful!" he cried out. "I command you to speak to me!" He spoke these words first in the Central Dialect (also called the Dialect of the Inner Chamber), then in the Dialect of the Builders, and the Changers, and—

"Enough!" the head rumbled, speaking in the Central Dialect, but with a stronger accent than Joachim had used. "I heard you the first time."

Joachim said, "I charge you to reveal the secret mysteries."

"Do you?" the head said, and the lips moved in a smile that was anything but gentle. "Joachim the Blind wishes to uncover the Hidden Truth?"

The dream scholar stepped back. He had the awful feeling that he'd somehow fallen into a trap. "What did you call me?"

"You heard me. What else would I call a man who scrambles around in old books while miracles splash outside his window at every moment?"

"What miracles? What am I missing?"

"Learn to see, Joachim. Teach your eyes to open the gifts of perfection."

If the head had been attached to a body Joachim would have grabbed the shoulders and shaken him. Instead, he curled his long fingers into fists to contain his fury. "You have no choice," he declared. "You must reveal the great secrets."

"But I already have."

All the fight left Joachim as he realized he might lose this great opportunity. "Please," he said. "I cannot study riddles. Tell me where to look and I promise you, I will pursue the truth as no man has done since the first ancestors rose up from the mud."

The eyes closed as the red lips turned in a smile. "Goodbye, Joachim the Baffled," the Kallistocha said. "I will see you when I see you."

"No!" Joachim cried, but a wind pushed him back, step by step, until he found himself outside the tunnel, back in the courtyard. Exhausted suddenly, he fell to his knees. The firefly light had vanished, and when he looked back at the wall there were no signs of an opening, let alone a spell, crude or otherwise,

He walked back slowly to his rooms just as the sky had begun to lighten and people had begun to move about and begin their tasks. In the student windows he could see sputtering candles, as if they'd

The Tarot of Perfection

"Wretched head of the once mighty and beautiful!" he cried out

burned all night; he could even hear the sighs of weary scholars, the slam of large books being closed.

Was it all a dream, he thought. Did he really discover a Kallistocha? In his study chamber he found his books on "The Exiles of Exiles," as some called them, but could find no indication of any heads walled up in secret university tunnels. He shook his head, closed his eyes, and soon was asleep.

From that day Joachim began to change. He taught less and studied even more fervently, and when he did give audience to the sages who came from all over the world, he spoke of such wonders, with theorems of such intricacy, that they felt themselves detach from the Earth and float into the geometric patterns of the spirits. Joachim the Bedeviled, some called him, but even they recognized that he shone more brilliantly than ever, but now from a great distance, like a star that coldly dominates a constellation out beyond the limits of the zodiac. And so he became known as Joachim the Beyond.

He continued this way for nearly twenty years. He slept late, and ate with his plate surrounded by books. At night, students might glimpse him on the rooftop, his face towards the stars or the phases of the moon. Often, he would stop in the middle of his work, push aside his books and diagrams, and walk out of the college. He would walk for hours, perhaps into the woods where he might suddenly pause to study the structure of a flower, or the remains of some dead animal. Or he might walk through the city, past mansions and hovels, through crowded markets, alongside taverns and cafes (though he rarely entered).

He was tall, this Joachim, and unlike many scholars did not stoop, or curve inward his wide shoulders, for he was likely to spend as many hours with his back straight and his head turned upward to the sky as he did bent over a book. His face was lean and delicate, his dark hair long and unruly, and he wore robes of purple and black, ordered for him by the college and laid out by his housekeeper. He was a well-known figure in his city, and as he walked by, women sometimes shook their heads, and laughed, and called him Joachim the Befuddled. But other women, those who longed for something more than thick husbands who mounted them like horses, would whisper (to themselves) "Joachim the Beautiful." But none ever dared speak to him.

One day his wandering took him to an open-air market beyond his usual paths. The wooden houses were old and slightly tilted, with jangly music pouring out from the windows. The "merchants" had spread out blankets covered with what looked like the remains of entire civilizations: tarnished knives, broken pots, stained and torn clothes, portraits of long forgotten families in odd styles of dress, grimy coins from no country anyone would remember.

Joachim might have passed through all these tawdry wonders and not seen a thing if not for a reedy voice near the end of the street. "Secrets!" it called out. "Revelations, mysteries, and wonders!" He stopped, turned about, and stared down at a skinny old woman sitting cross-legged on a blue blanket crudely painted with stars and flowers. She wore layers of brightly colored dresses and scarves, and she'd smeared her thin mouth a bright red. Her teeth were chipped and yellow. Her smile stiffened as Joachim stared down at her. "What are you talking about?" he said. "What secrets? What revelations?"

"Your fortune, brave sir. The mysteries of your future."

A fortune teller? Joachim looked down at the filthy blanket. Where were the maps of the stars, the charts of the planetary journeys? Where were the compass and the astrolabe? Where were the lists of progressions and regressions? All he could see was a stack of papers about the length of a man's hand. The top one displayed a clumsy design of blue and red swirls against a yellow background, and Joachim noted absently that at least the woman had got the basics right, blue and red for the powers of life, yellow for the mind, though what she did with such a picture he had no idea..

He was about to leave when her skinny hand took hold of the hem of his robe. "Only ten talers, sir," she said. "I know you won't regret it."

"I doubt that very much," Joachim said, but even as he spoke the words he noticed that some of the crowd had moved into a loose circle around him, some with cold stares, others with smiles that did not speak of friendship. He remembered stories of scholars who had entered the wrong tavern in hope of a simple drink, and never returned to their study rooms. Joachim was no coward. The daring of his ideas, his willingness to go out in storms to study the prayer forms generated in agitated trees, such things had earned him the nickname, Joachim the Brave. But he also understood the value of caution. He reached into his pocket, and amidst scraps of paper with fragments of formulae and notes in ten or twelve languages he found some coins to toss down on the blanket.

"Oh thank you," the woman said. She glanced around at the small crowd. "As generous as he is wise." To Joachim she said "Your generosity will cause the Goddess Fortuna to turn the wheel in your favor."

Joachim knew very well the image of this shadowy Goddess who cranks the great wheel of heaven, and he knew further that the picture symbolized the implacable rotation of the zodiac over a period of 25,920 years, and still further that no act of petty charity could alter whatever fate the wheel spit out for him. How could it be otherwise? If individual virtue or sin could alter the wheel the seven planetary spheres would soon crack and shatter. But he said nothing, only watched impatiently as the woman spread the papers in front of her. He was surprised to see that the pictures were all the same. "There you are," the woman said. "Pick two."

"By what standard?" Joachim said. "They're all the same."

"Oh sir," the woman said, "if you peek how can the God guide you to the correct choice?"

Joachim sighed. "Very well," he said, and pointed to one in the center and one on the right. When the woman turned over the pictures he realized he'd been looking at their backs, for each one apparently bore a crudely drawn image. They appeared to be reproductions, woodcuts perhaps. Of the two he'd chosen one appeared simple but he found himself staring at it. It showed a pair of golden chalices, or rather cups, for they were without decoration. Snakes wound around them in symmetrical spirals, with the heads emerging at the top to bend towards each other across the gap. It was hard to tell from the poor printing but a light seemed to rise up like a staff between the two snake-wound chalices, so that the whole image resembled that most secretive of forms, the caduceus of Hermes, God of sorcerers. Joachim could not imagine how it could appear in the hands of this foolish old fake of a seer.

The other picture also showed two cups but in a much more elaborate setting. A clumsily drawn angel held them, one in each hand, with water flowing in a sinuous path between them, at an impossible angle. The angel's expression was blank, and his robe bore no sigils, shields, or angelic "signatures" for Joachim to identify him out of the long catalogue of angels stored in their proper corners of his seven palaces of memory. The angel stood with one foot in the water of a swiftly flowing stream, the other foot on stony ground. It was hard to tell—Joachim found himself frustrated at the poor quality of the art—but the river resembled the reptile skin of the snakes from the first picture. He found himself wondering if all snakes were simply water that had taken on animal form. And the ground—its rough surface seemed to contain a secret fire.

He bent down to reach for the papers so he might look closer. "No," the woman said sharply, "it is dangerous to touch them."

"Nonsense" Joachim wanted to say, but he pulled back his hands. The woman went on "Something will come to you. Something wondrous. But you must be very careful for it may burn you as much as help you. Indeed, good sir, you will need all the wisdom you so clearly possess, for a weaker man would be swept away."

"Yes, yes," Joachim said, then impulsively "Show me some more."

"More?"

"Yes, more pictures."

The woman shook her head. "We must not trifle with this, good sir. We walk in the spirit realm, our fingers touch the very skin of fate."

Joachim laughed. "Are you telling me that if I look at more pictures I can change my fate?"

"Do not tempt the Gods."

Do not tempt pompous old women, he thought, but there were enough of her fellow beggars that he kept silent. He should just leave, and yet some impulse took hold of his hand, so that it suddenly darted down, like one of the snakes in the picture, and turned over one more stained paper.

The woman gasped, and a collective grunt sounded from the crowd. A tall fellow with hands that looked like they could crush the head of a bull stepped forward, but the woman waved him back.

Joachim paid no attention to any of this, so fascinated was he by this strange image. At first he thought it upside down, for it seemed to display a man standing on one foot but turned around. Then he saw that it actually depicted someone hanging by one foot from a wooden beam. A rope—or perhaps a snake—tied his right ankle to the shiny wood, while his left leg crossed gracefully behind the right calf. The arms were behind the back, with the elbows sticking out from the sides so that they formed a triangle, just as the legs formed the number four. Thoughts about the mysteries of trinity and quaternity tried to pull Joachim away but his attention stayed focused on the young man in the picture. Though still crudely drawn, the face was beatific, serene, with a golden light that filled the air around it.

The woman rocked back and forth, as if in pain. "Now see what you've done" she said. "They've caught you, and they'll never let you go."

Her moans shocked Joachim and he straightened up. "Don't be absurd," he said. With a nervous glance at the man with the huge hands he found a few more coins and dropped them on the blanket. The woman snatched up the coins, then just as quickly gathered up the pictures.

Joachim turned, took a step, and turned once more to face her. "These oracular pictures of yours," he said. "What do you call them?"

She looked startled, as if he'd asked something as obvious as "What do you call that bright disk up in the sky?" She said "Tarot."

"Tarot?" What an odd word. Eight or nine possible derivations from as many languages flashed through his mind but none of them seemed to fit.

"Yes, of course," she said. "Tarot cards."

Of course. Cards. He remembered times he'd seen the guards and cooks at the college tossing cards and coins down in frenzied competition. He smiled at himself, nearly taken in by a fortune-teller and a gambling device.

And yet, that night, as he sat at a long oak table lit by silver candlesticks, he set his spoon down alongside his bowl of leek soup, and asked the Grand Guardian, who sat to his left, "Robert, what do you know about Tarot cards?"

Robert lifted his head, elegant and silver-haired. "I'm sorry," he said, "I do not think I know that term." With a slight smile he added "But really, Joachim. Cards? Have you decided to enter a new field of study? Perhaps you will enrich our coffers."

"No, no," Joachim said. "Of course not." And the two men returned to their soup.

Over the next days Joachim found it difficult to concentrate. Instead of the book he was studying he would find himself searching for some reference to the angel with the two cups, or the caduceus formed by two vessels and a beam of light. He found himself staring at trees and wondering what it might be like to be tied and hung upside down by one foot from a high branch. When he went up to the roof to study the heavens he imagined he could see two giant chalices behind the constellations. From the right the Milky Way poured out like actual splashed milk, from the left came dark waters, waves and waves of darkness.

A week passed, and one afternoon Joachim cried out "Enough!" slammed his book, filled a small bag with gold coins, and strode out from the college. After a few false turns he found his way back to the market and the skinny old woman, surrounded by her fellow tradesmen and beggars. "Secrets," she called out. "Revelations, mysteries, wonders."

Joachim stood over her. "Do you remember me?"

The woman's mouth twisted in a smile. "Of course I remember you. The Hanged Man."

"What?"

"I told you they wouldn't let you go."

He said "I want to buy them."

Her eyes half closed, hooded, like the eyes of the serpents wound about the two cups. "Do you think I can just sell these? They are my life-blood, handed down from my ancestors. They are my lovers. I would die without them."

Joachim squatted down. "I understand your sacrifice," he said. "I can only offer this small recompense and beg that you forgive my shallowness." He held out the bag of coins. Like a frog's tongue at a fly the woman's hand darted out to grab the bag. When she opened it and saw the gold she gasped, then hid the bag in the folds of her skirt. She wrapped the cards in a filthy cotton scarf before she handed them over to Joachim.

"Thank you, wise mother," he said, though he made sure to check that she had not substituted blank paper for the genuine pictures. As Joachim walked off, the woman called out "Goodbye, Joachim the Bewildered. May you become the master and not the slave." The market people all laughed.

For three days and nights he studied the pictures, even ignoring a dinner to honor his forty years at the college. At first they thrilled him. There was the "Hanged Man," his face radiant below the mysteries of three and four. And there was the blank angel, one foot on serpentine water, the other on fiery stone.

And there were so many others, each one with hidden truths. A woman wrapped in swirls of blue, as if the sea itself had become her dress, sat between dark and light pillars. And here were pictures of coins, each of them with faces of men or women, that Joachim recognized as the markers of principles, whether lust, or charity, fury, or kindness. How good, he thought, that he had rescued these pictures—these "Tarot cards"—from the old fake, for he was certain she had no idea what they really meant. What an insult, he thought, to use something so precious for fortune-telling.

Look there, he thought, the man with ten sticks on his back, each one with leaves of fire, though none of them burned. No doubt the woman would have seen in this a prediction of "burdens," or "hard work ahead," and completely miss the truth, that the sticks extended from the Great Tree, that itself grew out of the Radiant Jewels of Creation. And what was the man but a sacred messenger, assigned to extend the jewels into the abandoned dross of the physical world? What holiness! And only he could see it.

And yet, as the hours flowed by, he became at first unsettled, and then more and more frustrated. At first it was simply the unanswered questions. Where did they come from? What did the name Tarot actually mean? But then deeper problems arose. The pictures were so crudely drawn Joachim could only assume they imitated some greater original. The picture—the "card"—with the two cups. Though it had led him to his vision of the chalices in the sky it seemed to conceal as much as it opened. And the others—how could he properly identify the angels and spirits when the artist's clumsiness had stripped them of meaning? More and more they seemed to Joachim like some great treasure covered in dust, with no way to clean them, so that all he could do was try to glimpse the treasure's outlines.

Where was the original? How could he find it? He could ask the old woman where she'd gotten them but no doubt she would spout some nonsense, such as a mysterious child handing them to her during a lightning storm at midnight. For if his books said nothing of Tarot cards, and a scholar as fine as the Grand Guardian of the Keys had never heard of them, how could a wretched fortune-teller possibly reveal anything of value? He would have to discover it himself.

Over the next few months Joachim wrote to all the best scholars in all the best colleges and libraries, pleading with them for information on the Tarot. Some didn't reply at all, others wrote polite regrets that they knew nothing. Only a handful had ever heard of the things, and these dismissed the cards as entertainment for the ignorant. No, no, Joachim thought, couldn't they see that they pointed to something? But pointed to *what*, that question maddened him.

One night he threw down the cards in disgust. One picture fell out apart from the rest, a simple drawing of a single wooden staff, vibrant and alive, its top aglow with a dark radiance. As he stared at it from above he thought he detected a hint of eyes in the glow, and luxuriant hair. And suddenly he remembered the Kallistocha, that smug angelic head perched on its angelic stick. Did the artist mean to show that? Was it possible that the Kallistochoi themselves had designed the originals? Were there no records in the libraries because the so-called Tarot actually predated humanity itself? He hurried downstairs to the stone wall where he'd found the doorway, but it remained as impenetrable as ever.

It was on the way back that an idea came to him. He would do it himself! If he could not find the perfect Tarot then he would create it. All that was implicit he would bring forward. All that was hidden he would reveal. In his hands (or at least under his instruction) the Tarot Of Perfection would lay bare the secrets of existence.

All night he worked, setting out sketches and notes and commentary, and then in the morning he marched over to the Guardian and demanded the name of the best artist among the students. Robert sighed but told him of a young man named Gregorio, who was already renowned for the "perfection of his craft." Joachim smiled and went to rouse Gregorio from his bed.

To Joachim's surprise, Gregorio actually had heard of Tarot cards. His uncle, it seemed, was a gambler and had played every card game ever invented. He once had spent a week on a stormy boat playing a certain game with Tarot cards. That's all he would ever say about it, except to add that he hoped never to play it again. When Joachim showed Gregorio the old woman's cards, the artist made it clear that such pictures hardly deserved the term "art," but he was more than willing to elevate the form.

"You will follow my instructions," Joachim said. "I want no flourishes or experiments to distract from the symbolism."

Gregorio bowed his head. "Of course, Maestro,. I await your directions."

And wait he did. At first Joachim flooded him with descriptions and his own sketches, but even though Gregorio followed them precisely the pictures never seemed to reveal what Joachim could sense just below the surface. He made the artist do pictures over and over, and tossed them aside, or tore them to pieces. And then he told Gregorio to keep his brushes ready for the moment when he, Joachim, discovered the missing element. Only, that moment never came. Joachim spent hours, days, weeks, writing and sketching, stabbing the paper, staring at the cards with clenched fists. Finally, he dismissed Gregorio. As he gave the artist a hefty purse he told him "The fault lies not in your hand, Gregorio, but in my mind."

There was no denying it. If he ever wanted to create his Tarot of Perfection he would have to find guidance beyond his own resources. For the first time since he was seven years old he planned to leave the college.

Robert, the Grand Guardian, tried to stop him. "Whatever resources we do not possess," he said, "we can summon for you."

"I am sorry," Joachim said, "but apparently some secrets do not travel. And some masters do not wish to be known, at least to messengers. I will have to seek this out myself."

Robert said "This is your home, your world. How will you survive out there?"

Joachim put a hand on his friend's shoulder. "Our home is in the stars," he said. He picked up the Tarot pack, now wrapped in a blue silk cloth painted with the sigils of the Kallistochoi. "And when I find the answer to *this*, then the map of our celestial home, the anatomy of our celestial bodies, will be laid open for all who have eyes."

Robert shook his head. "Joachim, this is—"

"Foolishness?"

"Yes, foolishness. These cards of yours—I do not know what spell that old woman cast on you, but these pictures are simply a game."

Joachim smiled. "Yes, they certainly are that. The most frustrating game anyone has ever played, for they show just enough to hint but never enough to reveal. Imagine, Robert, a great prince, a beauty of the Other World, who passes through and leaves behind his cloak. And then imagine that a beggar finds the cloak and wears it, with no thought of its origin. The sage who sees the beggar recognizes that a Great One has passed this way, but how can he tell, through the body of the beggar, the form of the prince? That is the game these cards are playing with me. But I promise you, I will win."

And so, Joachim the Beseecher began his fool's journey through the dust of the world. He began with temples and ancient libraries, and scrolls that no one had unrolled for centuries. He learned a great deal, such things as the language of clouds, or the dream-life of frogs, but after three years of holding his breath lest he blow away the very ink he had to admit that he would never find what he wanted in written works.

He began to search for hidden masters. He followed rumors, and absurd stories, and found himself on his belly in narrow tunnels, or blindfolded on long boat rides, all to spend swift moments with a half-naked man whose face and chest were covered in scars, or perhaps a twelve year old girl wrapped in so many layers of dresses and shawls and necklaces she could hardly move. But no one could help him.

Then one day an old man in a broken down temple told him of a woman who could bring the dead to life, who talked with God, and swam in the River of Flowers, all from the proper use of a set of very old paintings. For the first time in months Joachim allowed himself to hope.

The woman was called the Lover of Images, and to meet her Joachim first had to prove himself to a series of disciples, who all wanted secrets the way some men wanted gold. Joachim told one of them which trees began on Earth, and which seeds fell from Heaven during the War. To another he explained the oracular messages in earthquakes. Finally, word came that he might meet the Lover at a stone hut in the hills beyond a rough town at the edge of the sea. Joachim must arrive precisely on time, the disciple said, for the woman would not wait even a minute.

It took him a week of travel with little sleep and less food, but he arrived an entire day before the meeting. When he had found a room in a small inn a short distance from the meeting place, and was setting out his few possessions, one of the old fortune teller's Tarot cards fell from the pack and landed face up on the floor. He picked it up. It showed the cloaked woman between the dark and light pillars. A curtain ran between the pillars, as if to guard an entrance, but it was clear that nothing lay behind them but a pool of water and stony hills. Joachim glanced out the window at the rough ground, then back at the picture. He smiled. "It's you, isn't it? This is a degraded portrait of one of your ancestors." He bowed his head a moment, then returned the picture to the pack.

Unable to sleep that night he went outside and stared at the stars. Soon, he thought. Soon he would know how the stars were assembled, what lived inside their fires, what they said to the Sun each morning when it chased them from the sky. He held up the wrapped pack of cards. "When I know the language of *this*" he said, "I will know the language of heaven."

He set out an hour before noon, over twice as much time as he actually needed. He knew this because he had walked the path the day before, walked it twice in fact, and measured every step.

He was halfway there when he heard a noise in the bushes. At first he thought it was a weeping child before he realized that in fact it was some kind of animal, in pain. He glanced up the path, then towards the sound. There was still more than enough time. He stepped off the path and made his way across scree and rocks to where a wounded black and white goat lay on its side. Blood ran out from a gash in its belly onto the stones and dirt.

No, Joachim thought, *I don't have time for this*. He turned sharply around and took a step, but with a sigh he turned round once more and bent down to examine the wound. It was not deep, but if the bleeding did not stop the creature would die within the hour. When he touched the wound the goat kicked its legs, but feebly. Joachim stood, glanced at the sky. Less than half an hour to noon. *One minute late and she'd be gone.*

He looked all about until he spotted a spiky green plant with tiny white flowers. Joachim knew some fifteen names for this plant, but more important was the knowledge that a paste from the leaves would stop bleeding. He knew this but he had never actually seen it. He plucked the plant, pulled off the leaves, and stuffed them in his mouth. They were so bitter he scrunched up his face like a child. Good, he thought, bitter would stimulate the liver to cleanse any poisons in the body. The leaves were tough as well, and it took a long time, with many glances at the changing position of the Sun, before he could make a true paste.

Finally it was soft and moist enough to go over the wound. There was still time, he told himself. But when he tried to set the paste on the goat the poor creature tried to pull away, even to kick at him. He knew he would have to calm it down or the herbs simply would not stay on the wound long enough to help. He began to sing to it, a song from an old book that probably no one else alive had ever read. The song actually was in the language of sheep, but Joachim thought the goat might still respond to it.

And he was right, for the poor creature lay back and half-closed its eyes, and when Joachim applied the paste it didn't resist. He nearly jumped up to see if he still could make it, but what if the goat rubbed off the paste as soon as he left? So he remained on the hard earth, with one hand on the goat's head, and sang a song of lost sheep found by their mother, and wept for his own lost dream.

At last the bleeding slowed to a trickle and then at last it stopped. Joachim stood carefully, to not disturb the goat, who had fallen asleep, and then half-ran, half-walked, to the stone hut. When he reached it, a faint perfume drifted in the air, roses and spices. It made Joachim slightly light-headed, and he wondered what it must have been like to breathe in the full fragrance. But other than that trace of a scent to tell him she had come, there was no sign of the Lover of Images.

Joachim cried out in despair. What a fool he'd been! If only he'd let the damn goat bleed out its life! What value was a goat against the secrets of Creation itself? If he'd found the true Tarot, allowed its genius to infect him, if he'd created his Tarot of Perfection, he himself could have brought the goat back from the dead. He could have created a hundred goats, each one more beautiful and stronger than that wretched creature who probably would die from some other wound in less than a week. And suppose the goat was lost, sucked into death forever. Would the future generations who would live in a world enlightened by Perfection care for one moment that a goat had died to bring it about? Of course not. They would pray and give thanks that Joachim the Brilliant had made the proper choice. Wisdom over life.

He sat down now, as a great sob shook him. He knew he had made the only choice he could. Perhaps God could make decisions on the patterns of generations but he was a man, and it was the essence of humanity that we live, and choose, in the brief ignorance of our lives. He stood up and began to hobble down the hill. When he reached the place where the goat had lain he nodded at the blood-stained ground. He had lost his dream but he had made the right choice.

He returned to his room and went straight to bed. When the innkeeper knocked at his door for dinner he called "Go away!" and went back to sleep, not to awaken until after sunrise. Moving about the room to pack his few belongings, he felt like a phantom, as if his body once had contained the cosmos and now held only a whisper of dust.

When he was all packed he looked about the room and in doing so happened to glance out the small window that looked out behind the inn. A goat stood outside—*his* goat. It was some distance from the inn, but he recognized the black and white markings. And there was something in its mouth, a large leaf, or a piece of tree bark.

He stepped outside and walked over, half expecting the goat would bound away, but no, it stood motionless until Joachim had come within a few feet. At that moment he could see what the goat held. It was a piece of painted parchment. When he cried out, the goat dropped its treasure and ran off.

Joachim grabbed at the parchment as if a cruel gust of wind might take it from him. It was the Hanged Man! This was the very picture that first had suggested to him that the old woman's cards might hide some greater truth. There was the reversal of the body as it hung by one foot from a beam, there was the crossed leg, the arms behind the back. But what was vaguely suggestive in the rough card was clear and explicit in the parchment, for lights formed behind the Hanged Man in such a way that a knowledgeable eye could make out the constellations on mid-summer's night. Thus, it became an image of the structure of eternity seen within time, in particular that part of the earthly year when darkness is born out of greatest light, and the awakened soul descends into the secrets of winter.

Tears poured freely from his eyes. They were tears of sadness for the seventy-seven wonders he would never see, but mixed with joy for this single picture. And pride as well, for he had been right. If only he had a full set of such pictures he indeed could have created his Tarot of Perfection.

Where had the animal found this? Did the Lover of Images give it to her and somehow direct her to bring it to the inn? It didn't matter. He had the painting and that was enough.

He told the innkeeper that he wished to stay another day, then hurried to his room to study it. How elegant it was. But not quite perfect. Or rather, it was perfect for *him* because his eyes could drink in the hidden clues, but what of someone less knowledgeable? He began to sketch his own version, keeping all of the imagery, yet clarifying it with just a few touches, such as lines that extended from the arms and legs to make plain that the picture revealed mysteries of geometry, the principles of trinity and quaternity that formed the basis of spiritual and material creation.

Previously, when Joachim had tried to sketch the hidden symbols in the pictures his hand had proven clumsy. Now the muse did not just inspire, it possessed his very nerves and muscles. The brush glided over the page, and blankness gave way to…well, perfection. When he finished he set it down gently on the bed and just stared at it.

He ate a good meal that night, his first in many days. He even treated the few other guests to a bottle of the landlord's wine. As he sipped the harsh drink (aged about a week, he suspected) he thought of the superb vintages poured every night at the Grand Guardian's table. What would Robert think of this meal, he wondered, and laughed.

He slept deeply that night and awoke to look once more at the double gift, the original painting and his own enhanced version. Carefully he packed them away, then once more gathered up his belongings to leave. But when he glanced out the window there was the goat, with another parchment.

He ran outside in his bare feet, not even noticing the sharp stones. The goat waited until he reached out and took the painting before she ran off. It was the one he called The Over-Flowing Cup, a single chalice with water running over its mouth and onto the ground. But where the old woman's card poured dullness this one gushed radiance. The cup looked to be clear crystal, and inside swirled purple energy, but when it left the cup it became sparkly light. The ground below was desert, except that where the water fell and formed into four streams tiny flowers grew, peonies and poppies. The image spoke of Creation itself, when the darkness of the deep became the light of the living world.

He walked back slowly, his eyes on the picture, and when he began to draw his own version, changed slightly to make clear the transformations, a good two hours passed before he realized his feet were bleeding, and another twenty minutes before he got himself up to wash them.

The next morning the goat brought him The Generous Man, a picture of a merchant giving coins to two beggars. Now he could see that the three figures, the one and the two, signified the laws of reciprocity that governed the flow of life between the stars and planets.

Twice more the goat brought him pictures, but on the sixth morning, when he reached for the parchment, she turned and walked off. Joachim stared after her, horrified, until she stopped and turned her head to look at him. *She wants me to follow her* Joachim thought, and strode forward.

For several hours the goat led him at a steady pace, stopping whenever he grew tired, then resuming when he was ready to continue. The land changed from stone to dirt to lush heather and broom. Trees appeared, figs and pomegranates, though that seemed impossible in such a chill climate. Except it wasn't chill at all, the air was warm and fragrant. Joachim thought he should be tired, but his steps became lighter and swifter.

Finally, they came to a wide circular meadow, bright with flowers. In the center, an underground stream gushed into the open to separate into four channels that wandered into the trees. And there, right alongside the bursting water, perched on his ebony stick, smiled the golden head of the Kallistocha. "Ah," he said in that eerie musical voice, "Joachim the Bountiful. At last."

Joachim staggered forward. "You've been waiting for me?"

"Of course. Did you not command me to reveal secrets?"

"I thought you refused."

"I am not permitted to refuse. We could not begin, however, until Joachim the Blind learned how to see."

"And I have learned?"

When the Kallistocha smiled light streamed from his mouth. "Do you have the drawings with you?"

Joachim opened his bag. Almost surprised, he saw his drawings, along with the blank sheets and the pen and ink. He remembered now, he didn't want to leave them in the room. He took them out and spread them on the ground facing the angelic head.

"Very good," the Kallistocha said, and Joachim felt a thrill he had not known since he was a boy and would solve a problem none of the adults could comprehend. The head went on, "Now look."

Joachim turned about just in time to see the goat drop the sixth painting neatly onto a pile of parchments. Joachim cried out as he rushed over to look through them. Yes, it was all of them, each one like a curtain pulled back from a vision of Creation. Did this mean that the Tarot was indeed an invention of the Kallistochoi? To his amazement he discovered he simply didn't want to know. He had them, that was all that mattered. The Kallistocha said, "Now Joachim the Beginner can begin."

Joachim never knew how long he worked. He drew and pondered, and pondered and drew. It must have been many days, yet he never tired or hungered. The fragrant air nourished him, and if he became thirsty he simply leaned over and sipped from the underground stream.

Then it was done. Seventy-eight drawings, each one a small perfection. And when he laid them all out a greater wonder emerged. Here were the very strands of the cosmos, structures within structures, levels upon levels, from the sweep of the Milky Way to the flutter of a butterfly. He understood at last the formulas that called the stars to shine, the push/pull of darkness and light, how each birth and death followed a spiraling thread connected to all the others, and how it all went on forever and ever.

At first he felt like a bird that spirals in the bright air, just for the joy of the Sun. But then—slowly—as he stared at the pictures and understood pattern within pattern, something strange happened to him. Sadness pushed aside his exhilaration. At first he didn't understand it, tried to tell himself it was simply that he had finished the great work that had consumed him for so many months, and what could possibly follow it?

But then he realized. The sadness was in the work itself. It was all so *perfect*, but where was there room for discovery? If everything becomes known, what happens to the human hunger for something new, and original? If the cosmos was a perfect machine where did it breathe? The flowers at his feet, the goat, himself, even the Kallistocha, were they nothing more than minute calculations on an infinite abacus?

And what of human choice? When the Tarot of Perfection can reveal the place of every object and every moment, is free will a fool's fantasy?

For the first time in days, Joachim turned to the Kallistocha, implacable on his ebony perch. Joachim said "Is this all there is? Does perfect also mean empty?"

"Turn around," the Kallistocha said.

Joachim turned and found himself at the open doorway to a one-room building, with wood walls painted a soft yellow. Inside appeared to be a class of some kind, for men and women sat in loose rows of wooden chairs facing a tall thin woman in the front of the room. The woman wore a long dress of blue silk, tied with a snake-like belt. Red hair streaked with gold framed her excited face. Around her neck she wore a gold chain with a pendant in the shape of an eight-pointed star. She did not seem to notice as Joachim stepped into the building to sit down in the back.

"Today," the woman said, "we talk about the Hanged Man." And then she reached down to a stack of painted cards on a small wooden table. Joachim made a noise as she held up what was clearly a reproduction of the picture that he himself had drawn only days before.

"Look," the woman said. "See him suspended over the depths of the world, tied gloriously to his roots in paradise. See within him the threeness of heaven, the fourness of earth. And now listen, for I will tell you his story."

Story? Joachim thought. What was she talking about? The Tarot of Perfection was not about stories.

She said, "After the War of Angels, the victors walked upon the earth. There they ridiculed the Kallistochoi, who had taken no sides, and now were condemned to live forever as immobilized heads. One of the angels, a chief named Bright-Shining-In-the-Fire-of-Heaven, danced around the Kallistochoi princes, laughing at the weakness that had led them to choose earth over heaven. Finally, one of the Kallistochoi said 'How easy it is for you. But you have never put yourself in the way of temptation. Wrap yourself in a physical body, let yourself feel its pleasures and desires, and then see if the world doesn't touch you.'

"Bright-Shining brought himself before the Veil of the Creator and asked that She give him a human body so that he might test himself in the world. Soon he stood upon the earth, tall and beautiful, the body of a man with the mind of a Power of heaven. He felt grass and rock against his feet, gusts of wind upon his face. He smelled the perfume of flowers, the stench of animals. He ate every food he could find, raw or cooked. The world delighted and frightened him, and he understood how the Kallistochoi could have gotten lost. But he laughed, for he believed it could never happen to him.

"Then, on his third day, he saw a woman named Mother-Sheep-of-God. She stood among flowers, staring at the walls of a zigguratic city, and he thought that not even the Throne had ever known such beauty. Her clothes did not just lie against her body, they yearned for her, exalted in their closeness to her. And her smell!

"He went before her and announced himself as a great Sword of the Heavenly Arm. When she did not react, but only continued to stare at the city, he told her bluntly that he was an angel and she would become his lover.

"'Nonsense,' she told him. 'Angels are grand, and wise. They know the keys to the seven spheres. They know the secret Name of God.'

"'I know the Name,' he said.

"Finally she looked at him. 'Really? Tell it to me.'

"He laughed. 'I can hardly tell that to a woman.'

"She turned away again. 'Just as I thought,' she said. 'You don't know anything.'

"Furious, Bright-Shining shouted the Name at her. As soon as she heard it, Mother-Sheep tilted back her head and spoke it to the sky. In an instant the Name had lifted her beyond all reach, deep into the river of stars. Bright-Shining tried to grab her, but all he could get was her sandal, which in his rage he threw at the city. A crack opened in the wall, and out of it came a great flash of light. And then the light died, and the entire city vanished.

"Bright-Shining understood then that the woman had been staring at the Earthly Paradise, and that she herself had conjured it to appear, through ritual and sacrifice and meditative devotion. And because of him the chance to enter had been lost, not just for her but for all the generations who might have followed her.

"He fell to the ground and begged forgiveness. The Creator took pity on him. She suspended him, upside down, as a bridge between heaven and earth." Now the woman held up the picture once again. "Here he is, bound in heaven, radiant with earthly memory."

This is insane Joachim thought. She'd taken the geometric purity of the Hanged Man and made him into a fable.

A woman in the class raised her hand. "Why upside down? Why not the feet down here in the dirt and the head in the Palace?"

"Because we ourselves are backwards. We see the world the wrong way around. And there is another reason. We come into the world in just this way, head first, with our feet in the source of life. Thus each birth re-enacts the story of the Hanged Man. Every baby restores the link between heaven and earth, between the World Above and the World Below."

Disturbed, Joachim got up and left the classroom. He found himself back in the field, with the Kallistocha before him. "They understand some of it" he said. "Pieces. Fragments. But they arrive there through stories. The Tarot of Perfection is about forms and equations. What can stories do but insult the truth?"

The Kallistocha said "These stories maintain the world."

"What?"

The head cast its eyes down to the flowing waters. "Just as the underground river gives birth to the four streams, so the Tarot of Perfection gives birth to the stories that keep alive the universe. If no one told stories from these pictures the world would become as *perfect* as an empty cup."

A strange feeling came over Joachim. He said "You mean the original pictures, yes? The ones the goat brought, and the ones that were waiting here."

"No. I said what I meant."

"But I've just finished it. How could it keep the world alive if it did not exist until right now?"

The Kallistocha smiled. "The Tarot of Perfection has always existed. The stories it inspires have always entered people's minds, even those who have no knowledge of it. You think that you created it, but only because it chose to reveal itself in this fuller form, with you as its agent. The pictures that you used as your models? They exist only so that *you* would have a guide to bring the true pictures into the physical world."

Joachim found himself dizzy. In a tight voice he said, "If the Tarot of Perfection always existed, and the world itself was *created*…"

The Kallistocha said, "Yes. The Tarot of Perfection existed before the world. The world has the structure it does because the Creator consulted the Tarot to learn how to shape it. And now you must understand. It was not just the world's *form* the Tarot revealed, but much more, its *story*."

Joachim could hardly stand. "What you are saying—that God studied these pictures—*did the pictures exist before God?*"

"Yes. God is a story told by the Tarot of Perfection."

It was too much. All his life Joachim had sought secrets, wisdom, mysteries. But this—how could he exist with such knowledge?

And what of himself? Did he devote his life to something that was so far beyond him that he never understood its most basic truths? If the Tarot of Perfection only used him—and the creators of the earlier versions that inspired him—to reveal itself to the world, did he have any purpose other than a messenger? He said "What is my part? If the Tarot of Perfection exists forever—and what matters are the stories, not the ideas and symbols I believed were so vital—was I nothing more than a conduit? A hand without a mind? If these later generations understand the truths that I was blind to, have I actually contributed anything at all?" But even as he said the words, a different thought entered his mind. The pictures. The stories. As long as they were there, did it matter who had created them?

"Turn around," the Kallistocha said. Joachim did so, and found himself once again in the classroom. A young man in the first row raised his hand. "Master," he said to the woman, "all these stories and the wonders they reveal. Who was the first to tell them?"

The woman smiled, said "These stories we tell today come directly from the mind of our greatest teacher. Joachim the Benevolent. We owe him everything."

"Ah, of course," the young man said. "Joachim the Beloved."

"Exactly. Joachim the Blessed."

Joachim laughed. Even as the sound filled the air, he found himself back in the field, among the tributaries of the underground river, with the goat alongside him, and the Kallistocha nowhere in sight, and next to his foot his seventy-eight drawings. He looked at them and smiled. He *had* created something perfect, only perfection was not what he'd thought it was. It was not a set of architectural specifications, but an opening. He thought he had finished it but it would never be finished because it was not so much an object as an invitation. He sat down on the grass and stroked the goat, who closed her eyes. A smell of roses and spices surrounded him. Joachim lay down with his head on the Tarot of Perfection.

He slept for many hours, and when he woke up he picked up his gift of cards and brought them to the world.

For Mark Powell

The End

The Pickpocket's Destiny

Once upon a time there was a land called Harmonious Song. Harmonious Song was in fact the oldest of all the world's countries, the very first land to rise up out of the sea and rock. There the Gods first taught humans to shelter themselves, and which plants were good to eat, and later, how to follow the endless dance and battles of the stars and planets. The people of the land called themselves Singers, or Harmony's Children. For many thousands of years they lived in peace and prosperity, with one group after another building their temples and palaces and monuments on the rubble of the ones who had gone before.

And then one day, in the season when the Morning Star enters the Great House of the Heavens, and people know it is time to set their seeds in the ground, a huge fleet of black ships sailed into the harbors of Harmonious Song, and out of them poured soldiers, an endless swarm of them, with thick armor, and hard faces, and terrible weapons. They called themselves the Army of Love, for their masters had assured them that everything they did was done in the cause of goodness, all the burnt homes, the dead, the tortured, the stolen wealth and beauty. Their country called itself "Chosen," and declared, on all its banners, its money, and its engines of death, the blasphemous slogan "Beloved of God."

Harmony's Children did their best to fight back against the Army of Love, but they might just as well have been babies caught in a sandstorm. Many years passed, generations in fact, and the people of Harmonious Song suffered and suffered.

One day a woman who lived in a straw shack (as did so many others) gave birth to a loud baby boy who wailed and waved his tiny fists as if he would grab some treasure from the very air. It would have to be from the air, for the poor woman owned nothing, nothing at all. Nevertheless, she was happy to hear his cries, and to see him clutch the air as if he could pull down the sky. She'd given birth to five children before this one, and none of them had lasted more than a week. This one, she thought, will fight back against the hunger and sorrow, this one will grow strong and do great things. She named him Hungry For More, and instead of lullabies would whisper to him stories of all the wonders he would perform, and the wealth he would acquire, and how the whole world would love him.

But alas, in the country of Harmonious Song even a child named Hungry For More could find little opportunity to survive, let alone become rich. He grew up strong and handsome, with a quick mind and nimble hands, but when his mother brought him to craftsmen or merchants and begged them to take the boy as an apprentice none would have him, for they needed the places for their own children. Finally, the poor woman died, and the boy, desperate to live, resorted to the lowest of all trades. He became a pickpocket.

For several years Hungry For More made his meager way in the world. He was quick, and clever, and no one ever caught him, and so he made enough money for food, and clothing, and sometimes a warm room for the night. But he was not happy, for what would his mother think if she knew how he had betrayed all her ambitions for him?

One day, he picked a traveler's wallet and discovered a letter. Now, this had happened before, and usually Hungry For More would not read a word but make sure to leave letter and wallet somewhere where a diligent search might recover them. But this time, as he held the paper, his fingers tingled, and the more he tried to resist, the more he could not turn his eyes away. After all, he told himself, his mother had gone to great lengths to find someone who would teach him to read, should he waste such a hard-won ability?

To his amazement the letter spoke of a certain figure whom Hungry For More had heard about but never believed was real. She was called The Old Woman of the Silver Caves, and if indeed she was real she was the carrier of a tradition so ancient even the temple archives could not describe its beginnings. The Old Women were healers, and keepers of the wisdom of the plants and animals, but most of all (at least as far as Hungry For More was concerned), they were oracles. If you could find your way to her she could see directly into the hidden destiny of your soul. And not only did the letter speak of her, it actually described the difficult journey to find her.

The letter was sad, for the writer wrote that he had failed, the way was too hard, and he had to turn back. And yet, it spoke with great confidence of the path to the oracle.

Hungry For More read the letter three times to memorize it, then tore it into very small pieces. It was good, he thought, that he had stolen it, for what if the foolish man who'd kept it in his wallet had been accosted by some curious officer of the Army of Love? Fate had chosen him, he decided, to rescue the letter and its precious information. In fact, maybe the Gods had made him a pickpocket for just this moment! And if indeed he had fulfilled his destiny as a snatcher of wallets, then maybe he was free, or some greater purpose would unfold itself. And who better to reveal such a truth than the very oracle whose secret he had helped preserve? With the money he had taken from the wallet, Hungry For More took a room at an inn and ordered a luxurious meal. The next day he set out on his journey.

He traveled nine days, through forests and desert, over mountains and rivers, until at last he came to a tiny cave entrance hidden in a nest of bleak and lifeless hills. With a small torch he followed a winding path deep into the ground. It became very cold, and the tunnel became so low and narrow he had to turn sideways and bend at the knees to keep going. His torch went out but a silvery light filled the air, just enough that he could see the walls. They were rough and sharp, and if he just brushed against them they would scrape the skin and meat right off his bones. This is terrible, he thought, he could hardly breathe with the walls so close like this. He would have to turn back, he had no choice. But then he remembered his mother and all she had done to help him make his way in the world. He breathed very shallowly so as not to expand his chest against the sharp rocks, but he continued.

Finally, just as he thought he must certainly die in that wretched passage he saw a light, and when he turned a bend the tunnel finally ended and he emerged into a perfect little valley. The sun shone on a stream with sparkly water, trees hung heavy with fruit, wildflowers of every color covered the ground, and a sweet smell filled the air. In the center stood a small wooden house. It looked very old, the wood all discolored into subtle shades of blue and red, but it appeared strong too, as if it had stood there forever, and would stand forever more.

A white cow and a pair of black sheep grazed happily near the house. Hungry For More strolled past them with a cheerful wave. But as he got closer he discovered more fearful guardians. Green snakes slithered towards him through the flowers, their mouths open to show their sharp fangs. Hungry For More looked all around until he spotted a gnarly branch that had fallen from one of the trees. Quickly he grabbed it and waved it low to the ground. The snakes stopped, stared at it, convinced the stick was their king, and when he tossed it to the side they all swarmed off after it.

Hungry For More stepped forward again, only to discover a large red wolf right in front of him. It growled and rumbled, and flecks of foam dripped from its teeth. Hungry For More shook with fear, and he wanted to turn and run for the tunnel, but instead he began to wiggle his quick fingers, like dancers, in front of the wolf's eyes. "Aren't you something?" he said gently. "What a beautiful creature you are." The wolf stopped his growling as he stared at the elegant fingers. Hungry For More reached out and stroked him, and the wolf sat back among the flowers, then closed his eyes. "Good puppy," Hungry For More said, and smoothed the wolf's fur before he moved on.

"Well, well, well," a voice said. "A visitor. How lovely." Hungry For More walked round the corner of the house, and there, in a yellow rocking chair, sat an old woman. She wore a dark blue dress that seemed too large for her narrow body. The skin on her face and neck and hands was covered in tiny lines, and had stretched so thin that it seemed the sun could shine right through it, and light up her delicate bones. She was knitting a shawl that filled her lap with the image of the night sky, for the wool was dark and glisteny, with sparkling dots and swirls that mimicked the stars and milky way. The needles were gold and silver, and they moved so fast they sounded like crickets on a summer night.

She glanced at Hungry For More for just a moment, the way someone might look at a flicker of a fire just barely visible on the far horizon, and then she returned to the click-click of her knitting. She said, "It's certainly been a long time since anyone's been kind enough to visit us."

Hungry For More bowed awkwardly. "Great Mother of Wisdom," he said, "I come to you a weary seeker, blown across the world like dirt. I beg for your guidance." He'd practiced this speech many times, only to feel foolish in the actual moment of telling it.

She smiled slightly and said, "That certainly sounds troublesome. And you do seem like a nice young man. My animals like you, and we must always trust the animals. How can I help you?"

"I seek my true work in the world."

"Do you? And what work do you do now?"

"To my great and eternal shame, I am a pickpocket."

She made a noise. "Pickpocket! No, no, that is not a profession for someone as smart and talented as you."

Hope sparkled in Hungry For More's face like the stars in the old woman's shawl. "Then tell me. Tell me my destiny. What should I become?"

"A thief."

"What?" She was making fun of him! He wanted to grab her shoulders, shake her, yank her from her chair. He took a deep breath to control himself.

As if she didn't notice his fury she said simply, "You must give up the life of a pickpocket and become a thief."

Hungry For More sighed. Maybe she was right. Maybe *thief* was all he was good for. And yes, it would at least be an improvement on *pickpocket*. And so he bowed once more, said "Thank you, grandmother, for your wisdom," and made his weary way back to the tunnel.

Now he no longer lifted wallets but instead stole valuable objects, such as golden cups, or jeweled necklaces, from wherever some poor innocent might have left them vulnerable to his quick hands. To tell the truth, it was very rare that something so precious as a necklace came his way. Mostly he stole such insignificant items as a pair of boots left outside a door, or a chicken untended at the side of a market. Nevertheless, he did well, and soon he could afford a small house at the edge of a woods. He no longer slept to forget hunger, and even had a warm bed in his warm little home.

But still, he could not bear the thought of what his mother might say if she could see him at his work. So, after some time, he made his way back to the tunnel, back to the worn cabin in the valley. This time he brought honey-bread to distract the snakes, and a lovely piece of raw goat for the wolf.

"Wise mother," he said to the woman, who sat in her chair and knitted her shawl, which now tumbled over her lap to the ground. "I followed your guidance and became a thief. And I have to admit that yes, I have done well. But my heart is still troubled."

She glanced at him, the way someone might look at a fire that burns brightly in the distance. "Thief!" she said. "Well of course you are troubled. That is not a profession for a young man so clever and resourceful."

"Then tell me," he said. "What should I become?"

"A burglar." As Hungry For More threw up his hands the woman said "You can hardly just wait for people to leave things out for you. Yes, this is my advice to you. Become a burglar."

Hungry For More lowered his head. "Thank you, Grandmother" he said, nearly in tears.

Once again he returned to the world, and now he broke into homes at night, homes of merchants on their travels, or rich people who'd gone to country houses, or simply people who'd gone off to visit friends, never suspecting that they would return to a ransacked home, with all their valuables vanished into a burglar's bag. Hungry For More discovered he was good at such work. He taught himself to pick locks, and even to break windows without making any noise, and he quickly learned all the secret places where rich people hid their jewels or money. He bought himself a bigger house and furnished it with fine wooden chairs and a carved bed. When he went to sell his stolen goods and met the master thief's beautiful daughter he realized for the first time in his life he had enough money to think of a family.

One night he was throwing silver spoons and knives into his sack when a voice behind him ordered "Drop everything and don't move!" He turned, and there in a long embroidered nightshirt, stood the owner of the house, with a sword extended to within a foot of

Hungry For More's chest. The burglar stared at the sword tip, and the gloating face of the man he was sure had left the city with a caravan of mules. The man said, "Now you will learn what happens when you steal from innocent citizens."

Fury overwhelmed Hungry For More's fear. Innocent! How dare this pompous fool, who cheated people every day of his life, who became rich trading with the Army of Love, how dare he denounce a poor burglar who just wanted to make his way in the world? He crouched down, then sprung forward to butt his head against the man's belly. With a loud noise the merchant dropped the sword and staggered back.

Hungry For More grabbed the weapon, and in a moment had the tip of it against the man's throat. His breath came in great gusts, and he was about to pierce the skin and watch the man's life spurt into the air, when suddenly his mother's sad face appeared in his mind. He threw the sword against a far wall and ran from the house. The next day he set off for the Old Woman.

"Grandmother," he said, as she sat peacefully and worked at her shawl, "please help me. I followed your advice and became a thief, and then a burglar. Is this really my destiny? Just before I came here I almost killed a man. Please tell me. What should I do?"

She looked at him for several moments now, the way someone might look at a fire that consumes an entire hillside. Then she went back to her knitting, the gold and silver needles like lightning as they added more darkness and stars to the long shawl. "Become a bandit," she said.

"What?"

"A bandit. A robber. Someone who jumps out—"

"I *know* what a bandit is."

"Good. I was wondering about you for a moment."

"But a burglar is bad enough."

"Exactly," she said. "Sneaking around in darkness, snatching whatever people have left behind. That is certainly no life for someone so brave and intelligent as you. Bandit. That is what you must do." And she returned to her knitting, as serene as if she sat all alone among the wildflowers, with only the sheep and the cow, the snakes

The Tarot of Perfection

"Become a bandit," she said

and the wolf, to keep her company. With a deep sigh Hungry For More returned to the tunnel.

When he arrived home he went straight to the house of the master thief (where the daughter smiled shyly at him as she served wine and cakes). He bought himself a good strong sword and a pair of pistols engraved with pictures of ancient heroes. For several days he practiced jumping from behind trees or giant rocks. He would wave his weapons at the air, try to hold a menacing posture, try to speak in a deep and commanding voice. Finally he knew he must either do it or deny what the old woman had told him. And somehow, even though he hated the destiny she'd given him, and hoped his mother lay beyond all knowledge of it, he could not bring himself to ignore what the oracle had told him.

And so, on a moonless night, he took a piece of blue cloth, cut out eye holes, and tied it around his upper face for a mask. Then he waited behind a dense clump of trees until he saw a pair of merchants wending their way home from a party. He jumped into the road with his arms straight out so that the pistols came to within inches of each of their faces. "Stop!" he cried. "Give me everything you have or die in the dirt!" It was not a good speech, he thought, but it was the best he could think of. And it worked. The terrified merchants dropped their wallets, their rings, their various trinkets, and probably would have taken off their clothes if Hungry For More had not waved them on their way.

As he swept his prizes into a plain blue sack he tried not to think of the shame his mother would have felt at the sight of those two frightened fools, with pistols, *his* pistols, pointed right at their eyes. And yet, he could not deny a strange thrill that surged through him. The Old Woman was right! He'd *hated* always hiding, never daring to confront the people whose property he stole. He laughed. If he must live as a thief in this corrupt world then let him do so openly! He remembered suddenly how his mother had taken him from place to place, begging every merchant and tradesman to give him honest work, and no one had helped them. Very well, then, he thought. Bandit it is.

And so he began to prey upon the countryside. The Blue Mask, they called him, for the cloth he wore over his face. Merchants, nobles, even government officials, nobody was safe from him. Though sometimes the purses he stole were in fact less than he might have gotten as a burglar he pursued this new life with much more enthusiasm, and soon he was able to build himself a fine house, and give money to the poor. And when he asked the daughter of the Master of Thieves to marry him, she threw her arms around him, and in a voice filled with tears told him she was the happiest woman in the sad land of Harmonious Song.

One night he was hiding behind a thick tree when he spotted a pair of wealthy lords nervously looking all about as they hurried along the road. But when he jumped out and waved his pistols at them, they only laughed. They threw off their cloaks and stood revealed in their uniforms as soldiers of the Army of Love. In their flat dead accents they said "Now, you rag-headed piece of Harmonious garbage, you're going to get what you deserve. And maybe the rest of your filthy countrymen will learn a lesson."

Hungry For More fired his pistols but they had already jumped to the side and taken out their own guns, bigger and more powerful than anything a lowly robber could hope to acquire. Hungry For More dropped to the left just as high speed bullets whined past him. He knew they expected him to run, or try to fight both of them at once, so instead he crouched low and charged directly at the taller and stronger of the two soldiers. While the other stood there, afraid to fire for fear he would hit his friend, and the soldier under attack tried to aim his gun, Hungry For More slit the man's throat with a silver-handled dagger his wife had given him as a wedding present. In almost the same motion he flung the dead man's body at the other soldier. Before the frightened man could get back on his feet, Hungry For More shot him in the face.

He stepped back now to lean against a tree, too weak to stand. He'd just killed two men! More, he'd killed two soldiers from the terrible Army of Love, something no child of Harmonious Song had done in over a hundred years. He was not sure if he felt ashamed or exhilarated as he walked to a nearby stream and washed the blood from his face and hands.

After that, Hungry For More became even more clever and fearless. He evaded trap after trap, but when he could not do anything but stand and fight he attacked with such ferocity that no one could resist him. Then one night he came home to his wife unable to stop trembling. When she asked what had disturbed him so deeply he told her that when he stepped from hiding to rob a rich aristocrat traveling with his family the wretched man had begged and begged "Blue Mask" to kill only him and allow his wife and babies to survive. "Is this what I've become?" he asked his wife. "A ghost of death to terrify helpless people?"

"Go see the Old Woman," she told him. "Maybe she can reveal a deeper truth."

And so, once again, Hungry For More crossed the desert and mountains, the forest and rivers, and held his breath as he squeezed through the cave. Once again, he petted the sheep and the cow, and gave treats to the snakes and the wolf who now greeted him as a dear friend.

"How nice to see you again," the Old Woman said. Her gold and silver knitting needles moved so fast that Hungry For More could hardly follow them. The shawl now covered the ground all around her feet.

"Please," he said. "I was a pickpocket and you told me to become a thief. I was a thief and you told me to become a burglar. And then I was a burglar and you told me to become a robber. Now the very sight of me terrifies people who have never done me the slightest harm. Is this really my destiny?"

Her needles slowed as she looked up at him. She stared at him intently now, the way someone looks at a fire that rages across the countryside. Finally she said "No, no. I can see that you are brave and strong, and really quite a fine bandit. But there is a whole countryside to rob, and you can hardly do it all yourself."

He stared at her. "I am sorry, wise mother, but I do not understand you."

"Really? It's not so complicated. Here is what you must do. Choose five men who are brave, resourceful, and clever. Just like yourself. Train them in the ways of the bandit. I'm sure you know much more about that than I do. Then, when they have proven themselves, tell each of them to train five more and each of those to train another five. And let them all wear blue masks, so that everyone knows they belong to you, and follow your will. And when you have done all that, well, then you really will have made some progress."

Hungry For More could only stare at her, his mouth open. She glanced up, as if surprised he was still there. "Well, go on," she said. "There's really no time to waste, you know."

Wearily, Hungry For More made his way back through the tunnel, and across the countryside to where his wife waited for him. He could hardly keep tears from his voice as he told her his new destiny. But his wife stroked his hair, and his cheeks, and she kissed him and she said, "Now, don't worry. If the Old Woman tells you to do this, then of course you must do it. Hasn't she always been good to us? Without her help we never would have met. You would still be a pickpocket, if indeed you had even survived so long."

And so, with the help of his wife and his father-in-law, Hungry For More selected five men, strong, and fearless, and smart. Carefully he taught them to fight, and plan, and escape traps whenever possible. And then he sent them out into the world.

Years passed. The Brigands of the Blue Mask roamed the countryside at will, stealing from lords and merchants and tax collectors. They'd long ago lost track of how many men they'd killed—soldiers, private guards, men who wanted to prove themselves, or simply the greedy rich who could not bear the thought of life without their money.

Hungry For More and his wife lived in a large but simple house, their only indulgence a small collection of carvings from the long ago years before the Army of Love had conquered their country and banned everything harmonious. The rest of their money they gave to the poor and the families of any bandit who were caught or killed.

But still he was troubled. One day he and two of his lieutenants stopped a small caravan of tax officials and their families. The soldiers ran in fear, and the men nearly threw their money at the robbers, while the wives crouched down in their carriages. Only an elderly woman stood her ground. She held her cane tightly with both hands, and said to the bandit leader, "What have you done with your life? What kind of man doesn't dare to show his face to the world? Do you think your mother is proud of you?" One of the robbers raised his pistol at her but Hungry For More slapped his hand away. The old woman only laughed.

Over the next nights Hungry For More found it impossible to sleep. All night he turned in his bed, but every time he closed his eyes he imagined he could hear that old woman laughing. Finally, his wife took his face in his hands and said to him, "Why should you feel such shame? You have only ever done what the oracle told you to do. Go. Ask her the meaning of it or we will never have any peace."

Once again Hungry For More made the great journey. He traveled across wetlands and forests, he squeezed his way between the razor sharp walls of the cave, until he emerged once again in the hidden valley. The two black sheep and the white cow stopped their grazing and followed him, and even the snakes and the wolf ignored the delicacies he had brought them in order to slither or walk alongside him.

"Wise mother" he said to her as she knitted her shawl that poured out from the yellow chair like some vast lake of darkness and stars, "I have done all that you told me. I became a thief, a burglar, a bandit. Now I rule a great force of bandits, and no one may travel the roads or the woods unless we allow it. But still I am pained. Is this all my life will ever mean? Please. Tell me. I have always followed your words. What must I do now?"

"Now?" she said. She tied the end of her massive shawl, and dropped the gold and silver needles to the ground. Hungry For More felt the earth shudder beneath him. The Old Woman turned to face him. She folded her hands in her lap and stared at him a long, long time, the way one looks at a fire that burns the entire world. "And now?" she said. But her voice had changed, become younger, stronger. And then she stood up, and as she did so the years fell away like water, and she became young and beautiful and terrifying. With one hand she flung the great shawl behind her and it filled the sky, dark and glistening, alive with rivers of stars. "*Now*," she said, in a voice cold and hard as a winter's night, "*you and your invincible bandits will rise* up and drive the Army of Love from every speck and corner of this sacred land!"

And so they did. They fought for seven years, and after that the invaders who had ruled so cruelly for so many generations finally sailed away in their dark boats. The land of Harmonious Song once more became free, and Hungry For More became its king. As Destiny the First he ruled for many years with his wife beside him, both of them beloved for their wisdom and compassion.

When the queen finally died, Destiny left his throne, never to be seen again. Some say he never died, but lives forever with an old woman, a pair of black sheep, a white cow, a nest of green snakes, and a ferocious red wolf. But others claim he travels the heavens, where he robs the very stars, so that he can pour light down upon a dark and hungry world.

For Annie Ogborn, taxi driver, revolutionary, toy maker, and secret king of America

The End

The Girl Who Went to the Rich Neighborhood

There was once a widow who lived with her six daughters in the poorest neighborhood in town. In summer the girls all went barefoot, and even in winter they often had to pass one pair of shoes between them as they ran through the street. Even though the mother got a check every month from the welfare department, it never came to enough, despite their all eating as little as possible. They would not have survived at all if the supermarkets hadn't allowed the children to gather behind the loading gates at the end of the day and collect the crushed or fallen vegetables.

Sometimes, when there was no more money, the mother would leave her left leg as credit with the grocer. When her check came, or one of the children found a little work, she would get back her leg and be able to walk without the crutch her oldest daughter had made from a splintery board. One day, however, after she'd paid her bill, she found herself stumbling. When she examined her leg she discovered that the grocery had kept so many legs and arms jumbled together in their big metal cabinet that her foot had become all twisted. She sat down on their only chair and began to cry, waving her arms over her head.

Seeing her mother so unhappy the youngest girl, whose name was Rose, walked up and announced, "Please don't worry, I'll go to the rich neighborhood." Her mother kept crying. "And I'll speak to the mayor. I'll get him to help us." The widow smiled and stroked her daughter's hair.

She doesn't believe me, Rose thought. *Maybe she won't let me go. I'd better sneak away.* The next day, when the time came to go to the supermarket Rose took the shoes she shared with her sisters and slipped them in her shopping bag. She hated doing this, but she would need the shoes for the long walk to the rich neighborhood. Besides, maybe the mayor wouldn't see her if she came barefoot. Soon, she told herself, she'd bring back shoes for everyone. At the supermarket she filled her bag with seven radishes that had fallen off the bunch, two sticks of yellowed celery, and four half-blackened bananas. *Well*, she thought, *I guess I'd better get started.*

As soon as she left the poor neighborhood Rose saw some boys shoving and poking a weak old lady who was trying to cross the street. *What a rotten thing to do,* the girl thought, and hoped the children in the rich neighborhood weren't all like that. She found a piece of pipe in the street and chased them away.

"Thank you," wheezed the old woman, who wore a yellow dress and had long blonde hair that hung, uncombed, down to her knees. She sat down in the middle of the road, with cars going by on every side.

Rose said, "Shouldn't we get out of the street? We could sit on the pavement."

"I can't," said the old woman. "I must eat something first. Don't you have anything to eat?"

Rose reached in her basket to give the old woman a radish. In a moment the shriveled red thing had vanished and the woman held out her hand. Rose gave her another radish, and then another, until all the radishes had slid down the old woman's densely veined throat. "Now we can go," she said, and instantly jumped to her feet to drag Rose across the road.

Rose told herself that maybe she wouldn't need them. She looked down at the silver pavement and then up at the buildings that reached so far above her head the people in the windows looked like toys. "Is this the rich neighborhood?" she asked.

"Hardly," the woman said. "You have to go a long way to reach the rich neighborhood." Rose thought how she'd better be extra careful with the rest of her food. The old woman said, "But if you really want to go there I can give you something to help you." She ran her fingers through her tangled gold hair and when she took them out she was holding a lumpy yellow coin. "This token will always get you on or off the subway."

What a strange idea, thought Rose. How could you use a token more than once? And even if you could, everyone knew that you didn't need anything to get off the subway. But she put the coin in the bag and thanked the old woman.

All day she walked and when night came she crawled under a fire escape beside some cardboard cartons. She was very hungry but she thought she had better save her celery and bananas for the next day. Trying not to think of the warm mattress she shared with two of her sisters, she went to sleep.

The next morning the sound of people marching to work woke her up. She stretched herself, thinking how silver streets may look very nice but didn't make much of a bed. Then she rubbed her belly and stared at the celery. *I'd better get started first*, she told herself. But when she began to walk her feet hurt, for her sisters' shoes, much too big for her, had rubbed the skin raw the day before.

Maybe she could take the subway. Maybe the old woman's token would work at least once. She went down a subway entrance where a guard with a gun walked back and forth, sometimes clapping his hands or stamping his feet. As casually as she could Rose walked up and put her token in the slot. *I hope he doesn't shoot me,* she thought. But then the wooden blades of the gate turned and she passed through.

A moment later, she was walking down the stairs when she heard a soft clinking sound. She turned around to see the token bouncing on its rim along the corridor and down the stairs until it bounced right into the shopping bag. Rose looked to see if the guard was taking his gun out but he was busy staring out the entrance.

All day she traveled on the tube train, but whenever she tried to read the signs she couldn't make out what they said beneath the huge black marks drawn all over them. Rose wondered if the marks formed the magic that made the trains go. She'd sometimes heard people say that without magic the subway would break down forever. Finally she decided she must have reached the rich neighborhood. She got off the train, half expecting to have to use her token. But the exit door swung open with no trouble and soon she found herself on a gold pavement, with buildings that reached so high the people looked like birds fluttering around in giant caves.

Rose was about to ask someone for the mayor's office when she saw a policeman with a gold mask covering his face slap an old woman. Rose hid in a doorway and made a sound like a siren, a trick she'd learned in the poor neighborhood. The policeman ran off waving his gold truncheon.

"Thank you, thank you," said the old woman whose tangled red hair reached down to her ankles. "I'm so hungry now, could you give me something to eat?"

Trying not to cry Rose gave the woman first one piece of celery and then the others. Then she asked "is this the rich neighborhood?"

"No, no, no," the woman laughed, "but if you're planning to go there I can give you something that might help you." She ran her fingers through her hair and took out a red feather. "If you need to reach something and cannot, then wave this feather." Rose couldn't imagine how a feather could help her reach anything but she didn't want to sound rude so she put the feather in her bag.

Since it was evening and Rose knew that gangs sometimes ran through the streets after dark she thought she'd better find a place to sleep. She saw a pile of wooden crates in front of a store and lay down behind them, sadly thinking how she'd better save her four bananas for the next day.

The next morning the sound of opening and closing car doors woke her up and she stretched painfully. The gold streets had hurt her back even more than the silver ones the night before. With a look at her bananas, now completely black, she got to her feet and walked back to the underground.

All day she rode on the train, past underground store windows showing clothes that would tear in a day, and bright flimsy furniture, and strange machines with rows of black buttons. The air became very sweet, but thick, as if someone had sprayed the tunnels with perfume. Finally Rose decided she couldn't breathe and had to get out.

She came up to a street made all of diamond, and buildings so high she couldn't see anything at all in the windows, only flashes of colors. The people walking glided a few inches above the ground, while the cars moved so gently on their white tires they looked like swimmers floating in a pool.

Rose was about to ask for the mayor's office when she saw an old woman under attack by manicured dogs and rainbow dyed cats whose rich owners had let them roam the street. Rose whistled so high she herself couldn't hear it, but the animals all ran away, thinking their owners had called them for dinner.

"Thank you *so* much," the woman said, dusting off her long black dress. Her black hair trailed the ground behind her. "Do you suppose you could give me something to eat?"

Biting back her tears Rose held out the four bananas. The woman laughed and said, "One is more than enough for me. You eat the others." Rose had to stop herself shoving all three bananas into her mouth at once. She was glad she did, for each one tasted like a different food, from chicken to strawberries. She looked up amazed.

"Now," said the woman, "I suppose you want the mayor's house." Her mouth open, Rose nodded yes. The woman told her to look for a street so bright she had to cover her eyes to walk on it. Then she said, "If you ever find the road too crowded blow on this." She ran her fingers through her hair and took out a black whistle shaped like a pigeon.

The girl said, "Thank you," though she didn't think people would get out of the street just for a whistle.

When the woman had gone Rose looked around at the diamond street. *I'd break my back sleeping here*, she thought, and decided to look for the mayor's house that evening. Up and down the streets she hobbled, now and then running out of the way of dark-windowed cars or lines of children dressed all in money and holding hands as they ran screaming through the street.

At one point she saw a great glow of light and thought she must have found the mayor's house, but when she came close she saw only an empty road where bright balls of light on platinum poles shone on giant fountains spouting liquid gold into the air. Rose shook her head and walked on.

Several times she asked people for the mayor's house but no one seemed to hear or see her. As night came Rose thought that at least the rich neighborhood wouldn't get too cold; they probably heated the streets. But instead of warm air a blast of cold came up from the diamond pavement. The people in the rich neighborhood chilled the streets so they could use the personal heaters built into their clothes.

For the first time Rose thought she would give up. It was all so strange, how could she ever think the mayor would even listen to her? About to look for a subway entrance she saw a flash of light a few blocks away and began to walk towards it. When she came close the light became so bright she automatically covered her eyes, only to find she could see just as well as before. Scared now that she'd actually found the way she slid forward close to the buildings.

The light came from a small star which the mayor's staff had captured and set in a gold cage high above the street. A party was going on, with people dressed in all sorts of costumes. Some looked like birds with beaks instead of noses, and giant feathered wings growing out of their backs; others had become lizards, their heads covered in green scales. In the middle, on a huge chair of black stone sat the mayor looking very small in a white fur robe. Long curved fingernails hooked over the ends of his chair. All around him advisors floated in the air on glittery cushions.

For a time Rose stayed against the wall, afraid to move. Finally she told herself she could starve just standing there. Trying not to limp, she marched forward and said, "Excuse me."

No one paid any attention. And no wonder. Suspended from a helicopter a band played on peculiar horns and boxes. "Excuse me," Rose said louder, then shouted, the way she'd learned to shout in the poor neighborhood when animals from outside the city attacked the children.

Everything stopped. The music sputtered out, the lizards stopped snatching at the birds who stopped dropping jeweled "eggs" on the lizards' heads. Two policemen ran forward. Masks like smooth mirrors covered their heads so that the rich people would only see themselves if they happened to glance at a policeman. They grabbed Rose's arms, but before they could handcuff her the mayor boomed (his voice came through a microphone grafted onto his tongue), "Who are you? What do you want? Did you come to join the party?"

Everyone laughed. Even in the rich neighborhood, they knew, you had to wait years for an invitation to the mayor's party.

"No, sir," said Rose. "I came to ask for help for the poor neighborhood. Nobody has any money to buy food and people have to leave their arms and legs at the grocery just to get anything. Can you help us?"

The laughter became a roar. People shouted ways the mayor could help the poor neighborhood. Someone suggested canning the ragged child and sending her back as charity dinners. The mayor held up his hand and everyone became silent. "We could possibly help you," he said. "But first you will have to prove yourself. Will you do that?"

Confused, Rose said yes. She didn't know what he meant. She wondered if she needed a welfare slip or some other identification.

"Good," the mayor said. "We've got a small problem here and maybe you could help us solve it." He waved a hand and a picture appeared in the air in front of Rose. She saw a narrow metal stick about a foot long with a black knob at one end and a white knob at the other. The mayor told Rose that the stick symbolized the mayor's power, but the witches had stolen it.

"Why don't you send the police to get it back?" Rose asked.

Again the mayor had to put up his hand to stop the laughter. He told the girl that the witches had taken the stick to their embassy near the United Nations, where diplomatic immunity kept the police from following them.

"I have to go to the witches' embassy?" Rose asked. "I don't even know where it is. How will I find it?" But the mayor paid no attention to her. The music started and the birds and lizards went back to chasing each other.

Rose was walking away when a bird woman flapped down in front of her. "Shall I tell you the way to the witches' embassy?"

"Yes," Rose said, "Please."

The woman bent over laughing. Rose thought she would just fly away again, but no, in between giggles she told the girl exactly how to find the witches. Then she wobbled away on her wingtips, laughing so hard she bumped into buildings whenever she tried to fly.

With her subway token Rose arrived at the embassy in only a few minutes. The iron door was so tall she couldn't even reach the

The Tarot of Perfection

A party was going on, with people dressed in all sorts of costumes

bell, so she walked around looking for a servants' entrance. Shouts came from an open window. She crept forward.

Wearing nothing but brown oily mud all over their bodies the witches were dancing before a weak fire. The whole embassy house smelled of damp moss. Rose was about to slip away when she noticed a charred wooden table near the window, and on top of it the mayor's stick.

She was about to climb over the sill, grab the stick and run, when she noticed little alarm wires strung across the bottom of the window. Carefully she reached in above the wires towards the table. No use. The stick lay a good six inches out of reach.

An image of the woman in red came to her. "If you need to reach something and cannot, then wave this feather." Though she still couldn't see how the feather could help her, especially with something so heavy, she fluttered it towards the table.

The red-haired woman appeared behind the witches, who nevertheless seemed not to notice her. "I am the East Wind," she said and Rose saw that her weakness had vanished and her face shone as bright as her hair waving behind her. "Because you helped me and gave me your food when you had so little I will give you what you want." She blew on the table and a gust of wind carried the stick over the wires into Rose's hands.

The girl ran off with all the speed she'd learned running away from trouble in the poor neighborhood. Before she could go half a block, however, the stick cried out, "Mistresses! This little one is stealing me."

In an instant the witches were after her, shrieking and waving their arms as they ran, leaving drops of mud behind them. Soon, however, Rose reached the subway where her token let her inside while the witches who hadn't taken any money, let alone tokens, could only stand on the other side of the gate and scream at her.

Rose could hardly sit she was so excited. The subway clacked along, and only the silly weeping of the stick in her bag kept her from jumping up and down. She imagined her mother's face when she came home in the mayor's car piled so high with money and food.

At the stop for the mayor's house Rose stepped off the train swinging her bag. There, lined up across the exit, stood the witches. They waved their muddy arms and sang peculiar words in warbly high pitched voices. The stick called, "Mistresses, you found me."

Rose looked over her shoulder at the subway. She could run back, but suppose they were waiting for her in the tunnel? And she still had to get to the mayor. Suddenly she remembered the old woman saying that the token could get her off the subway as well as on. She grabbed it from her bag and held it up.

The woman in yellow appeared before her. "I am the South Wind," she said, "and because you helped me I will help you." Gently she blew on Rose and a wind as soft as an old bed carried the girl over the heads of the witches and right out of the subway to the street.

As fast as she could she ran to the mayor's house. But as soon as she turned the corner to the street with the captured star she stopped and clutched her bag against her chest. The mayor was waiting for her, wrapped in a head to toe cylinder of bullet-proof glass, while behind him, filling the whole street, stood a giant squad of police. Their mirrored heads bounced the starlight back to the sky. "Give me the witches' stick," the mayor said.

"The witches? You said –"

"Idiot child. That stick contains the magic of the witches' grandmothers." He then began to rave about smashing the witches' house and putting them to work in the power stations underneath the rich neighborhood. Rose tried to back away. "Arrest her," the mayor said.

What had the old woman in black said? "If you ever find the road too crowded, blow on this." Rose grabbed the pigeon whistle and blew as hard as she could.

The woman appeared, her hair wider than the whole wave of police. "I am the North Wind," she told the girl, and might have said more but the squad was advancing. The North Wind threw out her arms and instead of a gust of air a huge flock of black pigeons flew from her dress to pick up the mayor and all the police. Ferociously beating their wings the pigeons carried them straight over the wall into the Bronx, where they were captured by burglars and never heard from again.

"Thank you," Rose said, but the old woman was gone. With a sigh Rose took out the witches' stick. "I'm sorry," she told it. "I just wanted to help the poor neighborhood."

"May I go home now?" the stick asked sarcastically. Before the girl could answer, the stick sprang out of her hands and flew end over end through the air, back to the witches' embassy.

Rose found herself limping along the riverside, wondering what she would tell her mother and her sisters. *Why didn't I help the West Wind?* she said to herself. *Maybe she could've done something for me.*

A woman all in silver appeared on the water. Her silver hair tumbled behind her into the river. "I do not need to test you to know your goodness," she said. She blew on the river and a large wave rose up to drench the surprised girl.

But when Rose shook the water off she found that every drop had become a jewel. Red, blue, purple, green, stones of all shapes and colors, sapphires in the shape of butterflies, opals with sleeping faces embedded in the center, they all covered Rose's feet up to her ankles. She didn't stop to look at them. With both hands she scooped them up into her basket, and then her shoes. *Hurry,* she told herself. She knew that no matter how many police you got rid of there were always more. And wouldn't the rich people insist the jewels belonged to them?

So full of jewels she could hardly run Rose waddled to the subway entrance. Only when she got there did she notice that the streets had lost their diamond paving. All around her the rich people stumbled or fell on the lumpy gray concrete. Some of them had begun to cry or to crawl on all fours, feeling the ground like blind people at the edge of a cliff. One woman had taken off all her clothes, her furs and silks and laces, and was spreading them all about the ground to hide its ugliness.

Fascinated, Rose took a step back towards the street. She wondered if anything had happened to the star imprisoned in its cage above the mayor's house. But then she remembered how her mother had limped when the grocer had gotten her foot all twisted. She ran downstairs to use her magic token for the last time.

Though the train was crowded Rose found a seat in the corner where she could bend over her treasures to hide them from any suspicious eyes. *What does a tax collector look like,* she wondered.

As the rusty wheels of the train shrieked through the gold neighborhood and then the silver one, Rose wondered if she'd ever see the old ladies again. She sighed happily. It didn't matter. She was going home, back to her mother and her sisters and all her friends in the poor neighborhood.

For Jack Maguire

The End

The Fool, the Stick and the Princess

There were once three brothers who lived in a poor country far away. The two older brothers were very clever and everyone said they would do well in the world, even in a land with so few opportunities. But the youngest was nothing but a fool. He had never learned to read, and even the simplest tasks eluded him. Told to fetch wood, he would set out determined to get it right, but before he got to the back of the house and the woodpile he might see a rabbit and try to imitate its hop until he fell over laughing, the wood pile long forgotten. Or worse, he might see a rainbow and fling the wood in the air as he lifted his arms in happiness. The Fool, as everyone called him, simply loved rainbows. Whenever he saw one he would throw his arms high above his head, no matter what else was happening. People would shake their heads and worry what would become of him.

As time went on, the family became poorer and poorer, despite all the efforts of the mother and father and the elder brothers. Finally, the oldest brother announced that there were just no opportunities for an ambitious young man in a country where people told legendary stories about eating more than one meal a day. He must leave home and seek his fortune. He kissed his parents, told his second brother to take care of the Fool, and set out on a sunny morning across the cracked clay of their poor farm.

He had gone no more than a day's journey when he spotted something along the side of the road, half hidden under a burnt-out bush. At first glance it looked like a plain stick, about waist high, but the sharp-eyed brother noticed a glow of light all around it. "A magic staff!" he cried excitedly and seized it. Power surged through him and he shook the stick at the sky. "Now nothing can stop me!" he cried. "I will make my fortune and return home to rescue my family."

Just as he was striding off, he heard a terrible roar. He turned and saw an ogre about to rush at him. The ogre stood ten feet tall, with shoulders like rocks, and thick scales for skin, and teeth like sharpened iron stakes. Though he shook with fear, the eldest brother told himself he had no reason to worry. He pointed the magic stick at the ogre and shouted "Stop this monster from devouring me!" A blast of light streaked from the stick—but instead of striking the ogre it ran all through the eldest brother. In an instant his entire body had turned to stone. Furious, the hungry ogre lumbered away.

A year went by. When Spring came once more, the second brother looked one day at the scraps of bread on the table and shook his head. "It's no use," he told his parents. "Something terrible must have happened to my brother or he would have returned by now. We have become more wretched than ever. I must go seek my fortune." His parents begged him not to go. If he didn't come back, they said, and they died, who would take care of the Fool? But he only kissed them and shook his head sadly at his younger brother. Then he left.

Three days from home he came upon his petrified brother. The magic stick still lay at his stone feet. "Oh my poor poor brother," he cried. "He must have found this magic stick and tried to use it and it turned against him." He picked up the stick. The power in it made him tremble all over. "Well," he said. "Luckily I am much cleverer than my brother. Besides, he always wanted glory. I just want to feed my family. As long as I don't make any mistakes I can use this stick to make my fortune."

He had gone no more than a day's journey when he heard a roar. An ogre was rushing at him. Its mouth drooled with thick black slime. The brother raised his stick. He could see fire run along its length in its eagerness to unleash itself. "Prevent this creature from devouring me!" he ordered the stick. Just as the ogre reached him he turned all to stone.

Another year passed. One day the Fool said "Didn't my brothers leave some time ago? I remember something about that." His parents nodded. "They haven't come back, have they?" His parents shook their heads. "Oh," said the Fool, "I guess that means I'll have to go seek my fortune."

"No!" his parents cried. They knew he could hardly find his way out the door. But nothing they said could dissuade him. Maybe he'd forget. They tried to distract him, with stories, and games, and a bunch of flowers that his mother begged from a neighbor who had managed to grow a small garden. The next morning, however, the Fool tied a change of clothes in a large cloth and set out.

No sooner had he left the house than he saw a rainbow. "Oh look!" he cried, and raised his arms, flinging his bundle away from him. His poor father had to run after it or the Fool would have forgotten it entirely. As the Fool wandered up the road, his parents held each other and wept loudly.

The Fool had traveled several days, with detours to follow various small animals, when he came upon his petrified eldest brother. "How wonderful," he said. "Here we all thought something terrible must have happened, but instead someone's made a statue of him. He must be famous. How nice. He always wanted to be famous."

Several more days later, he discovered his second brother. "Now our family has really done well," he said. "Statues of both my brothers. Won't my parents be happy. Maybe someone will make a statue of me someday." As soon as he said it, the idea struck him as so ludicrous he bent over laughing. With his face close to the ground like that, he discovered the stick at his brother's feet. "Oh look," he said. "Just what I need to carry my bundle." He tied his cloth to the end of the stick and lifted it to his shoulder. A tickle ran all through his body. "What a nice breeze," he said to himself.

That night he used his stick to dig up some roots for his dinner. To his surprise they tasted like a marvelous feast, with flavors from roast quail to wild strawberries crème de menthe. "What amazing roots," he thought. "I'll have to tell my brothers about this." With the stick he drew an outline of a bed on the dirt. When he lay down on it he found it as soft as baby goose feathers. He smiled and fell asleep.

He had hardly set out the next morning when the ground shook with a great roar. "Thunder," he said to himself. "I hope the rain falls on something else and not me." Behind him, a sudden burst of rain like knives fell on the ogre who had just opened his mouth wide to bite off the Fool's head. As the rain hit him the ogre screamed, for ogres cannot stand water. He thrashed about but it was no use. The scales cracked, the skin underneath sizzled and burned. Finally the creature fell down dead.

"I wonder what all that noise was," the Fool said. He walked away without turning around.

For several weeks he wandered. Each day his stick dug up banquets in the form of roots, and every night he slept peacefully in his outline of a bed, untouched by animals or storms or even damp.

One day he came to a river. Beyond it he could see houses and fields, even a city, and somewhere near the city what looked like a tower of light. He wondered how he could get across. It was too far to swim and he could not see a bridge. "If only I was clever like my brothers and not such a fool," he thought, "I would know what to do." In a rare burst of annoyance he struck his stick against a tree. "I wish I had a boat!" he said. He heard a crackle, and when he turned around the tree had gone and in its place lay a fine rowboat. "How nice," the Fool said, as he got in and began rowing. "Someone just left this for strangers. What a generous land. Maybe here I can find my fortune."

When he reached the other side he found signs posted up and down the riverbank. Since he could not read he paid them no attention, and began walking towards the tower of light which shimmered and flickered in the bright sun. In fact, the signs were all about the tower.

The king and queen of this land had a daughter who was so beautiful that princes from lands as exotic as Cathay, Persia, and England all sent delegations asking for her hand in marriage. Some even came in person and bowed down with great flourishes (and expensive presents) to press their case. Her parents considered the princess a gift from heaven itself, for they could pick a husband who would bring even more wealth and power to their kingdom. Empire, they told each other. Through their daughter's marriage they would change from mere king and queen to emperor and empress.

Unfortunately, when they had calculated the best possible match for the princess, they discovered that the gods had played an awful trick on them. Their daughter refused to marry! At first, they thought they might have gone a little too far in their choice. The prospective husband was not exactly young, and the warts on his bent nose and saggy chin ruled out any suggestion of handsome. So they found a prince whose good looks caused young women to faint any time he walked down an open street (newspaper editorials suggested he wear a veil, or simply stay home, but the prince only laughed). Again the princess refused.

"What do you want?" her parents shouted at her. "Just tell us."

"I want to study," she said.

They stared at her. Study? They knew she spent a great deal of time with her books, rather odd books, in fact, but study? They'd always assumed she'd read all those books because she was bored and waiting to get married. Study rather than a husband?

They arranged one match after another. The princess refused to see them. Now they became truly angry. They told her they would choose a husband for her and she would marry the man, even if the palace slaves had to drag her from her precious library.

For the first time the princess became frightened. Until now she'd thwarted them by her will and by the good sense of prospective husbands who knew how miserable an unwilling wife could make them. But suppose her parents chose some brute who would relish forcing his wife to obey him? Suppose he took away her books?

Usually the princess did not study anything very practical. She preferred instead to ponder the mysteries of creation and the secret discoveries of ancient philosophers. Nevertheless, some of her books did contain a few magic formulas, if only to show the writer's disdain for such ordinary concerns. For days she searched through her books (she'd never gotten around to putting them in any order) until at last she came upon something truly useful.

While the palace slept the princess secretly borrowed a wheelbarrow from the gardener and carted all her books out to an open field. Standing in the middle of them, she cast a spell. A glass tower rose up beneath her, so steep and smooth that no one could possibly climb it. On top of it sat the delighted princess and all her books. Safe! She clapped her hands in joy. A moment later, she had opened one of her favorite works, a treatise on creation told from the viewpoint of trees instead of people.

Several hours later a noise disturbed her. She peered down the edge of the tower to see her parents there, waving their arms and stamping their feet. They screamed, they cursed, they threatened to tear down the glass mountain chip by chip. She paid no attention. Finally, her mother pointed out that she had taken no food with her. If she didn't come down and obey them she would starve.

Not so, the princess knew. As part of her years of study, she had learned the language of the birds. In a pure voice she sang out to them and they brought her whatever she needed. When her parents heard her song and saw the birds deliver her fruits and fish eggs and delicacies stolen from wealthy tables they finally knew she had beaten them.

Still they would not give up entirely. They sent out messages to all the princes and kings they could reach that whoever could climb the glass tower and bring down the princess could marry her on the spot. They even put up signs all about the land to announce this challenge. Secretly they hoped some lout would be the one to get her. It would serve her right they told themselves.

The Fool knew none of this, for signs meant nothing to him. Music, however— Just as the Fool started towards the glass tower the princess began her song. The Fool stopped and closed his eyes. Tears spilled out from beneath the lid to slide down into his wide smile. Never, never, had he heard such a wondrous sound. When it ended, and he opened his eyes, he saw birds of all colors and sizes, condors, parrots, humming birds, all of them in a great swirl around the top of the tower. Quickly he walked towards the light and the birds.

As he approached it he saw men, more and more of them as he got closer, most of them injured in some way, and all of them miserable. They hobbled about on crutches, they held bandaged heads in their hands, a few lay on the ground in the middle of broken contraptions. One man had strapped giant wood and cloth wings to his back, then jumped off a tree, hoping to flap his way up the tower. He'd only fallen on his head. Another had made shoes with wire springs so that he might bounce high enough to reach the princess. He'd only crashed into the side of the glass.

The Fool looked around at all these sad figures. "What happened to all of you?" he asked.

One of the men stopped groaning long enough to look up at the Fool's cheerful face. "What are you?" he said, "Some kind of fool?"

The Fool nodded happily. "That's right," he said. He thought he might have found a friend but the man only groaned more loudly and turned away.

"Well," the Fool said to himself, "if I want to climb to the top I better get started." He set the stick down on the base of the tower in order to brace himself. A step formed in the glass. He placed the stick a little ways up and then another step formed. "This is easy," he said. "I don't know why all those men made such a fuss. I'm just a Fool, but even I can find my way up a bunch of steps."

When he reached the top the princess stood there. She was furious! She pulled at her hair, she twisted her face in anger, she hopped up and down. Even so, the Fool thought her the most wonderful being he had ever seen.

"What are you doing here?" she shouted. "Why can't anyone ever leave me alone? How did you get up the tower?"

Her fury so startled the Fool he could hardly speak. "I...I just climbed up the steps. It wasn't very hard. Really it wasn't."

Now the princess stared at the glass steps. Then she looked at the Fool, and then at his stick, which shone with a soft pink glow. She nodded to herself. Again she looked at the Fool. She could see a light in him purer than the magic of his stick.

Still she refused to let go of her anger. "So," she said. "Now you expect me to marry you?"

"Marry you?" the Fool said. "*Marry* you? I could never think to marry someone as wise and wonderful as you. I'm just a Fool. I only came here because of the singing. I just wanted to hear you sing with the birds." He began to cry.

The princess felt her heart dissolve and flow out of her body. No, she told herself, she would not allow any tricks. "Right," she said sarcastically. "And I suppose you didn't see all the signs my father has planted everywhere."

The Fool said "I saw them, but I don't know what they said. I can't read."

The princess's mouth fell open. She stared and stared at him. How sweet he looked, how kind, how honest. "Will you marry me?" she blurted.

"What?" the Fool said. He looked around at the piles and piles of books, some as high as a house, some arranged like a table or a bed. "Marry you? I... How could I marry you? I just told you, I can't read."

"That's so wonderful," the princess cried. "I read more than enough for any two people. We will be perfect together." She began to sing the song a partridge hen sings when she has found the perfect mate. The Fool closed his eyes and became so swept up in joy he would have fallen right off the tower if the princess had not held on tightly to him. She stopped singing finally and kissed him. "We will be so happy," she said.

"Oh yes," he told her. "Yes!"

Before they went down from the tower, the princess looked at her beloved Fool and his ragged clothes. "Hmm," she said. To her he was perfect in every way, but she knew what her father would think of such a husband, and even though the king had said he would marry her to whoever climbed the tower she feared he would try to stop them. "Do you have any other clothes?" she asked him.

He looked at the bundle on the end of the stick. "Well" he said. "I did bring an extra shirt and trousers, just in case I had to give these to somebody who needed them more than me. But I'm afraid my other clothes have just as many holes as the ones I am wearing." He reached down and untied the bundle for the first time since he'd placed it on his stick. Then he gasped in surprise. His ragged clothes had vanished and in their place lay the softest and most elegant tunic and leggings anyone had ever seen, softer than silk, stronger than wool, with a river of colors woven into the fabric. The Fool scratched his head. "Now where did this come from?" he said.

Once the Fool had dressed, the princess called the larger birds, the condors and rocs and vultures, and asked them if they would carry her books down to the ground. Then she took her sweet Fool's hand and together they walked down the steps of the tower.

The king and queen were delighted to see their daughter married at last, and to such a fine prince—or so they thought, for when they asked him his kingdom he just waved his stick and said "Oh, over there," and each of them sat a vision of fields of diamonds growing like berries, and castles as large as mountains. They offered to have the Fool and their daughter live with them, but their new son-in-law said "No thank you. I promised my mother and father I'd come right home as soon as I made my fortune." He wondered why the king and queen laughed, but he thought it rude to ask too many questions (he so rarely understood the things other people said anyway), so he said nothing. They set out with seven horses, one for the Fool, one for the princess, one for the treasures the king and queen were sending to the Fool's parents, and four for the princess's books.

Just as they approached the river, the ground shook and they heard a roar like the earth itself breaking in two. The princess turned around and saw a whole army of ogres racing towards them! Word had gotten to the creatures of their brother's destruction and now they wanted revenge. *They'll tear us to shreds* the princess thought. *We have to do something.* But what could they do? There stood the river, too wide for them to swim across, and besides, what would happen to her books in the water? She looked up at the sky but there were no birds near enough to come to their rescue. Knowing that the ogres would reach them in just a few minutes, she began frantically to search through her books for the ones on magic. If only, she thought, as she raced from horse to horse, she had paid more attention to practical issues.

The Fool meanwhile paid no attention at all to any of these events. He did hear the noise and felt the ground shake but thought it might be a herd of animals running back and forth to enjoy the day. And he did wonder why his bride kept dashing from one horse to another, but trusted her totally, for after all, she was so much wiser than him. He might have wondered how they would cross the river, for someone had taken away the rowboat, except that right then, on the other side of the river, he saw his favorite sight in all the world (after his wife, of course). A rainbow!

The Fool did what he always did when he saw a rainbow, he raised his arms above his head to greet it. This time, however, he held the stick in his hand. The moment he lifted his arms, the entire river separated before him. The water rose up on either side, huge walls of water high enough to block the sky. You see, the Fool's stick was a very *old* magic stick, and it knew some very special tricks.

"Hurry," the princess urged as she spurred her horse, and the pack horses, across the passageway between the walls of water. The Fool laughed, thinking his wife wanted to exercise the horses, and so he galloped alongside her.

The princess looked over her shoulder. There came the ogres, filling the path, coming closer and closer. By the time she and the Fool and their horses reached the other side the entire army of ogres raced between the watery walls. *What can we do?* she thought, *they'll swallow us.*

The Fool glanced back, curious to see what his wife was looking at with such distress. All he could make out was a cloud of dust. "Now that's not right," he said to himself. "People depend on this river. What will happen if the water just stays piled up like that? I sure wish the river would come back down again." The moment he said it, the walls of water crashed down in a furious whirl of waves. The entire army of ogres washed away and was never heard from again.

Now they set out happily for home. Any time the Fool got lost (at least four or five times a day) the princess called a hawk or a raven to look ahead and return them to the path. They were two days from home when they came upon the Fool's second brother, still fixed in stone in the act of trying to cast a spell. "Look," the Fool said to his wife. "Not everyone in my family is a fool. My second brother has become so famous someone has made a statue of him." With his stick he tapped twice on the shoulder.

Instantly his brother came to life, falling to the ground where he looked up confused. "What..." he said. "Where am I?"

"Brother!" cried the Fool and gave him a big hug. "What a nice surprise. Look, this is my wife, she's a princess, imagine that. Your foolish brother married to a genuine princess. And look, here's our treasure, a whole lot of it, or so my wife tells me, and here are all her books." He helped his confused brother onto his own horse and walked alongside, caught up in a happy chatter. Just as the path turned around the side of a hill, the Fool glanced back. To himself he said, "I wonder what happened to that statue?"

A day later they came to the first brother. Once again the Fool tapped the shoulder with the stick, and once again his brother came to life. Now they all traveled together, and when the Fool's parents saw them they wept with joy. With one of the jewels from the treasure chest they bought food and laid out a feast. Just as they all sat down to eat, the oldest brother suddenly remembered what had started them all on their adventures. "The staff," he said, "what happened to the magic staff?"

"Do you mean my walking stick?" the Fool said. "When we came close to home I realized I didn't need it anymore, so I threw it away."

"You threw it away?" both brothers repeated. "Where?"

The Fool shrugged. He saw his wife look at him with laughter and love and smiled back at her. "I don't remember," he said. "I just tossed it in some bushes."

And there it remains to this very day.

For Holly Voley

The End

The Souls in the Trees

Once upon a time there was a woman named Julia who wanted to escape her life. It was not a bad life. In fact, it was quite good, and for a long time Julia tried to tell herself this, until that became impossible.

Julia lived in a nice house in a safe neighborhood. She worked at a good job, manager of an art gallery that sold small heads they pretended had been shrunken from the shoulders of ancient witches and warriors, but were in fact just painted glass. She had friends, and an older sister who got together with her once a month to eat lunch and gossip about the family.

Most of all, Julia had Mark. Mark was handsome with just a touch of homeliness, his nose a little wide, his chin a little small. He was successful without being driven, working for a pharmaceutical company, though not in research or advertising. He loved good food—it was Mark who made all the fancier meals—good jokes, good books and movies Most of all, he loved Julia. He was kind to her, and funny, and sometimes he would look at her with adoration while she washed dishes or made the bed. Julia's sister called him Prince Charming, and asked what store sold the glass slippers that had brought him into Julia's life.

So why did Julia lie awake at night, unable to breathe? Why did she wish she could fly away on a magic carpet, or throw on a cloak of invisibility and slip out of the house into a deep woods where Prince Charming could never find her?

One night she was cutting celery for a salad, and Mark was telling her about some lobbyist who'd tried to bribe an undercover agent, when suddenly she looked at him and imagined, *saw*, him turn into a beast, a thick muscled creature with fur and fangs, and vicious eyes. She would take the knife she held in her hands and drive it deep into his heart, and it would be okay because he was a beast, and she had to save herself, and even if, just before he died, he turned back into Mark, it would be sad, even tragic, but still okay, because she had broken the curse, she had saved Prince Charming from the Beast.

Julia didn't stop her work. The muscles in her arm tensed as she visualized the knife slamming into his heart, but still the blade moved down the stalk to leave behind half inch pieces on the cutting board. She didn't cry or shake, but she had to control the ragged shudder of her breath. What scared her was not that she'd imagined killing her husband, but that she'd imagined it so calmly.

The next day, she kissed Mark goodbye as he left for work, then packed a green duffel bag full of clothes, a couple of books, some jewelry, and then, at the last moment, the knife, because wherever you went there might be a beast.

Then she went to all the local ATMs and asked the ghosts who lived inside them to give her all the money they could spare. When the ghosts told her she had enough she drove away.

She drove all day, stopping only for gas, and bottled water, and a bag of mixed nuts and seeds (that she worried might leak a trail behind her if she was not extra careful). Should she use a credit card for the gas? But then the Beast (or the Prince) might track her, so she paid cash and decided not to worry about the money. At night she found a small town with a motel not part of any chain and slept very deeply.

Just before dawn she dreamed that she'd been asleep for a hundred years. Shopping malls and office towers had grown up around the motel, so that no one knew she was there. Finally, a prince who ran a wrecking company knocked down the wall and bent down to kiss her awake. But before his lips could touch her she turned into a beast and bit off his head.

She jerked awake, and for just a moment grasped for the knife, until she realized no one was there. Then she took a long shower, dressed, and got back on the road. She packed the knife at the top of her duffel bag.

That morning, when she stopped for gas, she discovered a piece of paper stuck to her foot. She plucked it loose and stared at it. "Dr. Apollo!" it proclaimed. "Master of Mysteries! Speaker of Silence! All truths revealed through the Harmony of the Seers!" She smiled. Maybe he could tell her the truth about Mark. She folded it neatly and put it in the glove compartment.

She traveled for two more days until she came to a small town she'd never heard of before. There were no motels but she discovered something better, a tiny house for rent, just a large room really, with a bathroom, and a kitchen where she could hardly turn around. The house stood all by itself outside of town, in the woods really, surrounded by tall leafy trees. Vines roamed the walls, and wildflowers grew all about the door. "Oh, I love it," Julia said to the rental agent, "it looks like an enchanted cottage."

The agent turned away. With her eyes fixed on the door, she said "Yes, it's very lovely."

Julia spent her first day at the cottage cleaning, for no one had lived there for some time. When she went into town to buy supplies people hardly spoke to her, and some actually moved away. Well, she thought, she'd wanted privacy.

She scrubbed and scraped, and when evening came she took a long shower in a stall so cramped she could hardly fit in it. Then she made herself a salad, and afterwards slept for many hours.

The next day she took a book and a chair outside, but after she'd read for awhile she put down the book and simply smiled at the flowers and trees. As afternoon came, however, she began to feel that old tightness in her chest. At first she panicked, for she thought *He's found me. The Beast is coming*, and where was the knife, she thought, and almost ran into the house for it. But no, she knew what the problem was, and what she had to do.

Julia got into her car, and with a twist in her face she drove fifty miles to a city where she could use a phone without fear of being traced. "Hi," she said when her sister answered the phone. "It's me."

"Oh my god," Jen said. "Julia! Where are you?"

"That doesn't matter," Julia said. "I just wanted to let you know I'm okay."

"What's going on? When are you coming home?"

"I'm not. Not for awhile, anyway."

"What do you mean? Mark is going crazy. We've all been so worried."

"I told you, I'm okay."

"That's all? For God's sake, Julia, what do you think you're doing? Scaring everyone to death—"

"There's just something I have to do," Julia said, then wondered what she meant.

"What you have to do," her sister said, "is come home. Poor Mark—"

Julia hung up the phone.

As she walked back to her car she wobbled a little, and when she grasped the wheel her hands shook so much she knew she better not drive. But then, slowly, the shakes gave way to a smile, and finally a laugh as she drove off. Poor Prince Charming, she thought, he'll just have to fend for himself.

On the way back to her enchanted cottage she stopped for a bottle of wine, and that night she stayed up, drinking, reading, and occasionally going outside to look at the Moon. It was a few days before full, but already it seemed brighter than she'd ever seen it.

Three nights later she woke up in the middle of the night, 12:42 according to the clock on the chair next to her bed. Lying there groggily, it took her a moment to notice the sounds. They were soft and hard to make out, but they sounded like weeping, like the slow steady sobs of women who had long ago gotten past the stage of anger as well as grief, and now cried because it was all there was.

She didn't know what to do. Should she go and investigate? She was a woman alone, very far from neighbors whom she didn't even know. What if there was a gang or something? People in town didn't seem very friendly, maybe a group of them—

This is ridiculous, she told herself. It probably was owls, or coyotes. She rolled over and tried to sleep, but it was hopeless. The sounds seemed to get louder, until they took all her attention. Finally, she got up and put on her slippers and the old pink bathrobe that Mark had given her their first Christmas. Then she grabbed the electric lantern and trudged outside.

"Hello?" she said, but not too loud. "Is anyone there?" No answer. "Hello?" she said again, and "Are you okay?" Nothing, just that steady throb of tears. They seemed to be coming from somewhere in the woods, and she took a step towards the tangled darkness before she caught herself and stopped. The full Moon shone down so brilliantly she could see thick shadows of branches but she still didn't dare enter the trees.

Once more she called "Is anyone there?" but all she heard were the sobs. Finally she went back inside and bolted the doors. She got back in bed and lay there, her breathing almost as tight as it used to be with Mark. Usually, Julia liked to sleep with the moonlight but now she got up and yanked shut the short curtains on her bedroom window, then got back in bed once more and turned towards the wall. Around dawn the sounds dropped away and at last she was able to get to sleep.

In the morning she went out and searched around the house, but the only footprints seemed to be her own. She decided to go into town, bring a book, and sit in the little coffee shop with a sandwich and a cup of tea. But wherever she went people stared at her, some from the sides of their faces, others openly. A couple of times she heard whispers and giggles as she passed by them. At the coffee shop she waited a long time by the cardboard "Please wait to be seated" sign on its aluminum stand before the owner, a bird-faced woman with straw-like hair, led her to a booth. When she sat down the people in the booth behind her, a man and woman in their forties, fell silent, and then the man said "Let's go. This should cover it."

Julia thought how they sure didn't like newcomers, but she hadn't really come for the social life. She'd been sitting there for ten minutes or so—her waitress had taken her order immediately, and brought the food almost as quickly—when she heard giggles from across the room. A moment later, a teenage girl, with a tattoo of a rose on her exposed midriff, came and stood over Julia. Her straight black hair was gelled into points, and she wore silver rings with cheap stones. She looked down at Julia with her face twitchy from holding in laughter, then blurted out "How do you like your new home?" Before Julia could answer, the girl hurried back to her whispering friends.

That's it, Julia thought. She left her half sandwich and still hot tea on the table with a minimum tip, paid at the counter, and soon was back in her car.

When she returned to the cottage everything seemed fine, the house all cozy, the flowers lit by the Sun. She should just keep to herself, she thought. She'd rented the place for its privacy, after all. She took a chair outside and sat with her book for a couple of hours, then made herself a vegetable soup. She went to bed early.

She woke at midnight, the sounds of weeping much more intense than the night before. "Who is it?" she called out, and "Where are you?" She should go look, she thought, but she didn't know if she dared. She imagined her husband, the Beast, setting a trap for her, seducing women and then tying them up to force them to cry until his wife would go into the dark woods to check. She grabbed hold of the knife, but then she put it down again, for of course it was silly to think like that.

It occurred to her suddenly why everyone in town had acted so strange. They knew about the sounds! Maybe it was all a kind of practical joke on the newcomer. She imagined a group of them getting together, maybe the girls from the restaurant, rehearsing it all, then parking their cars back on the highway so they could sneak into the woods behind the house.

Only, she did not really believe that even great actresses, let alone a bunch of teenagers, could fake such anguish. It was like nothing Julia had ever heard. She tried to cover her ears, turn on the radio, but the awful cries rode over everything she did. Finally the dawn came, and just as the day before, the wails diminished, then vanished.

Julia made no attempt to go to town that day. If they wanted to see how she reacted they would have to come look for her. That night the cries came back, but not as strongly as before. She couldn't shut them out, and she couldn't sleep, but at least she could read and try to ignore it. Just as the early light began to weaken the sounds Julia thought *maybe they're ghosts*. Or maybe innocent young girls whose wicked stepmothers had turned them into animals. She smiled as she put down her book and went to sleep.

After that the woods returned to quiet. For a week Julia woke up just before midnight to lie stiffly and listen, but nothing happened, and by the seventh night she once again slept peacefully. When she ventured into town again a few people stared at her but most ignored her.

A couple more weeks went by, and then one night she looked up at the swelling Moon and panic washed over her. Nonsense, she told herself. Whatever it was, it's gone. Maybe it had been some poor wounded animal, or bird cries. Five nights later, however, she jerked awake just before midnight, and a minute later the weeping began. *It's the full Moon*, she thought. It only happened on the three nights of the full Moon. All she had to do was go away for three nights a month and she'd never have to hear it again.

But oh, how horrible it was! Sad and anguished beyond all hope. She couldn't just abandon them. She pulled on her slippers and robe and rushed outside, where the Moon seemed to shine directly into the woods just beyond her home. Now she pushed forward, for a desire to know overcame her fear. She had not gone very far when she came to a circle of nine trees, their thin branches leafless and twisted together, with bare dirt in the center. The Moon shone directly down onto that empty patch, yet the trees themselves remained dark and lifeless.

Julia took a deep breath, then stepped into the circle. Suddenly she could hear voices inside the terrible wails. "Help us!" they cried to her. "Free us! Help us!"

"I don't know what to do," she shouted, but the voices just went on and on. The trees shook, though Julia couldn't feel any wind, and as she turned about it seemed to her that they were twining even more tightly together, to make it impossible to escape. As she squeezed through a gap, the branches scratched her face, but she ignored it and ran back to the cottage.

What was she going to do? She could simply go somewhere for the next couple of days, or leave altogether, maybe even go back to Mark (she half reached for the phone, then yanked back her hand). But those *voices*, that anguished "Help us!"

She jumped up and ran to the car, yanked open the glove compartment. Yes, it was still there, the flyer from "Dr. Apollo," the "Master of Mysteries." She never would have thought she'd consult a psychic, or whatever he called himself, but then, she never would have believed in ghosts, either, if in fact that was what they were. She wished she could call right away, but she doubted the "doctor" would appreciate a phone call in the middle of the night. At dawn, when the voices dwindled, she managed to fall asleep.

She woke with a jolt at 8:30 and grabbed the phone. It took several tries to press the right numbers, but then the phone rang and a second later a soft musical voice said "Hello. This is Dr. Apollo."

Julia hesitated, swallowed, said "I'd like an appointment."

"I know," he said. "And I think today would be good, don't you?"

"Yes. Please. Right away."

He gave her directions—it would take about an hour—and was about to hang up when she blurted out, "Do you handle ghosts?"

The laugh was as soft as the speech. "That would be rather difficult, don't you think?" And then the line went dead.

Dr. Apollo lived at the edge of a small city, in a stone house with blue shutters. There was no sign or name plate. A tall slender woman with a strong face and large hands answered Julia's knock. Long hair flowed onto the shoulders of a loose red and black silk dress. She wore long gold braid earrings, and a gold chain with a large onyx pendant. "Good morning," she said. "I am Dr. Apollo."

"Oh," Julia said, and almost stammered "I'm sorry," as if the woman might know Julia had assumed the soft voice was a man's. Dr. Apollo smiled, then led the way to a bare room lit by three bay windows shining on a wooden floor. There was no furniture save for a small round table, oak with a glass top, and two oak chairs. A picture was etched into the glass surface, the face of a beautiful woman with snakes wound in her lush hair. The only thing on the table was some small object wrapped in gold foil.

Probably it was the effect of the bright sun (or lack of sleep), but Julia imagined she saw specks of colored light move about the room. She blinked and shook her head, but she still saw them.

"Please sit," Dr. Apollo said, and gestured to one of the chairs. When they were both at the table Dr. Apollo leaned back and looked at Julia so long it was hard for Julia not to squirm. "When you called me," Dr. Apollo said finally, "I thought you the most cursed of women."

The Tarot of Perfection

She came to them disguised as a young girl, an apprentice

"What?" Julia said. Her hand went up before her face as if to shield her.

"But now I see that in fact you are the most blessed."

"What are you talking about?" Her voice sounded childish to her.

Dr. Apollo waved her fingers at the specks of light. "The Splendor are here."

"I don't understand you."

"I'm sorry, I thought you might know the term. It's a collective noun, like pride of lions, or murder of ravens. Splendor of spirits."

"Oh." Julia glanced quickly at the colored lights in the air.

"Exactly," Dr. Apollo said. "But that is not their form, more like the tracks they leave." She leaned forward. "Please understand. There are people who have labored for years to build up fortunes only so that they may have something to sacrifice, so that the Splendor may know they are serious. And here they are. For you"

"But you said I was cursed."

"A melodramatic word. Forgive me. It implies malevolence, and that is not the case here. Do you know what a *geas* is?"

"No."

"It's an old Irish word. It means a harsh obligation laid on someone, often by a magician or someone with divine power."

Help us. Free us. Julia said, "So someone has put this *geas* on me?"

Dr. Apollo shook her head. "I don't think so. I think the Splendor themselves have chosen you."

"But why? I mean, there's nothing special about me."

"Are you sure? But it doesn't matter, really. All of us are what we are."

And my husband? Is he a Beast? But instead of asking that, Julia only said "Do you know why I'm here, then?"

"No, I'm sorry. I'm a seer, not a mind reader. I can answer many questions, but not until people ask them."

"Oh of course," Julia said, and blushed. She told Dr. Apollo about the trees, and the voices, though not what first had brought her to the enchanted cottage.

"I see, I see," Dr. Apollo said, though in fact she had closed her eyes and begun to rock back and forth, with her arms wrapped around herself. If Julia had not been so desperate for an answer she might have run from the room. For nearly a minute this went on, and then slowly Dr. Apollo came to a rest until finally she opened her eyes. Or maybe tears forced them open, for she was crying now, fat tears that chased each other down her sharply angled face to fall onto the snake-headed woman in the glass.

Julia closed her own eyes for a moment, only to open them immediately, for she'd seen a horrific vision—a headless woman, standing upright in a long purple dress, with blood jutting from her neck.

"Yes," Dr. Apollo said to Julia's gasp, "a terrible story."

"Tell me," Julia said, though she was not sure she wanted to know.

"It happened a long time ago. Nine women gathered together to study sorcery. It was that very grove of trees they met, your grove."

"No," Julia whispered, "not mine," but Dr. Apollo only continued, "They were not evil, just reckless. Women in that time were allowed so little, and they wanted simply to prove that they existed. They did dangerous things, and made even more dangerous promises, and in their recklessness they attracted a genuine horror."

A beast Julia thought, *like my husband.*

Dr. Apollo said, "She came to them disguised as a young girl, an apprentice. They began to teach her, or so they thought. To impress her they committed greater and greater crimes, all done as if asleep, in a dream. They would wake up weak, nauseous, with blood on their hands and faces, and think how something was terribly wrong, how they should run from their lives before it was too late. Then night would come, and they would forget, and go breathless to the grove, to give another 'lesson' to their cold-eyed student.

"At last she pushed them too far. She induced the idea that they would truly impress her if they killed a young boy. They had picked out a victim, a servant's son, when something woke in them. They brought the boy to the grove but at the last moment sent him away.

And then they beheaded the woman. Though they destroyed her she cursed them. She trapped them in the trees, where they must remain forever until a woman frees them."

Julia wanted to roll her eyes, or laugh at this strange story. But she could hear the sad cries in the trees, and she could still see that headless woman, the jets of angry blood. She wished she hadn't come, wished she could just walk away from this odd woman with her "Splendor of spirits." And walk away from the house as well. It was only a six month lease, she could just drive off, as everyone in town seemed to expect her to do. But instead she said, "What woman? I mean, how will she know she's the one to do it?"

Dr. Apollo closed her eyes a moment, then said, "She will be a woman who has escaped from a beast."

Julia jumped up. *So it's true*, she thought, and wanted to run. "How much do I owe you?" she said.

Dr. Apollo sighed. "Nothing. I've caused you too much distress without taking your money as well." She picked up the foil-wrapped object and held it out. "Take this," she said. "For when you feel weak."

Julia took it gingerly and unwrapped the foil. It was a cookie, she saw, shaped like a snake. She put it in her bag. "Thank you," she said, then walked quickly from the room. In her car she thought again, *So it's true. I was right about him. He is a beast, and I escaped him.* But why did that mean she had to go help those women? If you escaped, didn't that mean you were free?

That night she went back to the grove, back inside the circle. She wore jeans and a tee-shirt because they helped her feel more determined, and she carried the knife held tightly in front of her, in case the branches tried to lock her in. And she put Dr. Apollo's snake cookie in her pocket, though she didn't feel hungry, let alone weak. "It's not fair," she said when she reached the trees. "I mean, I'm sorry for what happened to you—" (she thought how they'd brought it on themselves, but she buried the idea)—"But don't I get to live my life? I escaped the Beast. Don't I get to be happy?" The wails only swirled louder. "I don't even know what to do!" Julia said.

The branches twisted in the windless air like grief-stricken women waving their arms above their heads. Julia turned around in tight circles, the knife in front of her, moonlight on the blade. "Oh no," she said, "you're not going to close me in. I escaped the Beast, I certainly can escape you." And indeed, when she took a step forward two of the trees separated their branches, as if frightened of her, and she left the grove.

The voices surged at her as she walked away. "Help us! Save us!"

She turned and once more held up the knife. "What happens if I cut you down? Where do you go then?" She'd said it in anger, but maybe that was the answer. Maybe if she just chopped down the trees she would free them. But when she imagined it, when she saw herself swing an axe at one of the dead trunks, an incredible pain shot through her head, and she nearly fell to the ground. It struck her now that others must have tried to cut down the trees, if just to get rid of the noise. Just the fact that the trees still stood meant no one could do it.

"Help us!" they wailed, and Julia shouted back "I don't know what to do!" She hurried back to the house and locked herself in.

She fell on the bed, the knife still tight in both hands. Maybe Dr. Apollo was wrong. Maybe it made no difference that she escaped the Beast. Because if the trees would not let her cut them down, if they could do the same thing they'd done to anyone else who tried to get rid of them, then maybe she wasn't meant to help them at all. Maybe the best she could do was escape them, just like she'd escaped the Beast.

Dawn finally came, the end of the third night, and she knew she would have peace, or at least silence, for another month. As the cries faded away she finally fell asleep. The knife dropped to the floor.

Over the next week, Julia tried to put the whole thing from her mind. She tried to read, go for rides, clean the house. None of it worked. The house seemed dark and chilly, even when the Sun came through the windows. She felt very cold, unable to get warm even when she drove into town and saw everyone in shorts and sandals. She became scared that the women had stolen part of her and she would drift further and further from herself until her body moved aimlessly in the world and she too became trapped in the grove.

It was all so unfair. If a woman who escaped a Beast was supposed to end the curse, shouldn't she at least have some idea of what to do? Finally, it struck her. What if she *hadn't* escaped? She'd run away, yes, but did that actually make her free? Suppose he managed to track her down?

She remembered that evening in the kitchen, when she'd imagined sinking the knife into his heart. She'd scared herself then, and ran. But maybe the vision had been true. Maybe she was *supposed* to kill the Beast. How could you free yourself if you didn't kill the thing that wanted to devour you?

She was standing in the kitchen when this realization came to her. It was a sunny afternoon, just before another full Moon, with light scattered across the tomatoes and green peppers she'd cut up for a salad. Sweat broke out on her face and hands, and she had to grab hold of the sink edge to keep from falling. It was so obvious, why hadn't she seen it?

It was just such a moment when she'd first known the truth. She'd stood in the kitchen and understood that however Charming her husband might appear to her sister and everyone else, he was a monster, a Beast, and she should take the knife and…and cut out his heart.

She sat down at the small wooden table where she ate her meals. She discovered that she was holding the knife, though she did not remember picking it up. She stared at it, the way the light danced on the tip. Yes, she'd known what to do, she hadn't needed any Dr. Apollo. Kill Mark, escape the Beast, liberate the women in the trees. Of course, she hadn't known then about the women, but it didn't matter. She must have known unconsciously, because she could see it so clearly now, herself, the knife, the chopping board, Mark chattering alongside her. Or the thing that called itself Mark. She laughed. Maybe Dr. Apollo could tell her *that*, the true name of the Beast. But the name didn't matter. She'd seen who he really was that night, and knew exactly what she must do.

Only, she'd gotten scared. Run away. She could hardly blame herself. It was all so strange. She shook herself slightly, like someone trying to wake up. There was something—something wrong. Something wrong with her mind, the way she was thinking. She stared at the knife, squeezed shut her eyes, opened them again. How could she—

Pain shot through her head. She gasped, bent over. Without thinking she grabbed the knife, held it in front of her so tightly her arms shook, as if to fend off some invisible enemy. *Please*, she thought, *make it stop*.

Maybe it was Mark. Yes, of course, that must be it. She'd gotten away just in time, but it wasn't enough, she needed to escape him once and for all. How could she have doubted it? It was all so clear. And with that clarity, the headache suddenly vanished. She straightened up, took a long deep breath, and smiled. How good it was to know what to do.

With a cheerful hum she went through her clothes until she found a red silk scarf to wrap the knife. Then she dressed in the tee-shirt and jeans she'd worn to the grove the night she'd returned from Dr. Apollo—her "determined" clothes. She laughed. All set now, she grabbed her purse and keys, and set out on her mission.

She drove fast, and except for gas made only one stop, when she impulsively veered off the main road, found a consignment store, and bought a purple blouse to replace the dull tee-shirt. She didn't know why she did this, it just seemed a good idea. She didn't stop even once for food. She did buy a large bag of pretzels and a bottle of water at one of the gas stations, but both lay on the seat next to her, unopened. She didn't sleep.

Julia arrived at her house, the pale green raised ranch she'd shared with the Beast, at 1:22 AM. As she drove down the street, past rows of houses almost the same, she became scared she would find him gone. Or maybe with some new woman who didn't know what he really was. She imagined the woman's scream as she burst into the bedroom, and her very different scream after Julia had jammed the knife into the Beast's heart, after the woman had seen the face change into its true self. Then she would thank Julia for saving her.

But all Julia saw was Mark's car in the driveway, and no light in the windows. As she let herself in the back door a queasiness washed through her but she ignored it. This was not a time for weakness. She stepped silently through the kitchen and the living room.

How neat it all looked. No dirty plates in the sink, no magazines scattered on the couch. Was some woman cleaning for him? Or was he keeping everything just right in the hope she might return?

She stared at the knife in her hand. What was she doing? Why was she— As she tried to form the thought pain struck her again, and she had to hold onto the sideboard in the living room. *It's him* she told herself, *the Beast*. But it seemed almost as if some other voice was saying those words to her. She tried to think clearly, figure out what she needed to do.

You know what to do, the voice said. *Kill him*. She made her way into the bedroom. It must be warm, she realized (though she herself didn't notice), for Mark lay half tangled in the pale yellow sheet, the white summer blanket bunched at the end of the bed, as if he'd kicked it off. *Hurry*, the voice said, *before he wakes. Don't let him confuse you.*

At that moment, the Moon must have come out from behind a cloud, for light scattered across Mark's body. And with it came the wails of the women in the grove. It didn't matter that they were hundreds of miles away, she heard them as clearly as if she stood in the middle of the trees. They were frantic, keening now. *They're telling you not to stop*, the voice said. *This is your only chance*. Julia stepped forward, and as she did so the pain eased in her head, and as she raised the knife above Mark's it eased even more. *You see?* the voice said, *Do it*.

Julia was about to strike when a memory came to her. She and Mark were at the zoo, by the lion's cage, and there was a little girl, with her mother, and the little girl couldn't see above the people, and the mother wasn't strong enough to lift her up, so Mark hoisted her up on his shoulders. It was such a simple moment, but as she tried to hold onto it the pain cut through her head again, and the voice warned her *This is your only chance*, and the women's cries swirled all around her.

She thought, *I don't know what to do. I'm not strong enough*. And at that moment she felt a warmth in her pocket, and she remembered the odd little cookie Dr. Apollo had given her—"for when you feel weak."

With the knife still raised in her right hand, she jabbed her left in her jeans pocket and found the cookie. As the gold leaf paper fluttered to the floor the pain in her head cut her so sharply she thought she would break open. *No*, the voice warned her. *Stay with what you have to do.* Somehow she managed to put the cookie in her mouth.

It had a spicy ginger taste. She swallowed it in two bites. And then the pain was gone. And with it went not only the agony in her head, but also a kind of cloud, a confusion that felt like it had lived in her for many years, like a spell cast when she was a little child.

Alongside her, a woman's voice said "Kill him now, before he wakes up." Julia turned in surprise to see that there was someone else in the room. A woman in a long purple dress stood just to her left. It took a moment of staring at the woman's cold face to realize it was her own face. Except that the hair was longer, and the dress old-fashioned, and the eyes like polished stone, the woman looked exactly like Julia herself.

The woman opened her mouth to speak, then stared back at Julia. "You can *see* me," she said. Now the eyes shifted to the side, and Julia realized the woman was looking at the knife. A hand with long perfect fingers—Julia's hand, only better—reached out.

Julia lifted the knife out of reach. With both hands she held it all the way to the side, tensed her muscles, and then she swung it around with all her might, and all her heart.

The room shook with a cry of anger and pain. And then the entire head fell to the oak floor, and like fragile painted glass it broke into a hundred pieces. Dark jets of blood shot up into the air. They looked, Julia thought, like a dead tree.

And in that moment she found herself back in the grove. At first it all looked the same. There were the woven branches, the moonlight. But then she saw there were leaves, every one of them alive and young. And the sounds had changed. The insistent wails had vanished, replaced by the interlaced melodies of birds. She heard them, soft and beautiful, before she could spot the birds themselves, but then they all lifted above her head. They looked like crows, but instead of black their feathers were silver and gold. Or maybe the Moon just lit them with color, for they'd begun to fly up into the light, round and round in a tighter and tighter pattern, as if they traveled the inside of a cone. Their songs swelled with sadness and joy, and a gratitude that filled Julia's lungs and heart.

She watched them a long time, as they became smaller and smaller, their songs no more than fluttery whispers, until at last silent light swallowed them, and Julia stood alone in a soft grove of trees. She looked down at the knife now, still held loosely in her hand. Black stains shone dully along the blade. There were stains on her hands as well, and the purple blouse she'd bought on the way to Mark. "The woman who escaped the Beast," she said, and then she crouched down to use it one more time, to dig a hole in the moonlit dirt.

When she'd buried the knife, along with the purple blouse, and stamped down the dirt, she looked all around once more at the soft trees. She saw them then, colored specks of light, bright and sharp among the leaves. They darted all about, brighter than fireflies, far more of them than she'd seen with Dr. Apollo. "Splendor," she whispered, and as if she'd called them they began to circle round her, in and out of her hair, all over her face and hands. She closed her eyes, tilted back her head, and breathed in a music of light. She had no idea how long she stood there, how long they swirled around her, but when she finally opened her eyes they were gone. She stood a moment longer in the quiet moonlight, and then walked slowly back to her enchanted cottage.

What would he say? Would he tell her about a dead body, a headless woman, found in his bedroom? Were the sheets covered in blood? And if the police came, and took the woman's fingerprints, would they tell him his wife lay dead on the floor, and how did he explain it? Or would he simply say "I had the strangest dream about you." In the end he said only, "Julia! Oh my God, Julia. I've been so worried about you. When are you coming home?"

Maybe it was all just a dream. When she'd walked back to the cottage that night her car had stood in the dirt driveway. And yet, the hood was warm, and when she'd looked inside she saw the tee-shirt she'd taken off, crumpled on the passenger seat, next to the water and pretzels.

She drove more slowly this time, took a full three days to return to the house. She was about to open the door with her key when she decided to put it away and rang the bell.

Mark must have seen her, or else he'd been waiting for her all day, because he opened the door before the chimes had died down. "Hi," he said, and with a weak smile, "I haven't changed the locks, you know."

"I know," she said.

They stood there a moment, and Julia could tell he wanted to grab hold of her, pull her against him, and was blocking the door in the hope she would step into him. Finally, he just stood aside, and she moved past him into the living room. It was as neat as it had been the other night, but now the table was set, with the good silver, and candles, and a bottle of wine. She looked at him. He was so hopeful, so scared. She wished he could just kiss her, and she would wake up, and all the confusion would be gone.

She took a breath. "I might as well tell you right away. I'm not staying."

"Why?" he said. "What's going on? I don't even know why you left."

"I'm sorry, Mark. It's not you."

"Is it someone else?"

"No, no, it's nothing like that."

"Then what? What happened?" She could hear anger inside the pain, and it occurred to her that she would not have noticed that before. The idea gave her hope.

She said, "I can't explain it, Mark. It's just—I had to get away."

She could hear him swallow tears. "When you disappeared like that, at first I was scared, worried about a car accident, even murder. Then you called your sister, and suddenly I was really angry. I thought, what the hell is she doing? I thought there was a guy, or you'd gone crazy. But when you called, and said you were coming home—" The tears were putting up more of a fight, but he kept them down. He went on, "I figured you would come back, and hell, I don't know, that it would all be okay. I figured we'd just…"

It was hard to look at his face. She said sadly, "Live happily ever after?'

He smiled. "Yeah, I guess that was what I was hoping for."

"I love you, Mark."

"And I love you. Very much. Can't we just—"

"No. At least not now. I'm sorry. Maybe ever after will happen some time, but I just can't do it now. I'm sorry, Mark. More than you can know." She let him hug her now, a long time. And then she left.

For Deborah Nagle

The End

Carolina in the Morning

Once upon a time there was a girl named Caroline whose father came back wrong from the war.

Before her father went away Caroline and her parents lived very happily in a green house with yellow shutters, in a nice neighborhood at the edge of town. Sometimes her father would play a game with the radio, saying "Let's see what's on this morning." Then he would pretend to turn the dial, and would make various noises, as if they came from different stations. Finally he would sing "Nothing could be finer than to be with Carolina, in the mo-o-orning," and pretend it came from the radio. Between verses he would say "Listen, honey, they're playing the song written just for you. It must be number one, they play it on so many stations."

Her father used to tell her that people wrote that song because she was born with the Sun. Before her, everything was dark and cold, but when she came into the world light appeared for the very first time. Then he would hug her, and tell her that her hugs kept him alive, they were the best food he could ever have. Caroline's mother would laugh, and say "But you'll still have some pancakes, right?" Then they would all eat a wonderful breakfast. Afterward, Caroline and her mother would draw pictures, or run races in the hills behind the house.

When the war came, Caroline's father didn't want to go. It made no sense, he said. But he'd joined the army when he was younger, and now they were calling up anyone who'd ever served, so he had no choice. He went away, and when he returned everything changed. He sat in the corner and just stared out the window. If Caroline tried to hug him he snarled, like a frightened dog. Her mother tried to tell him he needed help, but he slapped her, or shoved her away from him.

He was very skinny, and seemed to get skinnier every day. It didn't matter what he ate. Sometimes he would eat everything on the table, even the food on Caroline's plate, ignoring her when she said "Daddy, that was *my* hamburger." Other times he just stared at the plate, or knocked it to the floor. It didn't matter. He just got thinner and thinner.

Sometimes his old self would come back. He would hug Caroline and tell her how sorry he was, or talk to Caroline's mother about plans for the future. Then something would annoy him—food overcooked, a sudden noise, even Caroline's laughter—and he would yell, and hit them. Once, Caroline woke up to hear her father singing, so softly it was almost a whisper, "Nothing could be finer than to be with Carolina, in the moorning." "Daddy!" Caroline called and jumped out of bed. He was staring out the window, but when he heard her he turned around. His face twisted, as if something had terrified him. He went to his bedroom and slammed the door, and when he came out he wouldn't look at her.

Every few days, at sunset, he became even more agitated than usual. He would rock back and forth in his chair, and rub his arms up and down as if he was trying to clean himself. Then he would jump up and run from the house. When he came back he was always very subdued, worn-out. If Caroline spoke to him he walked right by.

One evening she decided to follow him. She had learned to move very quietly so that her father wouldn't notice her during his angry spells. Now she stayed behind him, out past the edge of town to the top of a squat hill that overlooked a flat area with junkyards as far as Caroline could see. There were no buildings or trees on the hill, but Caroline hid behind an old stove that someone had left there.

A few minutes later a long black car with darkened windows came up the hill from the junkyards. "BTG" read the license plate, with curls of flame painted around the edges, and no other identification. It parked a short way from Caroline's father, and then a large thick man stepped out. He looked like a football player who'd let his muscles get soft but hadn't lost any of his toughness. He wore a black leather suit with a red tie, and snakeskin boots with pointed gold plates covering the toes. He had shiny black hair brushed back in an old-fashioned style, and a mustache that looked like it was made of tiny steel spikes.

He smiled as he looked out over the junkyards. When Caroline's father went up to him he made a big show of being startled, but Caroline was sure he'd seen her Dad off to the side. "Christ on a stick!" the man said, then laughed, as if he'd made a joke. "Didn't I tell you to leave me alone? I'm not going to get you soon enough? You want me to take you now? Come on, then, I got a jar in the back seat." When he said that, his tongue flicked out between his lips, and Caroline could see that the tip of it was in two parts, one black, the other red.

"You shouldn't take me at all!" Caroline's father said, in a voice that was loud with fake courage. "You have no right."

"What the hell do I care about right? Do I look like some kind of do-gooder?"

"But I never signed a contract!"

The man roared a laugh. "You think I need that? What, you think you're supposed to sign your damn name in blood or something? Hell, I don't do retail any more. I've got government contracts these days. Bulk sales and guaranteed delivery."

Caroline's father reached into his jeans pocket. "Here," he said, and held out his hand with something shiny in it. "Take this. It's very valuable." Caroline cringed back when she saw it was his wedding ring.

The man took it and tossed it in the air a couple of times before he put it in his jacket pocket. When he began to turn away again Caroline's father said "So you'll let me go?"

The man grunted. "Why the hell would I do that?"

"Because I gave you the ring." The man shrugged. *"Please,"* Caroline's father said. "I've got a daughter."

"Oh yeah? You offering her in your place?"

Caroline's father stared at him, and his face twitched. But then he said "No! That's not what I meant."

The man laughed, said "Yeah, sure it wasn't. See you around, pal." He turned back to his car. Before he got in, however, he turned his head towards the stove where Caroline was hiding, and sniffed loudly. Caroline grabbed some foul-smelling mud and rubbed it all over herself. The man sniffed again, shrugged, and got in his car.

Caroline's father stood a long time staring after the car, but when it was out of sight he stuck his hands in his pockets and walked down the hill. He seemed to get skinnier in just the hour it took him to walk home. As soon as she could, Caroline took a long shower, rubbing and rubbing her skin to get the mud off, and thinking about the man in the gold-toed boots sniffing the air.

Two days later Caroline woke up to find nothing left of her father but his clothes on the floor with a few rotted teeth, some fingernail clippings, and an oily black liquid that stank like rotten eggs.

After that, Caroline's mother began to drink. She was never without a bottle in her hand, and drank from the time she woke up until she passed out. In between drinks, she sometimes screamed at Caroline or hit her, but mostly she sat on the couch and talked to the floor, as if there was someone underneath it. One day, Caroline came home from school to find her mother throwing things wildly around the house while she screamed curses at some invisible enemy. When a bottle narrowly missed Caroline's head she realized she had no choice but to run away.

In the years before the war Caroline's parents had given her a generous allowance. She'd saved most of it, so that now she had enough for a bus ticket to the city and food for a few days. When she arrived at the bus station packs of wolves dressed in jeans and t-shirts and leather jackets smiled at her and invited her to come home with them for a good meal and a warm bed. They looked just like young men, but Caroline could see the wolf in them. If she let them they would devour her, or feed her to older wolves who liked to eat nine year old girls. But they couldn't hurt her if she didn't go with them, and so she hoisted her backpack on her shoulders and marched past them to the open streets.

Over the next months Caroline learned the secrets of survival. She made sure to keep herself as neat and clean as possible, and to walk with purpose, as if on an errand from her mother. She found out which homeless tribes liked children and would keep away the wolves, and which ones would sell you or eat you. Sometimes she slept with a tribe but more often she found an opening too small for an adult and shielded from any police or social workers who might be walking down the street. From another street child she learned how to use computers in libraries to break into police records systems and see if anything was being done to find her. When she saw that her mother had reported her missing she almost called her to tell her she was all right. For a few days she would stare at every pay phone she passed. But when she checked again, nothing further had been done to find her, and she decided it was better not to call.

In large restaurants, she noticed, people often asked for whole meals to be "wrapped" and then forgot to take them. You could pick up the bag and walk off, as if your parents had sent you back for it. And sometimes, if she went to a motel early in the morning, people drove off and left the door open. She could sleep for several hours and take a long shower before the maid would come to clean the room.

Most important for a child on her own, she learned how to hide. She found a large piece of cloth, so dull and ordinary, the color of dust, that when she crouched down and covered herself with it she might as well have been invisible. She cut the smallest possible slit for an eye hole. In the side pocket of her back pack she carried little bottles of different smells, such as old kitchen grease or gasoline, that she could sprinkle around so that even police dogs wouldn't notice her. And she taught herself to stay completely still and breathe without sound so that no one could hear her.

Every few months the tribes of homeless people would gather in an abandoned lumber yard at the edge of town. They would burn the leftover scraps of wood and beat on old oil cans while they cast pictures of government officials into the fire. The first time Caroline heard about this she avoided it, for fear of wolves, but when it came round again she decided to go. Maybe she could spot her mother among the drinkers, or maybe even her father. After all, he might just have left his clothes behind and run off, and now couldn't remember the way home again.

She'd been there a couple of hours, and was tired from all the noise and angry drunks, when suddenly everyone stopped whatever they were doing and began to shake in fear. "What is it?" Caroline asked an old woman who had crouched down behind a pile of rotten wood.

"It's *him*" the woman whispered. Her teeth began to rattle, and she clenched her jaw to stop them. "He's coming down the road. The fortune-tellers saw it in their cards." She looked up at the sky. "Please, please, don't let him take me."

Caroline looked around, saw scattered cards on the ground where just a moment before the fortune-telling ladies, in all their torn scarves and fake antique coins, had been promising happiness to lines of people. At each spot she saw the same two cards, a sort of horned monster holding people on chains, and a wagon or chariot pulled by black and white dogs.

Caroline knew she should wrap herself in the cloth and blend in with the dirt, but instead she walked quietly towards the gate. "What are you doing?" the woman said. "He'll see you. He'll know we're here."

Caroline put her finger against her lips and stared at the old woman, who shrank back. Near the gate, Caroline finally cast her cloth over her as she squatted down beside a pile of old metal and wood. A roar sounded from far down the road. Louder and louder it growled, until Caroline thought either the ground would open and swallow her or she herself would break apart. Just when she thought she couldn't stand it a large black car came around the curve and stopped just past the gate. "BTG" the license plate read. The door opened and a snakeskin boot with a gold toe appeared. And there he was, with his leather suit, his spiked mustache, his black and red tongue.

He walked into the lumber yard a few feet only to stop with his feet slightly apart, like a boxer, and tilt back his head to loudly sniff the air. Then he laughed. "What the hell are *you* people worried about? You think I'm running low on garbage? You think I'm going to grab you and shove you in my mouth? Christ on a stick." He laughed again. "I'll get you when I want you. Count on it." Then he sauntered back to his car and drove off.

It took the tribes a long time to come out of their hiding places, but when they did they seemed to try just to forget what had happened. They drummed more loudly, they drank faster and battled over the cheap wine, they grabbed each other and staggered behind the woodpiles where they gasped and screamed and howled at what Caroline guessed was supposed to be pleasure. No one would talk about the man with the red and black tongue. "Who is he?" she would ask people who would stare at her as if they had no idea what she was talking about, or else threaten to hit her.

Finally she found the old woman who'd warned her to hide. The woman was crouched down behind a broken gasoline pump, as if the rusty metal tank would shield her if the man came back. Caroline squatted next to her on the dirt. "Who was that?" she said.

"Shh," the woman said. "You don't want him to hear you. He'll come back and get you."

"That's silly," Caroline said. "He must be miles away by now."

"No no no," the woman whispered. "He can hear everything. He can hear you talking about him anywhere in the world. That's what makes him come after you. It's true."

Caroline thought how the man had already said he didn't want any of them, but she kept the idea to herself. She said "Where does he live?"

"Are you crazy? You can't go there. He'll grab you and eat you. And then he'll put whatever's left of you in a jar. You have to stay far far away from him."

Caroline reached into her backpack and took out an old chocolate chip cookie she'd found in the street. The woman stared at the half-melted chips. Caroline said "Tell me where he lives and you can have this." The woman tried to grab it, but Caroline held it out of reach. "You don't get it till you tell me."

The woman spoke so low Caroline could hardly make out the words. "He lives at the top of the world in a huge black house with red columns and a big fence. Follow the bird with the gold in its mouth and she'll take you there. But you mustn't go. You mustn't. No one will ever see you again." When Caroline held out the cookie the woman grabbed it and scurried away.

Caroline walked for weeks, with no idea where to go except up. She climbed hill after hill, through towns and villages, past farms and woodlands. Cars zoomed past her, and sometimes the drivers slowed, and she could see them squint in the mirror, but she kept her purposeful-errand look and no one bothered her.

One night, in a small city, she was so tired that when a band of homeless children offered to take her back to their camp in an empty building she went along. When she got there, however, loud boom boxes made her nervous. Sure enough, when she listened underneath the thumping music she could hear weeping children. *Wolves*, she thought. Her new friends were runners for wolves. Sometimes this happened to the children who were captured. First they resisted, but if the wolves hurt them long enough they changed, became wolves in training. Cubs.

For an hour Caroline pretended to party, laughing and dancing, though she made sure not to eat or drink anything. As soon as it seemed safe she asked for the bathroom, and let one of the cubs lead her to a fetid room with broken plumbing. When she went inside he stayed by the door, to make sure she didn't sneak out and run away. Despite the smell Caroline stayed in the room a long time, until finally the cub stepped inside to check on her. She hit him over the head with the lid from the toilet tank, then ran from the house.

As soon as she reached the street she heard voices and boots from around the corner. Quickly she cast her cloth over her and peeked out. Three wolves appeared. They wore heavy boots with steel toes, black leather jackets, and jeans with wide belts. The belts had ornate brass buckles, and in the center of each the letters "BTG." It took all of Caroline's discipline not to make a noise. Was she getting close? Or did he just have helpers everywhere? As soon as the wolves entered the house Caroline took off. When she was sure she'd gotten far enough away she made anonymous phone calls to the police and a local television station to report the house. Then she found a place to sleep. The next morning she continued her journey.

From the very start of her quest every time Caroline saw a bird she studied it to see if she could spot any gold in its beak. After so many days with nothing but ordinary crows and blue jays and wrens and sparrows she'd decided the old woman was just making something up, but she continued to look. And then the morning after her escape from the wolves she saw a glint in the sky. She looked up to see a large goshawk riding the currents above her. Pale gray, with black bars, and red eyes, its rounded wings stretched nearly four feet across.

Caroline began to cry, for she remembered a day long ago, when her father had taken her to a mountain lake, where he'd pointed out all the different birds to her. Goshawks were his favorite, he'd told her, because they flew so high no one could catch them. Caroline wiped away her tears so she could see more clearly. The bird looked tired, the wings heavy. For a moment it angled toward the Sun, and there it was again, the glint. A ring, Caroline saw. The bird carried a gold ring in its mouth.

There was no way she could keep up with the bird but at least she could see its direction . She slept that night among a small stand of dead trees. It was cold, and she found it hard to breathe in the damp heavy air. All night bad dreams twisted her face, but she made it through and woke up just in time to see the goshawk fly overhead in the other direction, with no gold in its mouth.

Caroline trudged uphill all day, on steep rocky ground, past barren trees and ruined houses she would never have entered, even to escape a storm. The air smelled of engines and rotting meat. Some time in the late afternoon the goshawk passed again. Its beak held a gold coin.

It was almost dark when Caroline came around a curve and there it was, at the very top of a hill. Caroline had never seen a black house before, and never a house that large. It looked like a hole in the sky. The red pillars reminded Caroline of temples she'd seen in a book long ago, when her mother used to sit Caroline in her lap and take her hand to trace the shapes of the letters. The pillars only made the house more squat and ugly.

There was no fence, but steel towers with cameras on top surrounded the house. There was no way to get up there without being seen, and no way to get inside the huge black door.

Caroline spent that night behind a large rock that she hoped would shield her from the cameras. The rock was part of a small circle of stones about the height of "Mr. BTG," Caroline's name for the man with the double tongue. The ground inside the stone circle actually looked a little more comfortable than any place around, level, without the broken glass and bits of metal that Caroline had to brush away from her hiding place. But there were ashes in the center of the circle, and even though they looked very old Caroline did not want to sleep there. So she hid behind the rock and ate the last bit of some roast pork chow fun someone had left behind in a restaurant, and drank from the bottle she'd filled days ago from a library water fountain. She thought of how her mother would take her to the library, and at night her father would discuss with her all the books they'd chosen. Finally she fell asleep.

She woke to the sound of trucks. From behind the rock she peered out at a line of delivery vans driving up to the black door. As the first truck reached the door Mr. BTG came out to supervise the delivery of his packages, some large, some small enough to hold in one hand.

For a couple of hours Caroline watched this procession. When it began to thin out she went down the hill, out of sight of the house. At a sharp curve, where the trucks had to slow down, she waited until she saw a van with no one behind it. As it passed her she jumped out and grabbed the handles on the back doors.

When the truck got to the top Caroline jumped off and crouched down on the far side, where Mr. BTG couldn't see her as he yelled at the delivery man not to break anything. Her whole body wanted to shake with fear but she clenched her fists, and pressed her lips together, and forced herself to stay still. When the last crate was safely inside BTG walked out to the truck to sign the invoice. At that moment Caroline dashed inside the house.

The house seemed to consist of one gigantic room, so big Caroline couldn't make out the end of it, with walls so high she could barely see the ceiling. In the center of the room there was a plain metal desk with a single drawer, and on top of it a keyboard and a flat screen computer monitor. Next to the monitor stood a large glass jar, empty. A black metal chair with red leather padding stood in front of the desk, with cases of beer and potato chips piled on either side.

A few feet away a large cage stood on the floor. Big enough for Mr. BTG himself to step inside, the cage held the goshawk, who flew nervously from side to side. It looked exhausted, its feathers burned at the edges, yet it seemed to avoid coming to a rest on the cage floor. When Caroline looked down she discovered why. The floor was strewn with the remains of dead birds. There were feathers of different shapes and colors, bones broken and whole, even crushed bird heads scattered across the floor.

Much of the rest of what Caroline could see was filled with shelves and shelves and shelves. In the back of every shelf stood empty glass jars. They looked very old, with a film of grease on them, and in some a smear of blood on the inside. In front of the jars every shelf was filled with endless collections. There were stamp albums, porcelain plates with scenes from old television shows, guns and knives and other weapons, cases of watches and old fountain pens, rows of Bibles, lunch boxes with pictures of cowboys and superheroes, antique dolls with their heads cut off, piles of polished bones, crosses and stars and other religious symbols. Among them all stood endless bowls piled high with gold—rings, pendants, ancient coins, whatever was small enough for a bird to have carried it away in its beak.

Caroline only had time to look around before she heard Mr. BTG heading back her way. She crouched down by one of the empty crates and covered herself with the gray cloth. Then she reached into her bag of little tubes of camouflage to scatter smells of grease and stale food around her. When that was done she made herself absolutely still.

BTG planted himself in the middle of the room and called out "Any damn fool stupid enough to stay behind? Figure to take something away with you? Let's look around." His right eye left his body and like a fly darted all about the room. When it came to Caroline's hiding place she had to control herself to stay still. The eye moved on, and soon returned to its master. Then his right ear flew around the room and it too hovered over Caroline but traveled on. Finally he flared his nostrils and sucked in air with a large noise. "Good," he said, obviously satisfied, and sat down at his desk.

Peeking out from the slit in the cloth, Caroline watched him type in his password. She was pretty sure it started with B and went on for a lot of letters, but he typed it so fast she wasn't even sure how long it was. An email program came up on the screen. Caroline noticed that a lot of the addresses ended with ".gov." but again, it all went by too swiftly for her to really see anything. Next came auction sites. One after another, he made constant bids, and as he did so, he talked to himself, ridiculed the competition, even spit on the floor. Finally he called up an auction page titled "Immortal souls," but now instead of bidding he sat back with a bottle of beer and laughed loudly at each offering.

He got up, stretched himself, then walked over to the bird cage. "Lock, lock, hear my word," he called out. "Let me at my ugly bird." The door swung open, and he stepped inside to where the hawk flew frantically about, trying to get away from him. BTG said, "where do you think you're going?" Quicker than Caroline could see, his left hand grabbed the bird by the neck. The poor goshawk cried out in pain and flapped her wings.

With the bird in his hand, BTG stepped out of the cage. He said "Feather, feather, slave to me. Go and fill my treasury." Then he flung up his arm and released the hawk. She circled up and up, through the shelves and stacks of boxes, past the empty jars and endless collections, until she reached a narrow window high on the wall.

As Caroline watched the bird, she thought *don't come back. Escape.* Was it possible the hawk was free? She wouldn't know for hours, she thought. If it didn't return for the rest of the day, then maybe— No. To Caroline's surprise, less than a minute passed before the hawk flew back through the window, so tired it could hardly flap its wings to keep itself from plummeting to the floor. In its beak it carried a gold locket. BTG let it alight on his arm. He took the locket, then flung the bird into the cage. "Lock, lock, hear my word," he said. "Imprison now this ugly bird." With a loud clang the cage door swung shut.

Without even looking, BTG tossed the locket over his shoulder into one of the bowls. Once again, he sat down at his computer. Whistling, he took out several bottles of beer from a case alongside his chair and twisted off all the tops. He drank one of them in one long swallow, and started on the next before he turned back to his computer to press control-s on his keyboard. The words "Permanent Guests" appeared on the screen against a background of flames. A moment later the words gave way to a list of numbers that filled the screen in a seemingly endless scroll.

He jabbed Enter and the screen stopped, with one of the names highlighted in black. A moment later a small figure of a man appeared in the jar alongside the computer. Caroline put her hand over her mouth to stop a gasp. The man twisted and grunted as if in great pain. He wore some kind of white robe, with gold decorations, and a white skull cap. Caroline thought he looked familiar, someone she might have seen on TV or magazine covers.

A faint voice, obviously in pain, spoke in a foreign language. BTG grunted. "What?" he said, "you think your pig Latin's going to impress me? Forget it, Pappie. I know how to speak it right, remember? I was there in the old days." He set the screen scrolling again. The old man disappeared from the jar.

BTG stopped at another file. This time the jar filled up with an old woman in a torn dress streaked in blood. Horrified, Caroline recognized the woman who'd told her how to find the house, "at the top of the world."

"It's not fair," the woman said, "I didn't do anything. I never harmed anybody in my whole damned life."

BTG laughed so loudly the empty jars shook on the shelves. "Damned. That's a good one. Maybe I should let you go for telling a good joke." He paused, then said "Nah. I'll just keep you."

"But why?" the woman said. "I didn't do anything."

"Why should I care what you did? What do you think I am, Santa Claus? You think I care if you were naughty or nice? I'm a collector. You just seemed like a good thing to round out my collection."

The woman fell to her knees and covered her face, weeping. Needles jabbed at her from all sides and she screamed. BTG listened blankly until finally he moved on to someone else. All afternoon he did this, while drinking beer and stuffing potato chips in his mouth.

Finally he got drowsy. He turned off the computer, leaned back in his chair, and fell asleep.

Very carefully, Caroline crept out from her hiding place. She had no idea how long he would stay asleep but all she needed was a moment or two. From her backpack she took out the little vial of sleep drops and emptied the whole thing into the open bottle of beer that stood on his desk alongside the monitor. Then she dashed back to her gray cloth.

A moment later, BTG shook himself awake like a giant dog. He scratched the side of his face, then reached out for his beer. He drained it all in one swallow. A good thing, too, because a moment later he gagged and tried to spit it out. Too late. Before he could even bend over to try and vomit he fell back in his chair, asleep.

Caroline dashed forward and slid the chair out of the way, careful not to touch him. She wasn't afraid he would wake up, she just didn't want any part of him against her hands.

She had to get into the computer. As soon as she hit the first key, however, the screen changed from a screensaver of flames to a box that asked for a password. B, she thought. And long, at least a dozen letters. Three words? Beginning with the letters B, T, and G? She tried Boss Tyrant Greed. No good. Boom Terror Guns. Nothing. Bite Tiger Girl, Bitter Tasty Garbage, Boy Tough Gorgeous, none of them worked.

She had to find it! What would she do if she couldn't figure it out? She thought of her father, and riddle games they used to play. Her whole body began to shake with tears. *No,* she told herself. She stood up straight and hit her hands against her thighs. Concentrate! The desk drawer. He probably kept his password there, in case he forgot. She grabbed the narrow brass handle. Locked.

Suddenly she had an idea. She ran over to the cage, where the hawk flew anxiously from side to side. Now she took a deep breath and said as firmly as she could "Lock, lock, hear my word. Freedom for this pretty bird." She almost burst into tears when the door swung open.

The Tarot of Perfection

There it picked something up in its beak and flew back with it. A key!

The bird flew out, circled Caroline joyously several times, then came to rest on her upraised arm. Caroline took a deep breath. With the tip of her fingers she stroked the bird's silky back, then whispered "Feather, feather, fly for me. Bring me back the mystery." She raised her arm, and the bird took off.

It climbed in circles, tighter and tighter, closer and closer to the window. Caroline held her breath. If it went out she didn't think she'd ever see it again. Just before the open window it veered to the right, to one of the shelves. There it picked something up in its beak and flew back with it. A key! With one glance Caroline could see it would fit the locked drawer of the desk.

"Thank you," she whispered to the bird, who'd once more perched on her arm. "Thank you, thank you." In a firm voice now she said "Feather, feather, go home free. Thank you for your gift to me." The goshawk circled her once and then spiraled up again, stopping only once, at one of the bowls, before it flew out the window and into the world.

Her hand shook so much she could hardly get the black iron key into the hole. But she did, and the drawer opened instantly. She leafed through what looked like contracts with various government agencies until suddenly there it was, a small piece of paper with three words on it. She laughed. Of course! It didn't actually say "password," but she was sure that was what it was. With great care she typed in "BetterThanGod." The screen went blank and then a second later changed to a long list of files.

If only they'd been names, but all there was was a string of numbers, with no system she could figure out. Caroline highlighted one at random and hit enter. It turned out to be a little boy, about Caroline's own age, dressed in the kind of clothes she saw in books about children hundreds of years ago. He cried out to her in some language she didn't understand, but she knew just what he was saying. "Help me. Please help me."

Caroline held her breath, pressed her lips together. *Please, please,* she thought, *make this work.* She touched the delete key. A box popped up. "Are you sure you want to delete this file?" She clicked the mouse on yes.

The boy vanished from the jar. Caroline stared at the empty space, terrified she'd done something awful. Then she heard a voice behind her. When she turned, there he was, alive and dressed just as she'd seen him. Weeping, he hugged her, kissed her on the cheeks, the forehead. Caroline pointed to the door. "Go," she said, and though the boy probably didn't know the word he ran off.

Just then Better Than God stirred and made a gurgly noise.

Caroline grabbed the back of the chair and raced with it as fast as she could to the open cage. Without ceremony she dumped the whole thing, man and chair, onto the pile of dead birds Then she cried out "Lock, lock! My command. Stop forever evil's hand." The door shut with a loud clang.

She was just back at the desk when she heard the confused sounds of someone waking up in a strange place, followed by "what the hell?" then "Hey! You little bitch. Get away from that desk. Come here and open this door. Bitch! Come here. Do you know who I am? Do you have any idea who I am?" He kicked the cage door. "I'll burn you!"

Caroline didn't turn around. Instead, she hit "control, a" so that all the files became highlighted together. Her hand shook as she hit the delete key. A box came on the screen. "Are you sure you want to delete the entire contents of Permanent Guests?"

Behind Caroline, Better Than God yelled "Don't touch that! I'll get out of here, you know I will. I've got friends. You have no idea what I'll do to you!"

Caroline clicked the mouse on "yes."

The room began to fill up with people. More and more of them at every moment. There were men, women, children, babies, all ages, all colors, costumes of every country and every age. They screamed in surprise, they yelled, the jumped up and down, they jabbered in every possible language. They pushed aside the shelves and boxes so that all the empty jars crashed and shattered, and all the stamps and guns and plates and lunch boxes and everything else was swept away in a rush of people.

One more thing, Caroline thought. As quickly as she could, before someone might knock over the computer, she inserted a virus into the running system. Now, if Better Than God got out and tried to restore his lost files the virus would wipe out his entire hard drive.

She was just in time. She heard a loud boom, and when she looked around discovered that the house itself had collapsed. The crowds of people now filled the hillside and all the land she could see. When she turned around the computer and desk were gone, and so was the cage with Mr. Better Than God.

So many people! She tried to look at faces, but it was hopeless, how could she possibly find one person among such a multitude? And then she heard it. In the midst of the cries and laughter, a sad voice sang softly "Nothing could be finer than to be with Carolina, in the m-o-o-o-rning."

"Daddy!" Caroline shouted. She pushed through the crowd and there he was, looking on all sides, searching. "Caroline?" he called, "is that you? Is it really you?" When he finally saw her he gasped then "Oh sweetheart," he said as he took her up and held her tightly. "You found me. You saved me."

"I love you, Daddy," she said. "I love you, I love you."

"You saved me," he repeated. "It was—I could see you from a long way away, but I didn't—I didn't think it was real. Oh, Caroline, you really did it. You saved everyone."

"I had to, Daddy," Caroline said. "I missed you so much."

Her father began to cry now, and held her tightly against him. When her hair was all wet he finally pulled away and wiped his face. "How do we leave here?" he said.

She took his hand. "This way, Daddy. We have to go down the hill."

They traveled two weeks until finally they saw the house. To Caroline's surprise it was clean and freshly painted, with a row of flower pots across the front. No sooner had they stepped on the path than Caroline's mother ran out to meet them. When they had all hugged and greeted each other she told them that the strangest thing had happened.

"I was sitting in the dirt," she said. "I was so—so helpless. Suddenly I heard a loud flapping. At first I didn't look up but when I finally did there was a great big goshawk flying all around me. I tried to push it away but it wouldn't go. But then I saw that there was something all bright and shiny in its mouth.. I don't know why, but I held out my hand. And this dropped into it." She pulled at a thin chain around her neck and out came the wedding ring Caroline's father had given to BTG all those months ago."

"Oh darling," Caroline's father said. "I'm so sorry."

"No, no," she said. "It told me you were coming back. I knew as soon as I saw it. Both of you. I knew you were on your way home to me."

She led them inside." In the living room Caroline saw a large charcoal drawing of her taped to the wall. All around it were photos of Caroline, many of them torn or burnt or stained with whiskey. Nervously, her mother touched the photos and said, "I found these when I was cleaning up. They made me miss you so much I drew the picture."

Caroline stared at the picture a long time, even though the eyes were so sad it made her throat hurt. Finally, her mother came and lightly touched her hair. "Come in the kitchen, sweetie," she said. "There's pancakes."

They ate breakfast, and hugged, and cried, and kissed each other, and when Caroline went back in the living room the picture was smiling. She knew then that they would all live happily ever after.

For Frankie Green

The End

Simon Wisdom

I

There was once a man named Jack Wisdom. The name may have been unfortunate, for neither he nor his parents were especially wise. Some unknown ancestor, they used to joke, must have done something smart, and now all they could do was try to survive having such a difficult name. Jack lived in a small town and worked for a nearby branch of a large company, where his bosses did not expect any great council or wise decisions, only hard work and loyalty. Jack was good at these things. His father used to tell him that because of his name people would expect too much of him, and that it was best to play it safe. Jack did as his father said, and as his bosses said, and after some years he became a technical specialist, with a large white house on a good street in the better part of town.

Sadly, he was lonely. He was in his thirties and had seriously dated only two older women, once in college and once ten years later. The first had left him to marry a law student, and the second—well, the second had just left him. Jack tried going out with women at work, or the daughters of his mother's friends, he'd even considered dating services, though such a practice seemed unsafe if not downright unwise, and so he'd never submitted his name. Then, when he was thirty-four years old, he met a woman who talked to squirrels in the park.

Jack had gone to a city halfway across the country on assignment from his company. He was there for weeks, and because his clients often needed time to try out his suggestions he often found himself with his afternoons free. At first he tried going to movies, or a sports bar to watch games on television, but both made him feel lonely. He didn't want to think what people might think of him, so he stayed away from such places. He tried watching television by himself in his hotel room but he became too restless. So he began to take walks in a large park a few blocks from his hotel.

One afternoon he saw, some distance away, a woman on a park bench leaning forward with her hands on her knees as she apparently talked to a pair of squirrels, one gray, one red, who stood upright on their hind legs to twitch their noses at her. Occasionally she would laugh, as if the squirrels had made a joke, while at other times she nodded solemnly. Jack was so surprised by this that at first he did not notice the sparkling lights, like fireflies, that darted all about her. After a few minutes the woman gave each squirrel a small piece of bread, and then with a wave of her hand sent them away. As the squirrels dashed off to eat their prize, the lights also left, spiraling above the woman to disappear into the sunlight.

The woman was tall, with long red hair, curly with a good cut but no special hairdo. She wore what looked like a heavy silk dress, deep red streaked with blue, and a blue shawl loosely draped over her shoulders. Around her neck a gold chain held a pendant that reminded Jack of the medical symbol of two snakes wound around a stick, except the snakes looked more real and the stick had a crown on top.

Once the squirrels had left, Jack wanted to go speak to her but he was afraid she would notice him staring, so he turned around and pretended to examine some flowers. When he finally looked again she was gone. That evening, Jack lay on his bed with the TV on, and his eyes on the ceiling, and he thought about the woman. You've got to be pretty squirrely to talk to squirrels, he thought. And what would that have made him if he'd talked to her?

The next day he went back to the park and she was there, dressed in purple this time, with a light gray jacket. She was talking to the squirrels again, and nodded, or gestured with her hand as if it was a real conversation. And once again, Jack turned and pretended not to see her as she got up and walked away. On the third day she wasn't there, and as Jack left the park he kicked a garbage can in his anger at himself for not speaking to her. That night he dreamt of her, strange scenes that lasted only seconds. She was fighting with him, or she was standing in a cold room, surrounded by people who were so pale and miserable they might have been dead. Or she was holding something over a fire, and he was screaming at her. He woke up angry, and then sad. For a moment he thought he saw those odd fireflies in the room with him, but it must have been an aftereffect of the dream.

Over the next two days Jack's clients insisted on showing him the sights. When he finally got a free afternoon again, he nearly ran to the park. At first he didn't recognize her, for instead of long dresses she wore jeans and a light chenille sweater, with her hair pulled back. In fact, it was only the squirrels that made him realize it was her. She leaned closer, as if they whispered secrets, and at one point he thought she was crying. When the squirrels finally scampered off he made himself walk towards her with what he hoped was a casual stroll. "Hi," he said. "Those have got to be the friendliest squirrels in the park."

She smiled up at him. "All squirrels are friendly," she said. "But they're still wild, you know. It's not good to think of them as pets."

He smiled back, hoping he would not appear either scary or pathetic. "You certainly seem to get along with them pretty well. It looked like you were having a great conversation." He laughed a little, to show he was joking, though not too much.

"Oh, they're good for news and gossip, but you know, they have their own point of view, they *are* squirrels after all, so you really have to sift through what they say for something useful."

She sounded so serious, despite a smile at the corners of her mouth, that he didn't know how to answer. He was never very good at small talk, anyway. So instead he just said, "Hey, look, do you think maybe you'd like to have a cup of coffee? I don't actually live around here, but I noticed a nice place a couple of blocks over."

The strangest look passed over her face, a sadness mixed with some kind of struggle. Jack was wishing he could just run away, maybe go bang his head against the wall for pushing too soon, when she sighed, then smiled sweetly at him and said "That would be lovely. Thank you."

"I'm Jack Wisdom" he said as she stood up.

"What a wonderful name. Mr. Wisdom. Is there a Mrs. Wisdom?"

"No, no, not at all. I mean, my mother, but…" He let his voice trail off before he sounded even dumber.

She laughed. "That's all right. I knew you weren't married."

"You knew?"

"The squirrels told me, of course. They're really very observant."

"What?" He looked around, as if he'd catch them spying on him.

She laughed again. "I'm sorry, I really shouldn't tease you. My name is Rebecca. Rebecca Vale."

"There's no Mr. Vale, is there?"

"Only my father."

"Good," he said, then quickly added "I mean, because I don't have any squirrels to give me that information."

As they walked out of the park Jack said "So you're a nurse?"

"No, I'm afraid that that's a job that has never appealed to me very much."

"I'm sorry. A doctor, then?"

She looked at him with a smile that might have made have made him feel foolish but instead lifted his body as he walked. She said "Not a healer of any kind. Not even a pharmacist."

"Oh sorry. It's just that necklace. Isn't it a symbol of the medical profession?"

"Yes, though in fact that's actually a mistake." She touched the pendant. "This is called a caduceus. In ancient times it was a symbol of prophecy. Of seers."

"Seers? You mean, like fortune tellers?"

"Afraid so."

He laughed, thinking she was teasing him again. "Great profession."

"Not really," she said.

From then on Jack spent every free moment with Rebecca. They went to movies, they walked around town, they even went to a museum where she surprised Jack with how much she knew about Renaissance painting. Sometimes that sadness would come over Rebecca, but then she would smile at him, or kiss him, and it would all be okay.

One evening they walked from Jack's hotel to a small park alongside the river, and as they sat on a bench watching a sailboat Rebecca said, "Jack, suppose you could do something really wonderful, something that would make you very happy. But suppose you also knew that it wouldn't last, that it would end horribly, that it would even destroy you. Would you do it?"

Jack said "I don't know. I guess it would depend on how good it is."

"The best," she said. "The absolute best."

"If it was as good as you, I'd do it in a second."

She began to cry and laugh at the same time. "Oh, Jack," she said, "I love you."

"I love you, Rebecca. I never thought I'd love anyone the way I love you." He kissed her, and hugged her, and kissed her again. Because he felt so good, and because he wanted to dispel any sadness in her he said "And I don't even care what the squirrels say."

She laughed and clapped her hands. "Right. What do a bunch of squirrels know anyway?"

The first time he went to her apartment he didn't know what to expect. He'd never been to a fortune teller's house before. To his relief there was no crystal ball, no weird symbols painted on the walls, no magic wands or lurid idols. There was, however, a small round table, oak, with two polished candlesticks, one brass, one silver, and in between them a deck of Tarot cards on a blue silk scarf painted with images of stars. Jack had seen Tarot cards before. Back home, at the annual Christmas party, one of the lawyers brought a deck and told fortunes for whomever wanted it. Jack could never decide what surprised him more, that a lawyer would do that, or how many people, sensible people, his boss included, lined up for readings.

"Wow," he said to Rebecca, "You really are a fortune-teller."

"Please," she said, "we prefer the term prophetic-Americans."

"So you really believe in all this stuff?"

She laughed. "I do it, of course I believe in it."

"So will you tell my fortune?"

"No."

She took his hands. "Sweet Jack," she said, "you are a man who found love when he didn't expect it. Isn't that enough to know?"

"I guess" he said.

"Good. Then kiss the fortune teller."

They got married the night before Jack was due to go home again. Jack could never remember if he'd asked her, or if it was the other way around. It didn't matter. nor did it matter that she didn't want a fancy wedding, didn't want any family present. She was the only one left, she told him, and there'd be plenty of time to meet his relatives later, when she'd come home with him.

When they were filling out the papers Jack suddenly thought about names. "Did you want to, you know, keep your own? It's okay. I know lots of girls, women, are doing that these days."

"Darling Jack," she said, "do you really think I would pass up the chance to be named Mrs. Wisdom?"

When they arrived at Jack's house the first time Rebecca told him how sweet it looked, "full of Jackness." Inside, she moved from room to room like a child in a playhouse. Except—in the living room she stopped and stared for several seconds at the fireplace.

"Honey," Jack said, "is something wrong?" For a moment he thought he saw those sparkling lights again, inside the fireplace, but if so they quickly vanished up the chimney. "It's nothing," Rebecca said, and began to talk about possible colors to paint the beige walls.

For two years they lived happily ever after. Jack's parents liked Rebecca immediately, and Rebecca was thrilled with her new family. Jack worried what people might think of his wife's profession, or if odd people would be showing up at all hours. To his relief, Rebecca said she was happy to take a break from her work and just enjoy life. Every now and then she would see someone, mostly longtime clients who depended on her, but she promised to see them when Jack was at work, and not to advertise. Jack never asked her about these people and she never spoke of them. Sometimes she would come home crying, or tight-lipped, and he wouldn't know what to do, how to help her. After awhile she would sigh, or rub her eyes, and then look at him with a soft smile, and everything would fine again.

One night in September Jack woke at three a.m. to discover his wife gasping for breath, shaking. "Bec?" he said. "What is it? Do you need an ambulance?" He grabbed for the phone.

"It's okay," she said. "It was just a dream. Go back to sleep."

He wrapped his arms tightly around her, held on until she stopped shuddering. "It's okay," he echoed her. "It was just a dream." After a minute she calmed down enough that he could let her go. She turned on her side, and Jack wondered, as he slid back into sleep, if she was still awake.

Four days later terrorists attacked. Everyone Jack knew was weeping with frightened eyes, except Rebecca, who immediately began to organize local relief contributions. Jack never asked her about her dream.

He also never asked for any predictions about his work. Occasionally he would joke about "getting a reading" but never actually did it. However, at dinner he would tell her about a problem, or pending decision, and the next morning she might casually make a suggestion. He never told her how these suggestions worked out, and she never asked, but once at a company picnic, when she met Charlie Perkins, Jack's boss, Charlie told her "Your husband's really something, you know? Any time we can't figure out what to do we just tell Jack and he comes back the next day with the right answer. I guess they don't call him Mr. Wisdom for nothing." Jack stared at the grass.

They were married for two years and seven days when Rebecca told Jack she was pregnant. He yelled and danced around and offered to go get a case of non-alcoholic champagne. Rebecca said very little, only asked Jack to hold her. Jack hugged her for a long time, then said "Sweetheart? Is this okay? I mean, the baby. I'm being a real jerk here, but I guess that's nothing new."

She shook her head. "You're never a jerk. You're sweet and lovable."

"I mean about the baby. I'm so excited I didn't even check how you're feeling about it. You okay? Because if not, and you want to, you know, do something, it's okay. Really."

"No, no," she said, then sighed. "Did you ever do something you know will turn out, well, bad, just because you know absolutely it's the right thing to do?"

He took her shoulders. "Sweetheart, nothing's going to turn out bad. I'll take care of you and if there's any problems we'll get the best doctors in the world."

"I'm not worried about that," she said.

"Then why are you so upset? You think I'll stop loving you cause there's a baby? I'll never stop loving you. Nothing can change that. I loved you the moment I saw you. I'll love you forever."

She stared at him. "You promise, Jack? Do you promise you'll love me no matter what?"

"Absolutely."

She closed her eyes. "Oh God," she whispered.

He held her again. "It's okay," he said. "you'll have a fine pregnancy and we'll have a wonderful boy or girl."

"Boy," she said, her voice muffled by his shoulder.

He let go slightly so he could look at her. "Are you sure?"

"Uh huh."

"Did you get an ultrasound? I mean, it's okay, but I would have liked to have been there."

She gave him that sweet smile of hers. "No medical tests," she said.

"Then how can you— Oh. Right."

She said "Can we go get that champagne now?"

The pregnancy went easily. Rebecca insisted on a midwife, though she agreed to see a doctor as well. The midwife, Jennie, said she'd never seen a baby so eager to be born. They named him Simon, for Rebecca's grandfather, though she'd never mentioned him before. From the first moments Simon looked at the world, and especially his mother, with curiosity and delight. Jack's sister said, "He has your eyes."

"Come on" Jack said, "he looks like his mother. Lucky kid."

"Oh, the shape of his eyes, yes. But that slightly bewildered look? Jack, that's you."

It wasn't until a few days after the birth that Jack admitted to himself how scared he'd been that Rebecca somehow would reject the baby. If anything, she went the other way, almost obsessed with spending every moment with him. And yet, at the same time, she got sadder and sadder. When she was not feeding or rocking Simon she would stare out the window, silently crying. Jack did everything he could to cheer her up. He brought her presents, he took her on weekend trips, he played with Simon with her, but none of it seemed to work. After four months he took her hands, and suggested, as gently as possible, that she see a psychiatrist. Post-partum depression, he said, was perfectly normal, it came from hormonal changes, and best of all, it was treatable.

Her smile was far sadder than tears. "Sweet Jack," she said, and touched her fingertips to his cheek. "This has nothing to do with my hormones. I wish it did."

It was late on a cold October night when the disaster happened. Curiously, Jack had been thinking of disaster when he went to sleep, for he'd been watching the late news, with reports of floods in Florida, earthquakes in California and Peru, and arsonists bringing down a library in Prague. When he woke up and smelled burning wood he thought he was dreaming. But no, it was part of the "awake-world," as Rebecca sometimes called reality. "Honey?" he said sleepily, and turned over to discover she was gone.

From downstairs he could hear her voice. She was singing, or chanting or something.

Simon, Simon

Rhymin' Simon

Take the time an'

Stop the crime an'

Set the children free

Jack said "What the hell?" and got out of bed. The first thing he saw when he came into the living room was the Tarot cards. They lay on the floor, fanned out in concentric circles of color and action. And then he saw his wife in the epicenter, crouched down in front of the fireplace, her back to him as she leaned toward the high flames. "Bec?" he said. "What are you doing?"

She turned, her face a mix of rage and despair. "Get away!" she yelled, then "Please, Jack. Trust me."

Only then did he see that she'd immersed her arms up to the elbow in the flames, and in her hands she held Simon, bathed in fire.

Jack screamed, leaped at her. With one hand she tried to push him away while the other held onto Simon. She was no match for him. He beat back her flailing hand and shook her away, then grabbed the baby from her. Clutching Simon against his chest he screamed "You lunatic!"

He thought she might try to fight him, or maybe run. Instead, she just stared at him. "Jack, Jack," she said, "I wasn't hurting him."

"Not hurting him? You were holding him in a goddamn fire."

"Feel him. Feel his skin, his clothes. Is he even hot?"

Jack started to shout again, but stopped. It was true, he realized. Simon slept peacefully against him, his beautiful soft skin pleasantly cool. Stubbornly he said "You were trying to kill him. I got to him in time."

She shook her head. "I was trying to save him. But you're right. You got to him in time, and now it's too late." She jumped up now and ran from the room. Jack didn't try to stop her.

That was the last time Jack ever saw Rebecca alive. He heard her weeping as he went first to their bedroom and then the baby's room to pack a suitcase, the whole time holding on tight to Simon, as if Rebecca might swoop in and snatch their baby the moment Jack set him down. But Rebecca never appeared, and when he'd taken what he thought were the essentials he grabbed his keys and the suitcase with his free hand, then ran from the house.

It was just six in the morning when he arrived at his parents' house. He didn't tell them what happened—he couldn't bring himself to reveal how crazy she was, as if they might say I told you so, even though he knew they'd always liked her. So he just said that she'd fallen into depression and had refused help and had tried to harm Simon.

Mr. and Mrs. Wisdom loved Rebecca but they loved their son more, and baby Simon most of all. Over the next days Grandma took care of the baby while Jack's Dad did his best to cheer him up, and every now and then suggest that maybe Jack should talk to her, maybe now she'd accept psychiatric help. Jack didn't answer.

Every day Rebecca called. The first time, Mrs. Wisdom picked up the phone and when she heard Rebecca's voice asking for Jack she got all confused, and said she would check if Jack was there. "It's Rebecca," she whispered to her son, who stared at the television as if it was a wall. Jack shook his head. The older Mrs. Wisdom told the younger that Jack wasn't there, she had no idea when he was coming back, and in fact had no idea where he was.

"And Simon?" Rebecca asked.

"He's fine," Grandma said, and wondered if she'd revealed too much. Or not enough. Could she have encouraged Rebecca to get help?

"Please tell Jack to call me," Rebecca said, and Grandma promised and hung up. After that, they screened all the calls and followed Jack's insistence that no one talk to Rebecca, though her messages begged Jack to call her.

"Shouldn't you talk to her?" his father said. "She really sounds sorry." Jack shook his head.

One evening, Jack's father took him to a basketball game. When the phone rang, and Rebecca came on the machine, Mrs. Wisdom was tempted to pick it up, to see if she could get through to her daughter-in-law that she had to take the first step of seeing a psychiatrist. Rebecca was obviously heartbroken, and Jack was clearly in pain. Just as she reached for the phone she realized Rebecca was saying something different this time, something crazy.

"Jack," Rebecca said, "Please listen to me. Please. You have to remember. Twelve years from now a man will offer to take Simon on a special trip. *Don't let him do it.* He'll seem so kind and wonderful, and promise you every safeguard. Don't listen to him. Don't let Simon go with him. Please, Jack, you have to remember. I don't care what you think about me, what you tell Simon about me. Just don't let him do it. *Remember.*" She was crying when she hung up the phone.

Mrs. Wisdom replayed the message three times. Rebecca sounded so desperate. But that very desperation, about something so obviously insane, was clearly a sign of her madness. Jack had a right to hear the message. Of course. But what would it do for him, except entrench him even deeper in anger? After the third time she sighed deeply and erased the message.

Two days later, on a Sunday morning, Jack was sitting at the kitchen table, feeding Simon pureed carrots and occasionally snatching bites of a bagel and cream cheese. His mother had offered to feed the baby so Jack could relax—working long distance seemed to tire him even more than going to the office—but Jack wanted to do it himself. It was late Autumn, and leaves swirled around the back porch. Jack's father stood at the window with his mug of coffee. He laughed and took a sip. "There's something you don't see every day," he said.

"What's that?" his wife asked.

"There's a pair of squirrels scratching at the back door like they wanted to come in." Louder he said "Sorry, boys. No nuts or berries available today."

Jack jumped up so quickly he dropped the spoon, and Simon began to cry. Jack handed the baby to his mother then rushed to the window. "Jack?" his mother said, "What's wrong?" and his father said "Son? What is it?"

Jack stood at the window, his mouth open as if he couldn't breathe. The squirrels turned toward the window, stood on their hind legs, and tilted their heads up to stare directly at him. "Oh my God," he said, hardly more than a whisper.

His father touched his shoulder. "Jack?"

The squirrels ran off now, along the pathway to the driveway and under Jack's car. Jack turned, stared at his father, and then his mother, as if they, not the squirrels, were strange and alien. Finally he said "It's Rebecca. I have to go to her. She's dying."

His mother gasped, and his father said "Dying? What are you talking about?"

Jack didn't answer, only ran for his keys. "Take care of Simon!" he yelled.

When he arrived home late that afternoon Rebecca's car was in the driveway, and he didn't know if that was good or bad. At the back door he dropped his keys twice before he discovered it was unlocked. "Bec?" he yelled as soon as he was inside the house. "Rebecca? Are you okay?"

The first thing he saw was the word "Remember!!" written in red marker all across the blue living room wall. He stared at it a moment, shook his head, and ran into the kitchen, the den— He found her on the floor of the bedroom, her red and black silk dress scrunched up around her knees, her face empty as the rumpled bed, her hair bunched up under her neck. He wanted to re-arrange her, set her out properly, but he knew from television that that wasn't allowed.

He didn't even realize he'd squatted down until he saw his own hand touch her cheek, her neck, her forehead. Cold. She was cold and thick and empty. He lost his balance and fell back against the bed. How long, he wondered, how many hours? He tried to remember how long it took for a body to get cold but nothing came to him. Was she already dead when the squirrels showed up? Is that what they'd wanted to tell him? He'd thought they were summoning him, but maybe it was already too late. He couldn't decide if that made it worse or better.

He needed to call someone. 911? Was it an emergency if it was already too late? And he needed to call his parents, they would want to know. And Simon. He had to tell their perfect son that his beautiful crazy mother would never see him again, never hold him— he shook the thought away. He didn't have to tell Simon. Not now, at least, not for many years. But he had to call the police, or the doctor, someone.

Abruptly he jumped up and rushed down to the basement, where a leftover half gallon of blue paint stood on a wooden shelf with a couple of brushes. Upstairs he painted over the giant command to memory with great slashes of green. No one would see her craziness, no one. Did she really think he would forget her? He wanted to shout "How could you think that? You were everything to me." But his voice wouldn't work, only his arms and shoulders as they obliterated the insults of madness.

At last he called 911, and then his parents. They didn't ask how he'd known.

At the funeral Jack's father and a cousin had to hold him up. At least it wasn't suicide. Brain aneurysm, the coroner said. Sudden, quick, and unforeseen. "It just happens," he told Jack. "It just happens. There's no way to predict something like that."

When they got back to the house Jack let his parents take care of Simon and set up for visitors. "There's something I have to do," he said. He searched the bedroom and everywhere else he could think of for Rebecca's Tarot cards. He wanted to tear them up, piece by piece. They were gone, or at least were no place he could find. Maybe, he thought, she'd come to her senses before the end.

Jack went home after that. His mother—once again the only Mrs. Wisdom—came for three months, leaving only when she was sure he was okay. Before she left she found a good day care for Simon, who was almost a year old. Jack resisted at first, said he was fine to work at home, but his mother told him he needed to get back with people. At the Happy Hands Center Jack's mother did almost all the talking. Near the end, as they were filling out forms, Jack suddenly said "You don't have anything to do with Tarot cards or anything like that, do you?"

Mrs. Beech, a large woman with heavy arms and tangled black hair, frowned at him. "Tarot cards? Now why would you think that?"

"Oh no, I didn't—" Jack stopped, not sure what to say.

"Maybe you'd be happier with a religious based center," Mrs. Beech said.

"No, of course not. I just—I had a neighbor who was always throwing Tarot cards, and it just seemed—I don't know, I guess a bad influence. I'm sorry, I shouldn't have said anything."

"Well, I can promise you we don't do anything like that here. We're pretty traditional."

"Good. Good. Thank you. Oh, one more thing. Simon has a kind of, I guess phobia, about squirrels."

"Squirrels?" Mrs. Beech said, and Jack's mother stared at him.

"When he was very little a squirrel scared him. He cried and cried. So if you see any squirrels around, could you chase them away?"

"Yes, of course," Mrs. Beech said.

Outside, Mrs. Wisdom seemed about to say something, then changed her mind. In the car she said "I'm so glad you're trying this.

You know, Jack, Simon needs to be with other children as much as you need to be with grown-ups. I know it's hard, but really, it's for the best."

And maybe it was. Simon emerged into childhood sturdy and curious, with a wide smile that attracted other children as much as adults. He had his mother's curly hair and large eyes, his father's wide hands. He seemed to like puzzles, or at least objects you could put together into some kind of shape. He could play for hours, it seemed, with blocks, or the soft colorful pieces of a baby jigsaw puzzle, arranging them into different forms, none of which made sense to anyone but himself. Though the other children liked him and often looked to him for directions he was just as happy all by himself. He learned to read very early, and soon the house was filled with books aimed at much older children. He loved fairy tales, and stories of dragons, and heroes who slayed monsters. And talking animals. At first, Jack tried to screen out such books, or cartoons. Soon he had to admit it was hopeless. From television to comics to toys the child universe was filled with jabbering animals. So he made sure Simon always knew the difference between fantasy and reality.

One night Jack dreamed that he went to check on Simon and lights flickered all about his son's head. In the dream, Simon laughed and grabbed at them, but they danced away from him. Jack ran at them, waving his hands as if they were flies or mosquitoes, and the lights streamed out the window. When dream Jack looked outside he saw a whole line of squirrels staring at the house. He yelled, and ran outside only to discover more squirrels out the front door and all around the building. "Leave us alone!" he yelled, and woke in his bed. Quickly he ran into Simon's room where the boy slept peacefully, hugging a stuffed elephant his grandma had given him. Jack made sure the window was shut, then looked outside. The trees and the grass looked clean and empty in the early dawn. For some reason Jack thought of "Remember!" scrawled across the living room wall. He shook the thought from his head like a dog shaking off water, then went to the kitchen to make a cup of coffee.

Simon excelled in kindergarten in all the ways a father wanted. The teacher, Mrs. Griswold, was amazed he could read whole chapter books. He was well behaved, and friendly, without seeming weak. He turned out to be a natural leader as well. "It's amazing," she told Jack one day. "The kids all seem to look to him to tell them what to do." She laughed, and added "To be honest, I think I'm feeling that way a little myself. Remember that field trip we took the kids on? To the petting zoo? Well, we came to a certain corner, with the bus, you know, and Simon suddenly said 'We have to turn here.' Well, of course I told him the driver knows how to go, and he was quite good about it, he just went back to playing Game Boy with Billy. But guess what? Two blocks later we saw a tree that had fallen across the road. Can you believe that? We had to backtrack to the corner where Simon had said to turn!"

That night, after he'd put Simon to bed, Jack sat at the kitchen table, wondering if he should take Simon out of school. He could home school him, maybe hire a tutor. But Simon was happy in school. He was smart, well-adjusted, everyone liked him—Jack rubbed his forehead. He was being ridiculous, he knew. School wasn't the issue. He went into his bedroom and picked up the framed photograph of Rebecca in the park. He'd taken it just after the wedding, when all the trees and sky seemed filled with light.

"Oh Bec," he said, "what have you done to our son? Is it true? Does he *really* have your eyes? I just want him to be happy. I want him to be normal. Is that so terrible? No squirrels, no Tarot cards, just a happy normal little boy." It struck him that she might have answered "But Jack, he *is* normal. Let him be who he is."

He closed his eyes and pressed the cool glass against his face. "God, Rebecca," he said. "I miss you so much."

II

Simon Wisdom was eight years old before he realized he was different than other children. Before then it had not occurred to him that other kids didn't know their grandma was about to call before the phone rang, or when Daddy needed help with something, or when something bad was going to happen in the world and you shouldn't watch television. Once, in kindergarten, he came home bruised where a girl named Susan had hit him on the arm. "It's okay," he told his angry father, "she just needed to hit someone." When his Daddy asked why, Simon said "Because her mommy's hurting her." Simon knew his Daddy was upset hearing this. He'd even known it would happen. He just didn't understand *why*. Didn't Daddy know what Simon was going to tell him? Didn't everyone know that Susan's mommy was hurting her? Daddy had said something about not knowing what to do, how he couldn't tell anyone because he couldn't explain how he knew. Simon couldn't understand that. He also knew that his Daddy was angry at *him* for some reason, but he couldn't figure out why.

It wasn't like Simon *always* knew what people were going to say. When Daddy asked him if he knew what everyone was thinking, Simon rolled his eyes and said of course not, how could he know that? But when he did know he just assumed everyone else did.

He was eight when he found out that his "talent," as Daddy called it, could get him in trouble. His teacher had sent him home with a perfect score on his multiplication test, with a note to his Daddy saying how proud she was of Simon's progress. Jack stared at the paper until Simon asked him, "Aren't you happy, Daddy? I got a hundred."

Daddy said "Seven times eight." When Simon didn't answer right away, his father sighed. "Simon," he said, "you don't really know this, do you?"

"I got a hundred."

"Yes, but you got it by reading the teacher's mind."

"Reading...?"

"Knowing what was in her head. You don't really know the times table, you just knew what was the right answer."

Simon moved back slightly. His father spoke calmly but his body vibrated with anger. Simon said, "But that's what you're supposed to do. Get the right answer."

"From the question, Simon. Not from the teacher's mind. It's…it's a kind of cheating." He said the word really hard, as if he wanted slam his hand on the table..

"It is not!" Simon's own hands clenched into fists. "I'm not a cheater, I'm not."

"If you read the teacher's mind that's cheating."

"No! I did what everybody does."

"That's not true. Most people don't get the answers that way. They have to study for them." He took a breath, controlling himself. "What you did, Simon—it's not fair."

"Yes it is!" Simon yelled, and ran to his room. Even as he said it, however, he knew his father was right. He thought about things kids said, and the way they got scared of tests, and for the first time in his life he considered the terrible possibility that he might be very different from other kids. Maybe that was why his father was so angry.

His father left him alone in his room a long time, and when he came back downstairs his father was reading a book. It occurred to Simon that if he concentrated really hard he might know just what Daddy wanted him to say. But that too would be cheating, and suddenly it was really important to Simon that he not do that. So he just said "I'm sorry, Daddy. I didn't know I was cheating. I won't do it again."

Daddy put down his book. "Come here, Sweetie," he said, and when Simon walked up Daddy hugged him so hard Simon couldn't breathe. When Daddy let go, Simon could see he was crying, and said quickly "I'm sorry."

"No, no," Daddy said. "I'm not angry at you. I was just—I was thinking about your mother. She would have been very proud of you."

Simon was surprised. He knew his father thought about his mother sometimes (Was it wrong to know that? Was it another kind of cheating?), but he almost never spoke about her. And there was a kind of anger in Daddy's voice, and Simon didn't understand that at all. Wasn't it good that his mother would be proud of him? He waited, but his father said nothing more, so he just said "I promise I won't cheat again. Ever."

"I'm sure you won't," Daddy said. "You're a good boy."

Simon wondered that night if he missed his mother. Could you miss someone you'd never known? Sometimes he dreamed of her. At least he thought it was her. In the dream he would see a woman far away, like the other side of the school parking lot, but when he would try to run to her so many buses would block the way she'd be gone by the time he could go there. Once he dreamed that he was walking with his grandma in the city, and he saw, across the street, a woman bent over a table, playing cards with somebody. Simon was sure it was his mother, and wanted to go see, but Grandma refused to listen, saying they'd be late for a party if they didn't hurry. In the dream he began to cry, and when he woke up he was gulping air and holding on tight to Mr. Axle, his favorite teddy bear, who was dressed in yellow overalls and carried a soft red wrench.

After Daddy explained about knowing the answers Simon wondered if his mother didn't want to see him because he'd cheated. Or maybe because he wasn't like other kids. Could Daddy have told her? It was so unfair. He didn't know it was cheating. He'd thought everyone knew those things.

From then on, Simon did his best not to know things that other people didn't. Most of the time it was easy, you just didn't pay attention, or you thought about television or something. But other times, especially when his father, or someone he liked at school, was unhappy, Simon had to hold back from helping them by telling them what they needed to know. He reminded himself that it was cheating, and no one likes a cheater, but sometimes it made him feel kind of throw-uppy, or feverish.

Three months later, a boy in Simon's class disappeared. His name was Eli, and he sat a couple of rows over from Simon but that day his seat was empty. Simon kept staring at it, even when the teacher told him twice to pay attention. As the day wore on, Simon started to squirm in his seat, for it seemed he could hear Eli's voice in his head, crying and crying. He tried to make it stop, for wasn't it a kind of cheating, even if it was just crying and not anything you could read? He tried, but he couldn't do it, it just got louder and louder. Now it seemed like Eli was calling him, not with his name or any words at all, just with a great pain that begged and begged for help, for someone, anyone, for *Simon*, to find him and help him.

Simon could find him. All he had to do was follow the noise in his head. He could tell the teacher, and the teacher would call his Daddy, and they would all go get Eli so he could stop crying. Only, that was cheating, so Simon held his fists tight against his body and did whatever he could to ignore the sounds.

School let out early that day. Lots of parents came and picked their kids up instead of sending them on the school bus. Even Simon's Daddy came, and said that they were going right home instead of to Day Care. Simon hardly paid attention, the noise in his head was so loud and he didn't want Daddy to know it was happening. He hated Eli, he wished he could grab him and yell at him to shut up, to leave him alone.

The crying stopped a few minutes after dinner. One moment it filled Simon's body, it filled the whole room, and the next it was just gone. For the first time Simon made a noise. He couldn't help it, it was like someone had hit him really hard in the belly, a pain so sharp he let out a scream before he knew he was doing it. His Daddy jumped up from his chair, said something that Simon didn't hear, and a moment later was helping Simon stand. Simon hadn't even realized that he'd fallen, or that he was on all fours and trembling, like a sick dog. His father led him to a chair.

"What is it?" Daddy said. "What's wrong?" Simon didn't answer. When is father went to call the doctor he said "I'm okay, Daddy. I just felt sick suddenly. But I'm okay now." His father looked at him a moment, then put the phone back on the wall.

Two days later the police found Eli's body in a burned out old house at the edge of town. Simon never really found out what happened but everyone at school was talking about "scary things" that someone had done to him, and a couple days later two state troopers, a man and woman in gray uniforms, came to assembly and warned all the kids against going away with anybody, even if he said their mothers or fathers had sent him. The grown-ups had their own assemblies as well. Twice that week his father went to a town meeting. He told the baby sitter not to open the door for anyone, for any reason. Both times he came home upset.

A week went by and everyone began to calm down. Kids went back on the school buses, all the teachers didn't stand around at recess, looking around nervously as if they were constantly counting to make sure no one was missing. Simon too began to feel better. For days all he could think of was Eli crying and crying and crying. He imagined his voice, very far away, saying "Why didn't you help me? You were the only one who knew."

On the day Simon stopped hearing traces of Eli his father looked distracted when he picked Simon up from after school care. Usually Daddy would ask him about school, or tell him what they were going to have for dinner (he wasn't really a very good cook but Simon would do his best to sound excited), but now he just drove. He seemed to have trouble breathing. When they got home, Daddy pulled into the driveway too fast and had to hit the brakes to stop from going into the garage door. He said a bad word, then took a deep breath. "Simon," he said, then stopped. Simon held himself really tight inside to stop from reaching out to touch what it was that Daddy wanted to say. After a moment, his father said "That little boy—Eli. Did you know—did you know anything about him? Where he was?" He stopped, then said "What was happening to him?"

Simon shook his head. "No!" he said loudly. "I'm not a cheater."

"I didn't say that" his father half yelled, as if they were in a noise contest. His face twitched. "I just meant—if you could have done something—"

"I'm not a cheater!"

"I didn't say you were."

"You said it was cheating to read people's minds."

"Well, yes. Yes, I said that. But—"

"I don't know anything. Okay? I don't know anything about Eli. He wasn't even my friend."

His father stared at him, then sighed. "Sometimes in extreme circumstances it's all right to do something that otherwise—"

"I told you, I don't know anything. Why can't you listen to me?" Simon began to cry, then rubbed the heels of his hands against his eyes, as if trying to push the tears back inside.

"Stop that," his father said, and grabbed his arms to pull his hands away from his face.

"I'm not a cheater, I'm not." He pushed hard against his father's grip.

Daddy wrapped Simon in a tight hug and held on until Simon stopped fighting him. "No, of course you're not," he said. "You're a good boy. I'm very very proud of you."

From then on, Simon began to have bad dreams. There were giant bears who took people prisoner in underground cages, or trees that gushed fire. Worst of all were the pieces of children. Simon would dream that he was walking somewhere—in the schoolyard, in the village where his grandparents lived, in the street behind the day care house—and at first everything would be fine, he'd be on his way to get a comic, or to pick up a baseball. Then slowly he would discover he was lost, in a place he'd never seen before. It would be late, with shadows that covered the bottom half of his body so he couldn't see his feet. As he began to get scared he would look for markers of some kind, signs of safety or the way home. At first he would seem to get help. A branch would point along the trail. A candy wrapper would contain some message, even if he couldn't figure it out. Then the objects would change, become fragments of clothing covered in blood and grease, a basketball shoe that looked as if a dog had ripped it with its teeth. Soon he would see actual pieces of children, a finger, bent as if it beckoned to him, a scarred knee. Most terrifying of all were the tongues that twisted about like agitated snakes.

There were never any faces or mouths but they made noise, a wailing sound, like children lost for a hundred years. Often he woke up at this point, for he would imitate the sound while asleep, and then his Daddy would rush in to wake him.

Over the next two years Simon became more and more what his father and the doctor called "troubled." He began to fail tests and have problems at school, sometimes for not paying attention, sometimes for talking back, or fighting. It seemed like he got in fights a lot.

He lost most of his friends. Kids who used to run up to him in recess now walked away when they saw him. It was so unfair, he thought, wasn't he trying so very hard not to cheat? They were just stupid, he decided. They couldn't read anybody even if they wanted to.

Before he found out that knowing things was bad, and everybody would hate him if he did it, he never really thought about it. Sometimes it happened, and maybe he could help someone, but most of the time there was nothing special. Why should he care if a kid next to him at lunch was hoping for a peanut butter and jelly sandwich but got tuna instead? But now he thought about it all the time. He had to make sure it didn't happen, and that meant he had to watch himself at every moment. Sometimes he got so tired he wanted to cry, but sleep was even worse. The dreams were there, like nasty dogs and wild animals waiting just outside the house.

His father took him to lots of doctors. There was Howard Porter, who'd been Simon's doctor his whole life, but then there were others he'd never met. Some talked to him, or asked him to draw things, or play games, or tell them about the dreams. Others attached funny wires to his head with gooey stuff, or made him lie very still inside a big noisy machine that they said was like a spaceship, except that was really dumb because it didn't go anywhere. He called these "wire doctors," because of the things they stuck on him. He liked them better than the play doctors. The tests were weird, but he didn't have to do or say anything.

With the play doctors he had to answer lots of questions, and that meant making sure he didn't cheat and know the right answer. One of them, Dr. Joan, asked him about his mother. Dr. Joan was pretty, with short blond hair and brightly colored dresses, but she never seemed very happy. She would lean forward and smile a lot, but she also would rub her hands as if trying to clean them, or tangle and untangle her fingers. Simon knew it was not polite to stare, but he wished she would keep them still.

Most of all, he didn't know how to answer her questions. Was he angry at his mother? Did he hate his mother? Did he hate his father? Did he love his father? Did he know his father loved him?

Other doctors gave him medicine. They said it would stop the dreams, make him less "angry," help him pay attention at school. The problem was, they also made him sick. It didn't matter which one it was, he would throw up and get a fever. They tried different colored pills (one of the doctors called them "magic beans," whatever that meant), they tried shots, but it was all the same, until finally his father cried, and hugged him, and promised not to give him anymore.

His grandmother took him to churches where the priests sprinkled water on his head and said what sounded like magic words but Grandma later said was just church talk. One priest held the sides of his head so tightly Simon worried his fingers would leave marks, then flung his hands away and yelled "Be gone!" None of it made any difference.

Throughout this time the only kid who stayed his friend was "Popcorn Jimmy," called that because his mom always packed a bag of popcorn in his lunch. They'd been friends since early in day care, and even though Simon was just as mean to Jimmy as to anyone else, Jimmy still hung around with him. "Weird and weirder" some of the kids called them.

One day at recess, when Simon was eleven, he was off by himself, kicking pebbles, when he heard a whimper. Surprised, he looked around and saw that no one was there. He heard it again, and knew somehow it came from the other side of the school. At first he was horrified that he had left a crack in the wall he tried to keep up against cheating. Then he realized, the voice was Jimmy. He ran as fast as he could, nearly knocking over a girl playing kickball. When he got to the other side of the school he saw Allen and Allen, two older kids who were gang types and thought of themselves as tough. They were shoving Jimmy between them and laughing. Jimmy's bag of popcorn lay scattered on the ground. "Leave him alone!" Simon yelled, and ran full force into the taller boy. Both he and Allen fell to the ground, but Simon got up first and threw a handful of dirt into the other Allen's face.

The Allens made noises of getting even, and said "Fucking weirdos," and laughed like they were in control. Then they strolled off, their hands in their pockets.

Simon helped Jimmy get up, then watched as Jimmy brushed himself off. "Hey, thanks," Jimmy said.

"Those guys are jerks," Simon said. He handed Jimmy the empty popcorn bag.

"Yeah." Jimmy looked around. "Hey, you want to go sit on the tree?" He nodded towards a tree that had fallen on the edge of the playground.

"Sure." Simon didn't really want to sit. He wanted to run away. He also didn't want Jimmy to feel bad so he sat alongside him. They both stared at the ground.

"Hey," Jimmy said. "How did you know—you know, what those jerks were doing?"

"I didn't cheat!" Simon said.

"Hey, man, I didn't say anything." Jimmy started to stare at Simon, then turned away. He laughed suddenly. "Look at that," he said, and pointed to where a pair of squirrels, one red, one gray, were eating the spilled popcorn. Jimmy laughed. "That's cool," he said.

Simon stared at the squirrels, his hands all sweaty. He knew his father hated squirrels, or was scared of them or something because he would shout and chase them away whenever they came anywhere close. Simon himself never thought much about them. Now he felt all strange inside as he watched them gnaw at the popcorn.

"Hey," Jimmy said, "you okay?" but Simon paid no attention, for the squirrels had lifted their heads, together, and it looked just like they were staring at him. He felt all strange inside, and for a moment became scared that he was dreaming again, and any moment now the popcorn in the squirrels' mouths would change to fingers, or tongues, and he would hear that terrible noise of all the sad children.

Lights darted about the squirrels' heads. It was hard to see at first in the sunshine, but they were all zipping in the air like fireflies, but they weren't, they were just lights. Simon watched them and sadness filled him, for he remembered the lights now, he used to see them sometimes when he was little, before he found out he was bad and had to control himself. The squirrels looked at him, and the lights jumped, and Simon knew the squirrels wanted to tell him something, but that was weird, and he better not let his Dad know.

Jimmy touched his arm. "Hey, you want to go back? The Allens are so stupid they probably forgot about it."

Simon pushed him away. Immediately he turned to say he was sorry, but something changed when he did that. He couldn't say what, it was like something broke, and when he looked back the squirrels had run off and taken the lights with them.

After lunch the next day Simon grabbed Jimmy and said they should go round the side of the building. "Don't forget your popcorn" he said, sing song, like a joke. The whole time they played, throwing pebbles at a tree, Simon looked around. No squirrels came. All that afternoon he wanted to hit Jimmy, or someone, but he kept himself still.

At night he dreamed of the woman again, the first time in months. He was on a field trip, to a museum or some other dumb place. The teacher (Mrs. Bowen, from all the way back in second grade), took them to a giant dinosaur skeleton, so big the bones looked like a city seen from far away. "In winter," Mrs. Bowen said, "the children let the dinosaur eat them so they can stay warm in its nice cozy belly. Then in Spring the dinosaur regurgitates them, like popcorn, so they can play in the sun. That's called tran-sub-station."

From somewhere to his left, Simon saw a flicker. When he turned he saw the dancing lights, just a few, and beyond them, under a doorway marked "Emergency Exit," stood the woman—his mother?—dressed in a guard's uniform. He tried to run to her but there were so many kids in front of him, pushing, yelling. The woman was saying something, and he was so frantic to get to her that he didn't see what happened to the children. For just a moment he could hear her—"Remember!"—but anything else got drowned out, for suddenly there was that sound he hated more than anything in the world, the terrible crying. He knew what had to come next, the pieces of children. Yes, there they were, scattered all over the shiny museum floor. "I'm sorry," he said in the dream. "I'm sorry, I'm sorry, I'm sorry." He woke up to discover he was hitting his father, who was trying to pin down Simon's desperate arms. His father was crying himself now, and when Simon finally calmed down his Dad held onto him for a long time.

After school that day, Simon rode his bike to several stores until he found the right brand of popcorn. Then he headed for the schoolyard, where some kids were playing soccer. He sat down on the fallen tree. As soon as he opened the bag they were there, the red and the black, both on their hind legs with their front paws out. He tossed some popcorn on the ground and they grabbed them up a piece at a time. When he threw some more, however, they ran off a few feet, then stopped to look back at him.

He followed them into the small patch of woods that ran from the school yard to behind the drugstore. The trees were thick, with branches and thorns constantly in the way. The squirrels stopped by an old oak hemmed in by upstart trees. Even though it was Spring, a mass of rotting leaves lay at the base of the trunk. In his head, Simon heard "Dig." He began to pull out clumps of leaves while the squirrels ate the popcorn that had spilled from the bag. Simon had no idea what he would find but it gave him a kind of peace to stick his fingers in the dark dirt. A few minutes must have passed when he touched a flat hard surface.

He moved the dirt away to find a blue cloth wrapped around a package about five inches long and a couple of inches thick. The cloth was stained but very soft. It looked like there were designs painted on it but Simon couldn't tell with all the dirt. Excitedly, he unwrapped it.

Picture cards. They were just a bunch of people in dumb costumes doing dumb things. He realized what they were. Tarot cards. A couple of girls at school had brought some and were showing them around the cafeteria, with lots of giggles and dumb faces. They went around to kids and waved the cards in their face and said things like "Let me tell your future" in a silly woo-woo voice. They even went up to Simon, who'd never needed a bunch of cards to know what was going to happen. He needed something to *not* know, and so he knocked the cards out of Ellen Lorenzi's hands. From the floor where she gathered up her cards Ellen said "I'll tell your future, Simon Wisdom. You're a stupid jerk and you'll always be a stupid jerk."

Now, as he held the old cards in his hand, Simon first thought he would throw them as far away as he could. Instead, he really looked

The Tarot of Perfection

"Are you a prince and a princess?"

at them. They were worn, and a little ragged, yet still brightly colored, each one like a miniature story. Here was a picture of a man walking away from a row of brightly shining glasses that seemed to hold something rotten in them even though you couldn't really see it. And here was a man hanging upside down by one foot tied to a tree branch. Light surrounded his face and he looked happier than anyone Simon had ever seen.

He sat down on the pile of leaves. The pictures made him a little dizzy, as if he was jumping from one place to another, like a character in a video game who can't stay on one level. When he closed his eyes the pictures all spun around him and he had to lie down on the leaves. Even though they were dirty and wet they felt like a soft bed where he could sleep and not be afraid of his dreams.

He must have fallen asleep, for he found himself in a dark grove of trees, tall and laced together like a fence. At first he felt trapped but then the squirrels appeared, and he followed them to an opening, a sort of gateway. It led to a dirt path, and at the end of the path a garden, with red and white flowers and high plants that moved in the breeze. The air was fresh and sweet, a mix of flowers and fruit. Simon breathed deep and closed his eyes.

When he opened them he cried out, for in place of the squirrels two children had appeared, a boy and a girl. They were younger than him, about eight years old. The girl wore a white dress, and her hair was so pale it might have been strands of silver. The boy wore a gold-colored loose t-shirt over black pants. His short hair was thick and curly and blond.

Simon thought he should be amazed by their sudden appearance. Instead he just said "Are you a prince and a princess?" and immediately thought how dumb that sounded.

They only smiled. "Something like that," the girl said.

"But you're also the squirrels?"

The boy nodded. "Yes. You get to see us as we really are."

"Cool."

They each took a hand, and the three of them walked along the path to the garden. There were roses and lilies and flowers of every color and season, and broom and heather, and green and brown and red herbs, and even patches of yellow grain. A waterfall fed it. The water came over a cliff far in the distance, gushed into a stream that vanished under the dirt to make the ground vibrate under Simon's feet. Though it all seemed to go on for miles it also felt small and friendly. Simon didn't understand that, how something could be both big and little at the same time, but he didn't care. He didn't feel like a bad person here. He was happy.

He found a bench made of interlocking vines and lay down to casually shuffle the cards. The children stood on either side, swaying slightly. They made him think of two trees, silver and gold. He laughed. First they were squirrels, then children, then trees. What a funny dream.

He closed his eyes and all at once he felt a warm and loving pressure, and he knew who it was, it was her, the woman, and he was sure now, she was his mother. She didn't hate him at all, she loved him. He wanted to open his eyes and jump up to her but he was afraid she would go away again. So he just lay there, and smiled, until finally he fell asleep.

He woke up in the woods a few feet from the pile of leaves and dirt, his back against a scrawny tree. He was all dirty and there was a cut on his elbow. He didn't care. He looked down at the Tarot cards scattered in his lap. So that's what they're for, he thought. Not to tell the future but to give you a safe place to get away. He wrapped the cards in the blue cloth and stuck them in his backpack. Maybe he shouldn't tell his Dad, he thought. He might say something about the squirrels, and Dad had a real thing about them. Anyway, when he looked around the squirrels were gone.

When Simon got home his Dad was at the kitchen table with some papers in front of him. Looking at the dirt and grass stains, Dad said "Where have you been?" He had that tightness in his voice and Simon didn't have to cheat to know Dad was worried he had gotten in another fight.

"Out in the woods," Simon said.

"By yourself?"

"Yeah."

"You look like you've been digging for buried treasure."

Simon rolled his eyes. "Yeah, sure. Everyone knows there's no buried treasure around here. We're not exactly living on a desert island, you know."

Dad smiled. "Of course," he said. He looked at Simon a little funny. "Are you okay?"

"Yeah, Dad, I'm good. I'm really good."

Dad said nothing for a moment, and his eyes got wet. When he spoke his voice shook a little, but all he said was "Well, why don't you go upstairs and take a shower." He stopped, took a breath, then in that same funny voice said "I'll start dinner. And make sure you put those clothes in the hamper."

Simon hid the cards in a box of old toys under the bed. In the shower he found himself laughing as he remembered how the squirrels had changed into those weird kids. What a funny dream. And then he realized, it was true. He *did* feel good. He felt better than at any time since his Dad told him he was cheating. Even the scar on his side didn't hurt.

Jack Wisdom had no idea what had changed in his son. He didn't dare to ask. Maybe like people said, all the nightmares, the anger, were just a phase, because suddenly it was if he'd gotten his son back. Simon smiled and laughed a lot, his grades began to come back, he even started making friends again. Jack told himself he didn't dare ask what had happened because he didn't want to make Simon self-conscious, or in some way jinx it. In fact, maybe he didn't really want to know. Better just to give thanks.

Simon never visited the garden again, never dreamed of the squirrels who became a boy and girl. He went back to the dead tree a couple of times, but didn't see them. It didn't matter. Every night, before he went to sleep, he took the cards from their hiding place and looked at them. Sometimes he quickly went through the whole deck, jumping from picture to picture like some quantum superhero jumping between universes. Other times he slid them in and out of each other, like a silent shuffle, then selected one at random. Each time he looked at them their stories changed, a computer game that endlessly re-programmed itself.

They all had titles at the bottom. Mostly they just said the suit and number, like "Four of Swords," but there was a group with fancier titles, "The Tower," or "The Hanged Man." Some of them showed naked women, and even though they didn't look much like the *Playboy* pictures some boy had brought to school in his backpack, Simon figured that was another reason not to tell Dad about them. At first Simon thought there were twenty-one of the special cards, since that was the highest number, but then he saw that one of them, the Fool, was numbered zero, so that made twenty-two. He liked that, he didn't know why. Twenty-two just seemed like a special number.

Actually, card zero was his favorite. Partly he just liked the title, "The Fool." All the others had really serious names, like "The Emperor," and they looked kind of serious, but here was a *fool*, and he looked so happy, even though he was walking at the edge of a cliff and might fall off at any moment. Simon just knew nothing bad could happen to the Fool, and nothing bad could happen to himself either as long as he had the cards. There were some scary pictures, or sad ones, such as a woman sitting up in bed, weeping in a dark room. The card was called "Nine of Swords," and there were in fact nine silver swords mounted like a kind of ladder on the wall behind the woman. When Simon looked at the picture he felt so bad for the woman. He wanted to put his arms around her and tell her he loved her.

There were angry cards, too, even a "Devil." It was okay, though. As long as the Fool was there you couldn't get caught in any of the bad places.

Later in his life Jack Wisdom would think of March 2 as the day he doomed his son. It was a Saturday, a month after Simon's birthday. Simon was on a play date, at the house of a boy named Jerry Lowe, and Jack was in a bad mood. Charlie, his boss, had sent him home for the weekend with a file that might as well have been marked "Danger! Headache!" The company had started a new product line a few months back and now some no-talent group of upstarts had filed a lawsuit claiming patent infringement due to a vaguely similar product they hadn't even brought to market. Charlie was sure they could win, but was it worth it? Maybe the other side would take a settlement and disappear. "This is driving me nuts," Charlie said to Jack.

"Maybe you can figure out what we should do." When Jack said he wasn't a lawyer Charlie said "Sure, sure. But you know how you used to sometimes come up with answers when it came down to a coin toss? This is one of those times, Jack."

So there it was. What they needed was Rebecca and she was gone, so really, it was simple, right? Out of luck. Except, Jack had a terrible suspicion that all he had to do was put the files on the table, maybe tell Simon Daddy was confused and trying to figure out what to do—maybe make a game out of it—and his wonderful boy would just tell him. It would be so easy, and he'd probably get a bonus, or become part of the inner circle. But he couldn't do it. Simon had just come through such a bad time, he was just starting to look like his old self again. Even this play date would never happened three months ago. Simon's emotional health had to come first, and that was all there was to it.

Simon threw down the sheaf of papers in disgust. He got up, walked to the kitchen, opened the refrigerator, stared at some leftover spaghetti and meatballs, then slammed the door shut. He needed to distract himself. A minute later he found himself in Simon's room. He smiled, took a deep breath and smelled the faint presence of his son. There was the rumpled cowboy blanket (he could never get Simon to make his bed properly), Mr. Axle, and the elephant Jack's Mom had given Simon. Schoolbooks and a few papers lay scattered over the small oak desk under a poster of a rock group in ridiculous outfits. A few comics lay on the floor, overshadowed by a stack of fantasy books and sea adventures.

He bent down to pick up one of the books—"The Tattooed Parrot"—and as he did so he spotted the cover of an old wooden box under the bed. He pulled it out and saw to his surprise and delight that it contained a bunch of Simon's old toys. Jack had no idea they had kept them. He grinned as he picked up a couple of building blocks, then the green snap-on driver of a firetruck. Jack smiled. This was just what he needed.

Then he saw the blue cloth, and his stomach wrenched before he even knew what it was. By the time he'd begun to unwrap it he knew, but he prayed he was wrong. There they were, worn and bent, even a little food-stained. Strawberry jam. Simon's favorite snack. When he was supposed to be doing his homework, or even playing Gameboy, or when Jack saw the flashlight and thought Simon was sneaking a few extra minutes with a book, he was looking at Tarot cards! After everything Jack had done to protect his child—just when he thought they were safe—this *infection*—

Jack grabbed whole bunches of them and tore them in half. He took the cards and the cloth and stomped downstairs to throw them in the fireplace. It took him three tries to light a match and hold it steady enough to set them on fire. He sat on the floor and cried as he watched first Rebecca's cards and then her scarf disappear into fire and dust.

He was at the table with a beer when Mrs. Lowe called, her voice trembling with bad news. "It's Simon," she said. "I don't know what happened. Everything was fine. Really. The boys were playing that Conqueror game, and suddenly Simon just yelled and fell over. I'm so sorry, Jack. I'm sure nothing happened."

"How is he?"

"I'm not sure. I don't think he's in pain. He just shakes his head when I ask him. You'd better come."

Could it be the cards, Jack wondered as he drove through red lights to Carla's house. But how—? And even if it was, it showed how dangerous they were. He found himself furious at Rebecca all over again. He'd managed to save their son from the fire, but not her sickness,

The first thing he saw, as soon as he entered the house, was Simon's scar. Redder than it had been in years, it shone like a lantern in a fog. To Jack it represented the destruction of everything he had tried to do for twelve years. It was just a moment, and then Jack saw past the scar to his precious son, curled on the couch and staring back at him with wild eyes. "Daddy?" Simon said. "What did you do?"

Jack bent down and pressed Simon against him. So hot— "It's okay, baby," he said. "Daddy's here." After assuring Carla she'd done nothing wrong, and he would pick up Simon's stuff another time, Jack led his son to the car. He called Simon's doctor, Howard Porter, from the cell, and by the time they got home there was a message about bringing the fever down. It took Jack a half hour to give Simon a cold bath and a pitcher of ice water. As soon as he could he called Howard, but even as they talked he could hear his son moving about overhead. He knew what Simon was searching for. Should he run out and get a set of Tarot cards? No, he told himself. Simon had to get over this—this thing. If he really thought a set of cards would help his son he'd track them down that moment, break into a store if he had to. Only, they wouldn't be hers, would they? Maybe he should get an exorcist, he thought. Can a dead woman possess her son?

The fever passed but not the agitation. Simon's nightmares came back, more frantic than ever. He would cry out at night, fling his arms about in his sleep. Jack never knew what Simon was dreaming, for now, when he woke Simon up his son refused to tell him. Jack told himself it was the onset of adolescence, but he didn't really believe it.

The friendships that Jack had been so thrilled to see quickly dropped away as Simon became even more aggressive. Even Popcorn Jimmy stopped coming round. Simon lost his appetite and sometimes refused to eat or threw the food on the floor. Jack would yell at him, order him to his room, then sit at the kitchen table and cry. Once, they were eating pizza, and Simon actually seemed to have an appetite when all of a sudden he threw up on the table. Jack ran over with a pot as Simon continued to vomit until all the food was gone, and Jack feared blood would follow. Jack tried to steady his son but Simon pushed him away.

Simon gripped the sides of the table as if he'd fall over otherwise. He looked up at his father with shadowed eyes. "Daddy," he said, "what did you do to me?"

"It was only a pizza," Jack said.

"*What did you do to me?*" Simon shouted, then ran upstairs.

Jack slumped in his chair. He should clean up the mess. At least he was capable of wiping up vomit. Instead, he just sat there and whispered "I don't know what I did. Really. I was trying to save you."

III

On the day that Simon got expelled from Middle School for the second time in three weeks jack received a letter from a Dr. Joseph Reina. The letterhead said "Reina Institute For Pediatric Neuro-Psychiatry," with an address in Wisconsin. "Dear Mr. Wisdom," it began, "I hope you will forgive this unsolicited letter. My Colleague, Dr. Howard Porter, and I were discussing cases recently at a conference, and he mentioned your son's deeply troubling condition." Anger surged in Jack that Howard would treat Simon as some kind of interesting study. Almost immediately, hope pushed the anger aside, for the letter went on to say that Dr. Reina had seen such cases before and had good results with an intensive treatment he had developed at his institute. Then it listed Simon's symptoms, the nightmares, the outbursts, the behavior changes, even what Dr. Reina called "a fixation or terror of the paranormal." The letter ended with the news that Reina was about to visit the area on personal basis and a request to come examine Simon, free of charge.

Jack didn't know what to do. Something in him wanted to tear the letter into small pieces and call Howard Porter to scream at him. But maybe Dr. Reina could really do something. He called Howard and asked him about Reina.

"I don't know that much about him," Howard confessed, "but he seems to know the field really well."

"You don't know him but you told him all about Simon?"

"Yes, it's a little strange, I know. He just seemed to understand, and I found myself telling him. Maybe he can help. I've got to be honest with you, Jack. I've run out of ideas."

"Why didn't you tell me about him?"

Howard paused, then said "I'm not sure. I guess I was embarrassed I told him so much. I know your concern for privacy."

"You think I should let him examine Simon?"

"Yes. Yes, I do."

The letter listed a website, Reinainstitute.org. Jack called it up and saw photos of a large stone building in a woodland setting, more like an elegant estate than a hospital. It didn't say much about Dr. Reina's methods, but there were photos of smiling kids, and letters from grateful parents, and endorsements from prominent pediatricians. Jack emailed Dr. Reina immediately.

Joseph Reina arrived just five days later. He was a tall man, handsome with graying hair around a young face so that it was hard to tell his age. He wore a dark gray suit with a blue striped tie, "banker's clothes," the would have said at Jack's office. He had a large gold ring on his left hand. His fingers were very long, Jack noticed when they shook hands. For just a moment Jack had the strangest reaction, a queasiness and then a desire to push the man away and slam the door. All that vanished when Dr. Reina smiled at him. This man was so warm and caring, he'd come specially just to help Simon. What kind of person would Jack be if he didn't trust him?

Jack had hoped Howard Porter could sit in on the consultation but that morning an emergency had summoned Howard to the hospital. Maybe it was for the best. Simon might have refused to cooperate if too many grown-ups ganged up on him.

When Simon first came downstairs at his father's summons he shrank back, and Jack feared he would run back to his room. Instead, Simon only squinted, as if he had trouble seeing Dr. Reina clearly, and when the doctor smiled and held out his hand Simon seemed to relax and walked right up to him.

Jack was about to sit down next to his son when Dr. Reina said it was best if he talked to Simon alone. "I'll be right upstairs," Jack said to Simon, who looked very young and frightened. The thought *Something is wrong* came into Jack's head, but then Dr. Reina nodded to him, and trust dissolved Jack's fears. "Just tell him whatever he needs to know," he said. Simon nodded. *Help him*, Jack thought as he left the room. *Please help him.*

Upstairs in his bedroom Jack saw a pair of squirrels on a branch outside his window. Dots of light bounced around them as they stared at him. He opened the window and threw an old ballpoint pen at them, and they ran down the trunk.

The session lasted nearly two hours. Jack sat on his bed the whole time, hands together between his knees. When Dr. Reina called him it was all he could do not to leap downstairs three steps at a time. Simon was still sitting on the couch, his head down. Jack thought,

What have I done? but when he looked at Dr. Reina the man was smiling, and Jack thrilled at the possibility of good news.

When he let the doctor wave him into the kitchen the news sounded anything but good. "The situation is serious," Dr. Reina said. Simon suffered from a deep inner conflict that was causing his psyche literally to attack itself in a kind of auto-immune response.

"What conflict?" Jack said.

"We will not know this until I begin treatment. Of course, with your permission."

Jack was having trouble breathing. "You think you can help him?"

"Oh yes. I can work with Simon to relieve his inner pain. I assure you, he will become once again the strong and healthy boy you have missed."

"That's incredible," Jack said. "That would be so wonderful."

Dr. Reina held up a finger. "I must warn, Simon is in a critical condition right now. He must come to my Institute immediately."

"Yes. Yes, of course."

"I return in three days. I will come for Simon then. You must have him ready."

Jack thought of people he'd have to call to get away at such short notice. "No problem," he said. "We'll be all set to go whenever you tell us."

"No, no," Dr. Reina said, "Simon must go with me alone."

Jack leaned back. "He's never been separated from me. Never."

"Exactly." Dr. Reina nodded, as if Jack had given a correct answer. "You are deeply entwined in his psychic world. He needs to break from that world so he can heal himself. Don't worry, he will not become distant or hateful. On the contrary, I assure you he will return with his love for his father liberated."

"Maybe I could get a hotel room somewhere near your institute."

"No. Simon must make a full break from his current psychic universe, and at the same time know firmly that his home awaits his healthy return. You are the essence of that home."

"Wow," Jack said. He sat down on one of the oak table chairs. *Don't do it*, he thought, and, *Something is wrong*. But Dr. Reina looked so solid, so confident. And what had Jack ever done but hurt Simon? He said "All right. I'll have him ready Monday morning."

After Dr. Reina left, Jack called Howard Porter. "That's wonderful," Howard said. "I knew he could do something. I just knew it."

"But Howard, we don't really know anything about him."

There was a pause. Howard sounded confused when he said "Yes, I guess that's true." Then he seemed to brighten as he said "I just have a hunch. This could be a real breakthrough."

Jack promised to let him know as soon as there was news. He hung up and took a deep breath. Time to tell Simon.

Jack found his son in his room, sitting on the edge of the bed, bent over with a book about a lost land of pirates. Jack sat down next to him. "Simon," he said, "what did you think of Dr. Reina?" Simon shrugged. "He wants to help you." No answer. "He says he *can* help you."

Simon whispered "No one can help me."

"That's not true. You're going to get better. I promise. And I think Dr. Reina's the one to do it." He paused. "Monday," he said finally. "He's going to pick you up and you're going to travel with him to his institute."

At last Simon looked up. "No, Daddy," he said, "please don't make me." He sounded six years old.

Jack hugged him. "He's going to help you."

Simon struggled free. "No! You can't make me."

"I can and I will. This is ridiculous. He says he can help you."

"Please."

Jack stood up. "I'm in charge. It's my responsibility to make sure you get better, and that's what I'm doing. After dinner we'll start packing."

That night, Simon met an old man in the attic. He was lying in bed when he heard a sad voice call his name. He walked up polished steps to a wide attic room lit by thick candles mounted on gold sticks shaped like trees. There were shining tables and carved chairs whose arms were shaped like animal heads. In the corner an old man sat all by himself on a plain wooden chair. He wore a white shirt and pants that reflected the candles like a landscape of mirrors. He wore no shoes and his feet were worn and bent. His hands resting on his knees were slim and graceful. Currents from the candlelight lifted his thin white hair. His lined face looked impossibly soft, like a child who'd grown instantly old. He said, "You mustn't go. You have to break the chain."

"I don't know what you mean," Simon said.

"You do, you do," the man told him.

Simon began to cry. "I don't want to cheat. Please don't make me." He ran downstairs and threw himself in bed with the covers held high. He lay there a long time, then went to wake his father.

"What is it?" Jack said immediately.

Simon told his father what had happened, then said "I don't want to go, Daddy. I'm scared."

His father sighed, said "Simon, it was just a dream."

"No! It was real."

Jack got out of bed. "Come on," he said. "I want to show you something." They went to the end of the hall where a small door opened to the unfinished crawl space that was too low for an attic and only served to store old computers and other things Jack intended to sell or recycle. "You see?" Jack said. "No fancy attic, no old man. It was just a dream, Simon. That's all it was. You're going to go to Dr. Reina's institute so you can stop being scared of your dreams." Simon ran back to his room and slammed the door.

On the second night before he had to leave Simon found a factory of dead children. He was lying in bed, tired but scared to fall asleep when he heard that sound of agonized children. "It's not fair," he whispered, and "Go away. Leave me alone." The sound grew louder until Simon knew it would not stop until he went to look for it. He put on his bathrobe and moccasins and went out the back door.

He walked for a long time, shivering in a chilly wind, until finally he came to a large brick building, very old, with chipped paint and broken windows. The sound of weeping children filled the sky.

Run Simon thought, but instead he found a metal door that creaked open when he pulled with both hands.

Inside he saw a giant room, very long and wide with a high ceiling and steel-beamed walls. Dust and a smell of grease filled the air. It was hard to see in the dim light from the doorway but after some time he could make out two long rows of metal tables, and on each one—each one— Heads! They were filled with children's heads! Like products waiting to be picked up and delivered to customers!

Simon gagged. He thought he would throw up or faint. He had to feel his way back to the doorway, for the awful sight filled his mind, the heads floating in the air, blinding him. Just as he found the way out the heads all spoke, fifty or a hundred voices. Don't go!" they cried out. "Break the spell!"

Simon ran all the way home. This time he went straight to his father.

"Simon," Jack said, "it was a dream."

"No!" Simon screamed. He showed his father the dirt on his feet and bathrobe.

"Oh sweetheart, you must have been sleepwalking. That's—that's a new one."

"I wasn't sleepwalking. I saw it." He got down on his knees and clasped his hands together, as if in prayer. "Please, please, please," he said. "Don't make me go."

Jack began to cry. He pulled Simon's hands apart, gently lifted him off his knees. "I'm sorry. We have to do this. You've got to get help. I don't want to send you away, please believe me. You're my boy, I love you. But I don't have any choice."

On his last night at home Simon Wisdom met a woman made of light. He had fallen asleep after an hour reading a book while his father sat on a chair alongside the bed. When Simon woke up, his father had gone, and there was a soft light in the chair, as if the full moon had taken his father's place. Simon smiled at this funny idea, and was about to go back to bed when he heard a soft voice from downstairs, reciting a poem

Simon, Simon,
Rhymin' Simon,
Take the time an'
Stop the crime an'
Set the children free.

Simon tiptoed past his father's room and on downstairs to the living room. A woman sat in Grandma's angelback chair (it was really called a wingback but Simon used to think Grandma looked like a queen of angels and the sides of the chair were the tips of her wings). The chair was pink with green threads, and the woman wore a green dress, soft and long, like an angel's robe. Tiny lights seemed to sparkle all around her, and for a moment Simon thought she actually was made of different colored lights, like on July fourth, when they would make a flag or even someone's face out of fireworks.

He felt calm as he sat down across from her. She was so pretty, and she looked at him so kindly. He wanted to go hug her or even sit in her lap. But if she was really made of light she might disappear if he tried to touch her. So he just sat politely and said ""Why did you call me that? Rhyming Simon."

"Oh," she said, "because you're such a perfect poem."

Simon didn't know what to say to that, so he just said "I'm Simon Wisdom."

The woman nodded. "I know. I'm Rebecca."

Simon's throat made a noise. He said "That was my mother's name."

The woman nodded. "Yes."

Now Simon did jump up but the woman—his mother—held up her hand. "I'm sorry," she whispered. "I wish, I wish I could hold you, but it's not allowed." Then simon knew it was true, that she wasn't really there, and he began to cry. "It's all right," his mother said. "I'm so happy to see you."

"My Dad wants to send me away. Can you tell him not to do it? Please. He won't listen to me."

"Oh darling, I can't. I've tried, believe me, but your father doesn't know how to hear me. Please don't be angry at him."

"But I'm scared. I don't like Dr. Reina."

The lights in her face dimmed a moment, then grew bright again, only it was the kind of cheerfulness that grown-ups put on when they want to pretend everything is fine. "I'm going to tell you something important," she said. "If you do what I say you'll be safe." Simon nodded. "When you go with Dr. Reina you need to do two things. First, pay attention."

"Pay attention to what?"

"Everything. Things will not be as they seem. Look carefully, and listen, especially at night. Do you understand?"

"I think so."

"Good. I'm very proud of you. And now the second thing. Make sure you do not eat or drink anything. Anything at all, not even a drop of water."

"What if I get hungry?"

"Don't give in. It will go away. If he watches you wait until he's distracted, then get rid of some of the food so he will think you ate it."

"What if he doesn't get distracted?"

She smiled, and it was such a happy sight. "The squirrels will take care of that."

"Oh wow," Simon said. "You know about the squirrels?"

"Oh yes. They're old friends of mine."

"So I didn't dream it? They really used to be a boy and a girl?"

She nodded. "A magician changed them a very long time ago."

"Can't they change back?"

"Maybe they will, darling Simon. Maybe you can help them."

"Wow," Simon said.

It would be dawn soon. The morning light began to dim Rebecca's face. She told Simon to close his eyes, and when he did he felt warm arms hold him against a soft full body that smelled of flowers, as if she lived in a garden. He kept his eyes closed until several seconds after the arms let go. When he finally opened them he discovered, just as he'd thought, that he was alone. He went back to bed where he fell into a peaceful sleep until his father came to wake him.

To Jack's surprise Simon woke up in a good mood. And hungry. He asked for pancakes and eggs and then a grilled cheese sandwich, and he drank three glasses of milk. Jack thought, maybe he was okay, maybe he could stay home. As if the very thought threw some kind of switch in Jack he found himself furious, and wondered if Simon was playing some kind of trick on him. With great effort he calmed himself. He didn't want the last time he saw his son to be filled with anger.

Dr. Reina arrived at 9:30, strong and positive in an off-white suit and a red tie. He smiled at Simon, who stared at the floor, and shook hands with Jack. "Everything all packed?" he said. Jack nodded. To Simon, Reina said "Well, young man, it looks like we're going on a trip. I hope you like sitting up high in a big car because that is what we are going to do." He seemed so cheerful and positive, Jack was sure he had made the right choice. And yet, there was a panic in him that he had to fight to suppress.

He held Simon for a long time before he finally let Dr. Reina lead him out to the car. He could still change his mind, he thought, as the door closed, as the engine started, as the thick wheels began to carry his son away from him. Instead, he just waved goodbye, even though Simon sat very still in the front seat and didn't look back. "I love you!" he yelled after the car. "I love you, Simon!"

Just as the car turned the corner, Jack saw a strange sight. Two squirrels ran down the road, side by side, for all the world like dogs chasing a car. Jack thought he should be angry, go chase them or something. Wasn't that the very last thing he wanted to see? But that part of him that was in full panic somehow calmed down, just a little. He walked back to the house and sat down and closed his eyes. For the first time in many weeks, Jack Wisdom felt a stir of hope.

IV

Simon was never sure how long the journey lasted. His father had told him it would take two or three days, and they would stay in hotels along the way. Maybe they did that, he sort of remembered big buildings and very clean rooms, but when he tried seriously to remember doing those things they stayed detached, like something you saw on television. The only thing he knew for sure was that he didn't eat anything.

They arrived at the Institute on a cloudy afternoon. The sky pressed the long stone building into the earth. Looking at it, Simon found it hard to get up out of his seat. Dr. Reina came and opened the door for him. He held out his hand and when Simon took it a small shock went through him. "You may leave your bags in the car," Dr. Reina said. "Someone will bring them to your rooms." Simon looked around. Where was everybody? Where were the other children, the doctors and nurses? There was a wide lawn, and flowers along the front of the building, and large trees towards the sides, oak and silver birches. It all looked cared for, yet somehow ragged, as if wilderness would rise up and reclaim the land, and the Institute, at any moment. And everything was silent.

Inside there were wide windows with black and white tiled floors, and ivory painted walls, with occasional carved chairs or small marble statues of children. It was all very beautiful, and at the same time cold and kind of *slippery*. "Where are all the other children?" Simon asked.

Dr. Reina nodded. "A good question. Now I will tell you a secret. You, Simon, are the only one here. Do you see now that you are very special?"

"I don't understand."

"I wish to give you my full attention. Just you and I, working together to make all the bad dreams and bad feelings disappear." He spread wide his fingers like a magician releasing a bird. "Gone forever. Do you see?"

"I guess."

Simon's room was large, slightly bigger than his Dad's bedroom at home, with a wooden bed covered by a green bedspread, a large oak desk and a high backed plain wooden chair. There was a small bathroom off to the side. There was so little in the room, just those few pieces of furniture, no telephone, computer, or television. Simon wished he'd brought a gameboy or a book, for there was nothing to do except look out the window at the long side lawn and some distant trees. At least there was a painting to look at, the room's only decoration. It showed a tree with white flowers. When Simon glanced at it it seemed cheerful, but as he held his eyes on it the tree appeared over-ripe, almost diseased.

"Can I call my Dad?" Simon said.

"Later," Dr. Reina said. "First you must settle in. Rest. Have dinner. This is very important."

"I want to speak to him. He's going to worry."

Dr. Reina held up a finger. "Simon," he said, "your father has given you to me. You must follow and do what I say so that healing will come."

"When can I call him?"

"We will see tomorrow. And that is all we will say about it for now." He smiled. His teeth were very white. "Now you must be hungry. Rest, please, and soon we will eat." He left the room and closed the door behind him.

As soon as he was alone, Simon took out his cell phone to try to call his father. "No signal" read a box, and below it a picture of an old-fashioned phone with a red X over it.

He tried to open the window but it wouldn't move. Could he break it with the chair? Where would he go? He started to cry. No, he told himself, and wiped his eyes. Crying like a baby wasn't going to help. He needed to pay attention. That's what his mother had said. Pay attention and not eat anything.

He lay on the bed, trying not to cry, until Dr. Reina returned, in a white suit. "Come, Simon," the doctor said, "it is time to eat." At that moment Simon discovered he was terribly hungry. He jumped up, filled with desire for fried chicken, or hamburgers, or ice cream. Or chocolate cake! Wouldn't it be wonderful to eat a big gooey slice of cake?

Simon followed Dr. Reina down a long corridor lined with statues. They looked like children in odd poses. Simon ignored them, drawn by the smells of hot food. The dining room was large, with big windows overlooking the lawn, and several long tables with red lacquered wooden chairs. Simon looked only at the table in the center, for it was filled with everything he wanted, chicken and cheeseburgers and hot dogs and ice cream and the biggest gooiest slice of cake he'd ever seen. He felt a big surge of happiness and would have hugged Dr. Reina if he hadn't wanted to start eating right away. Dr. Reina said "It's all for you, Simon. Special just for you."

Simon was about to pile food on his plate when suddenly he heard a soft whisper inside his head. It said

Simon, Simon,

Rhymin' Simon,

Take the time an'

Stop the crime an'

Set the children free.

But I'm so hungry. I'll be sick if I don't eat something.

"Pay attention," the voice said. "Do not eat or drink. Anything."

Simon put his hands under the table and clenched his fists. His body shook a little as he said "I'm sorry. I don't think I'm very hungry right now."

Dr. Reina stared at him with a look that made Simon turn away. "Not hungry? After so long a journey? This is foolishness, Simon. We cannot begin your cure if you refuse to eat. Your father will be very disappointed in you."

Though delicious smells filled Simon's whole body he said "No thank you. I'm not hungry." As soon as he said the words he discovered it was true. The hunger had vanished, and now the smells disgusted him.

Dr. Reina pointed a finger at him. "You must eat."

Right then, Simon head a scratching noise at the window. He looked and almost shouted with joy. The squirrels were there. They stood on the windowsill and clawed the glass as if they were trying to break in. *She sent them*, he thought. His mother.

Dr. Reina was furious. "Get away!" he shouted, and swept his arm across his body. The squirrels continued to tap tap at the window. Dr. Reina opened the window to grab them, but they only ran to the next sill. He rushed to the doorway. "Stay here," he ordered Simon. "I will chase away these pests. It is your father's wish. And it is his wish also that you eat, so you can make yourself strong." He ran down the hall.

Simon dashed to the window and was about to climb out when a soft voice said inside him "No, you cannot escape that way." When he looked at the squirrels the red one nodded his head. The voice said "Use your napkin to put some food on your plate, then drop it out the window. Make sure you don't touch it."

With the white cloth napkin Simon grabbed a chicken wing, a cheeseburger, and a hot dog. Even through the cloth the touch made Simon a little sick. He thought of the pieces of children from his dreams, the fingers and tongues. "Yes," the voice said, "nothing here is what it seems. Hurry." When Simon had dropped the food out the window the voice said "Now pour some of the drink into your glass, then throw it out of the window. Don't let a drop touch you." There was a large pitcher on the table with red fruit juice. Very carefully Simon poured some into his glass then walked it to the window and spilled it out.

He was just back in his seat when he saw Dr. Reina come round the side of the building, shouting something Simon couldn't understand. The squirrels ran away while Dr. Reina shook his fist.

When the doctor returned a minute later Simon was at his place, his hands folded neatly on the table. Dr. Reina still looked angry, but when he saw that some of the food and juice were gone, he smiled. "Good, good," he said. "You have eaten. Soon we can begin your treatment." Then he narrowed his eyes and looked at Simon who did not dare to look back. He picked up the plate, stared closely at it, even sniffed it. He did the same with the glass. When the doctor went and looked out the window Simon had to fight the desire to run. To his surprise, Dr. Reina smiled happily, then patted Simon's shoulder. "Good boy," he said, and Simon shivered. Dr. Reina said there was nothing more to do that day and sent Simon back to his room.

Simon sat in the chair or walked back and forth or lay on the bed. Every few minutes he would look out the window to see if he could spot the squirrels but there were never any there. "I want to go home," he whispered. "Please, please, can't I just go home?"

When night came Simon put on his pajamas and got into bed. He didn't dare to wash his face or brush his teeth for fear he would swallow something.

He began to feel sleepy, and even though he was scared of what he might dream he thought how at least sleep would take him away for awhile. Then he remembered his mother telling him to pay attention. He shook his head, and just as the hunger had vanished earlier so now did his tiredness. He lay in bed and waited. At home he would sometime lie awake for fear of his dreams, and listen to the wind in the leaves, or occasional cars, or the furnace or hot water heater in the basement. Here there was nothing.

It was difficult to feel time here, but after what seemed like an hour he heard the sound of someone crying, far away. He listened to it for a long time until finally morning came and the sound stopped, and for awhile Simon slept.

He woke up to daylight but no sense of how much time had passed. He had just gotten dressed when Dr. Reina opened the door. "At last you awake," the doctor said. "You were very tired, I think, to sleep so long, almost the whole day." Simon glanced out the window. Was it really that late? Dr. Reina said, "You must be very hungry."

Just as the day before Simon thought he would fall down if he didn't eat something. How could he be so foolish as to go days without food? When they came to the dining room, and he saw watermelon and cookies and macaroni and cheese and barbecued stead he wanted to grab all of it at once. But just as the day before he made himself sit and say "No, thank you. I'm not hungry," and the hunger immediately vanished, replaced by disgust at the piles of food.

"You must eat," Dr. Reina said, and leaned forward so that his face seemed to float inches away from Simon's eyes. "You eat and become well." Then, just as the day before, the squirrels appeared, and Dr. Reina, enraged, ran to chase them away. Simon put food on his plate, filled his glass, then dropped it out the window. When he looked down to see if the food had disappeared, or the ground had covered it it all just lay there. Yet when Dr.Reina looked he once again nodded his satisfaction.

That night the crying was louder. Simon tried to ignore it, or cover his ears, but it beat at him. And didn't his mother tell him to pay attention? To stop the crime. If some child was hurt she wanted Simon to set him free. So he got off the bed and put on the moccasins his father had bought him for the trip, and stepped into the hallway.

The house confused him, there were so many turns and corridors, all with a hazy light, though he couldn't see any lamps. What if Dr. Reina jumped out at him? He practiced excuses in his head—sleepwalking, curiosity—but wherever the doctor was he apparently paid no attention to the sad cries that filled his empty hospital.

At the top of a flight of stairs Simon came to a room with a dark red door. When he touched the handle it was very hot and he jerked his hand away twice before he could open it. Inside, instead of a hurt child, he saw only rows of what looked like very old wooden stands, each with a stack of small papers on top. No, not papers. Cards. Despite the urgent cries that still surrounded him Simon could not resist going closer. Yes, they were Tarot cards. A whole roomful of them. He reached out for the nearest pack.

And stopped. Something about it felt wrong. Even more scary than the poisonous food. He stood there for what seemed a very long time. Finally he dropped his arm and looked closer without touching. The top card on each pack was the Fool, his favorite. On each one the head had been cut out, slashed away with a jagged scissors or knife.

Simon ran from the room so fast he nearly down the stairs. If someone had asked him why it scared him so much he couldn't have answered, but he knew he had to get out of there. On the ground floor he discovered he could find his way back to his room as easily as if he'd left a trail of bread crumbs. When he lay down he discovered that the crying had stopped, but as soon as he closed his eyes he immediately saw those cards with the heads cut out so savagely a wild beast might have attacked them. *I want to go home,* he thought to himself, *I just want to go home.*

The third day was a repeat of the others. Simon wondered how Dr. Reina let himself get tricked like that, but he didn't care. He was just hoping he could do whatever it was he needed to do.

That night the crying was worse than ever. Simon got straight out of bed and tried to follow the sound. He came to the room with the Tarot cards and kept going. At the very tip of the house he saw a door as dark blue as the other was red. The crying was so loud here that Simon felt like he would shatter from the sound. He stared at the door a long time before he reached for the handle. It was cold, colder than the red had been hot, but he managed to get it open.

At first he thought the room was empty. It was dark, lit only by the light from the stairs, but Simon couldn't see any furniture, let alone crying children. When his eyes adjusted to the dimness he saw in the center of the room a single metal stand, dark and plain. It stood about as high as a grown-up, and on top of it was something like a ball. *Run,* Simon thought. *Get away.* He cried out, for he realized now that the thing on top of the column wasn't a ball. It was a head. The head of a child.

Simon made a noise, and right then the crying stopped. Simon almost fell, for he'd been bracing himself against the sound as if against a powerful wind. But who had been doing it? Simon looked around. "Hello?" he called.

"It's you," a voice said. "You're next, aren't you?" The voice was young and old at the same time, and sadder even than when it was crying.

Simon looked around again but he knew now he wouldn't see anyone. He walked up to the head. Like the voice it was old and young, the features those of a boy about Simon's age, yet with wrinkled, cracked skin. There were marks on the cheek and a dark smudge on the forehead. Somehow he looked familiar and Simon wondered if he'd dreamed about him. He said "Who are you?" It seemed safer than anything else he might ask.

"I thought I was the last," the head told him. "I'm almost done, and I hoped, I hoped so much—the world has changed I could tell that, and I thought, I hoped, he wouldn't find another one. That it would be over, finally, finally."

"What would be over?"

"This. What he does to us."

"I don't understand," Simon said, though he was terribly scared that he did. "Do you have a name?"

"I think I was named Phillip. It was a long time ago. You see? I'm almost finished."

"I'm Simon."

The head—Phillip—squinted at him. "There's an old poem." Softly he recited "Simon, Simon…" The voice trailed off.

"I know that," Simon said. "My mother said it. I think it was my mother. It was kind of in a dream." He didn't recite the rest of it.

"Come closer," Phillip said. "I want to look at you." Simon hesitated, then walked up. "Is it possible?" Phillip said. "Do you have protection?"

Protection. Maybe whatever terrible thing was going to happen he was safe. Then, suddenly, Phillip began to wail, and Simon realized there would be no safety. "Oh no, no," Phillip said. "There's a hole in the shield. Someone—a woman—tried to protect you but she wasn't able to finish. Now nothing can stop it."

Simon couldn't stop himself. "Stop what?"

"I'm getting old," Phillip said. "I'm wearing out. Tell me, does Reina seem at all weak to you?"

"Dr. Reina?"

"Doctor. Yes, that would be a title he would use. Have you seen any weakness?"

"No. Well, maybe. Not really weak, you know, but he sort of misses things." Simon told him about throwing the food out the window and Dr. Reina not seeing it.

"You didn't eat anything? Or drink?"

"No. Nothing. I was really hungry but then it went away."

"Oh, thank God," Phillip said. "Then you still have a chance. Listen to me, Simon. Whatever that food looked like it wasn't real. Reina feeds you pieces of himself. His body. And if you take any of it you belong to him."

"I didn't!" Simon said. "I didn't even touch it."

Phillip didn't seem to hear. His eyes flickered and he spoke softly, with a shake in his voice. "Then he comes to you. With that stone knife. Oh God. He cuts and cuts, a piece at a time, until there's nothing left but the head, and then he writes things on your face, and oh God, the last thing is the picture. He cuts it and burns it into your forehead."

The Fool Simon thought. That was why all the Tarot decks had the faces cut out of the Fool. Sickness came over him and he almost fell. "I want to go home," he said. He started to cry. He was trying to be strong, but it was all so scary and worse even than any of his dreams.

"You can't," Phillip said. "None of us can. You're on the other side now."

"Why? Why does he do this? Who is he?"

"He used to be a man. Many centuries ago. Then he discovered the great secret. He could live forever if he created the heads."

"Then why does he need me? If he's already got you." Maybe Dr. Reina would let Simon go if he realized he still had Phillip.

"I'm weakening, and so *he's* weakening. That's why you were able to trick him. My time is almost up and he needs a replacement."

"I'm sorry," Simon whispered.

"No, no, no. I want to end. Finally. But you! You must save yourself, Simon. If you can keep him from taking you, *he* will finally end. So many years, so many children."

"What do I do?"

"I don't know. No one has ever escaped him. Ever."

"I'll run away. I'll climb out the window or something. I just have to get to a phone and call my Dad."

"You don't understand. This is not really a place. It's hard to describe. It's his world."

"No!" Simon said. "You're lying. You just don't want me to get away because you never could. I'm going and you can't stop me." He ran for the door. He just had to reach his Dad. His Dad would send the police or something.

Behind him he heard Phillip's sad whisper, "Go, Simon. Maybe you can do it."

Simon turned around. "I know you," he said. "I mean, I've met you. Before I came here. But you were old."

Phillip's eyes opened wide. "I don't know," he said. "Maybe—maybe that was who I was would have been. If Reina hadn't caught me. I'd been allowed to live, and grow old. He began to cry now. "Go!" he said suddenly. "Run!"

Simon ran down the stairs so fast he hit the walls of the stairwell 4 times on his way to the ground floor. Out. Get out. Get to the woods. Find a phone. Call Daddy.

He hit the front door and fell back before he could open it. Then he was outside the house and he just had to keep going, run for the woods. It was daylight, and that didn't make any sense, but he couldn't think about that. There were the trees, they looked a couple of football fields away. His sneakers slapped the dirt, faster and faster.

"Simon!" Dr. Reina's voice filled the sky, shook the ground. "*It is time for you to begin your treatment.*"

Simon couldn't help it. He had to see. He turned and there was Dr. Reina, in his white suit, his face bright and his hair sparkly. In his left hand, loose at his side, he carried gray stone knife. It looked very very old. The sun flickered off red spots along the blade. Dried blood. Phillip's blood. The blood of all the children over so many years.

"Come, Simon," Dr. Reina boomed out. "Soon we will make you a healthy boy."

Simon ran for the woods.

Jack Wisdom knew something was wrong almost immediately, but it took him three days to admit it. As soon as the car had gone around the corner, he'd wanted to run after it, open the door and pull out his son, before—before it could swallow him. That was the image that filled his mind, Dr. Reina's Mercedes like some monster that would gulp down his helpless little boy.

Ridiculous, he told himself. If he seriously thought that Simon was in danger he wouldn't have let him go, right? If he really thought he'd made a mistake he would get in his car and chase him down, or call the cops, not fantasize a sprint down the block like some character out of a comic book. Separation anxiety, that's all it was. Possessiveness. Maybe he didn't want Simon to get better. Maybe he was scared he'd lose his tight hold on his son. Maybe he was jealous. *Selfish bastard*, he told himself. *Care more about yourself than your own child.* But that wasn't how he felt. How he felt was terrified.

For two days Jack used anger at himself to ignore the alarm bells that rang up and down his body. The surges of panic that almost doubled him over. The tears that finally caused his boss to tell him to take some time off. The prayers that ran through his mind when he was watching tv, or washing dishes. He found himself thinking of that horrible night when Rebecca had tried to kill their baby. Strangely, it wasn't the horror of the fire or his wife's insanity that caught him up, it was the peculiar poem or lullaby she was chanting.

Simon, Simon

Rhymin' Simon

Take the time an'

Stop the crime an'

Set the children free

What the hell was that about? And why was he thinking of it now, when he'd forgotten all about it for twelve years?

Strangest of all was the sense that Simon was actually very close. Right in the next room. Just outside the door. On the other side of the wall. He would wake up in the middle of the night, think *Simon*, and reach out to touch his son.

On the third day he woke with a certainty that Simon was not only close but in danger. He could almost hear him crying to go home. Just a dream, he told himself. Simon was safe. It was hard, but it was for the best...

No, he thought. Simon was *not* safe. He sat up and grabbed the phone.

For two days Jack had made no attempt to call the Institute. Whenever he thought about it he told himself that Dr. Reina had asked no contact in the initial stage of treatment. Now he had to admit that the real reason was fear he might hear exactly what he was hearing now. "The number you have dialed is disconnected out not in service." Jack's hands shook and he had to steady himself to dial again. He tried two more times, then information in case the number on Dr. Reina's card was out of date or misprinted. No listing. He had the operator check every variation he could think of, as well as other towns in the area. Nothing. "Oh God," Jack said as he hung up the phone. "Oh shit."

He ran to the computer, slammed the keys for web site. No such address. This too he tried over and over, and then search engines for the Institute or Dr. Reina himself. Nothing.

He called Howard Porter, asked him for everything he knew about Reina and the Institute. Howard started to speak then stopped himself. "Jesus, Jack," he said. "I don't—I don't think I really know anything about him. Jesus Christ."

Jack began to cry. "How could we do this?" he said. "How the hell could we do this?"

"I don't know. It's like I was hypnotized or something."

If Jack hadn't needed Howard so much he might have wanted to travel over the phone lines and strangle him. Instead he said "What am I going to do, Howard? That sonofabitch has got Simon. I don't even know what he is, but he's got my little boy."

"I'll be right there," Howard said. "You better call the police."

Jack and Howard Porter spent all day with the police: local, state, FBI, and on the phone with the cops in Wisconsin, who knew nothing about Reina or his Institute. In the middle of his panic Jack worried they would blame him, maybe even charge him with something. He kept expecting them to say "You gave your son away to some pervert with a fake website and a fancy brochure?"

In fact, they were kind, patient, and thorough. They also were helpless. There were no files on Reina, no information about his supposed Institute. When Jack and Howard worked with the sketch program to come up with a picture it brought no connections from the State or FBI's lists of pedophiles. The police managed to track down the organizer of the conference where Howard had met Reina. They too knew nothing, were not even sure how they'd come to invite him to speak. One of the organizers laughed nervously as she talked to the detectives. She said "I don't know how we could do that. Accept a speaker no one really knew anything about. It was like we were hypnotized or something."

After nearly twelve hours Jack finally allowed the police to fill him with hopeful reassurances and send him home. They told him he should eat, get some rest. They would call him as soon as they had any news.

At home, Jack stared at the telephone. Should he call his parents? They would want to know. They'd be home, watching that talent show they liked so much. He picked up the phone and put it down. What good would it do? He'd just worry them.

Worry! Worry was what you did when your son's grades went down. This was so far beyond worry— He what his mother would tell him to do. Pray. He'd been sitting in the kitchen, and now he walked stiffly to the living room, as if God might appreciate the more formal setting. He got down on his hands and knees alongside the couch, in imitation of how his mother had taught him to kneel by the bed at night. Hands clasped he said "Please God. Spare my son. I know I don't deserve your help. I haven't gone to church or anything for years. But please. Not for me, for him. He's just a little boy. Whoever this Dr. Reina really is, don't let him hurt Simon. Please."

He stayed there for a little while, then got up. He didn't know how to pray. He'd never really done it, not seriously. Was it even fair to ask God for help? Should he offer something? Jesus, he thought, he'd already given up his first born.

In a wild gesture of despair he spun around. His eyes fell upon the photo of Rebecca on the piano. Even in his time of deepest anger he'd never taken it down. He picked it up in both hands, sighed at the memory of her eyes. She was sitting almost formally on the bench he'd put in the backyard in honor of their first meeting. Both feet were on the ground, her hands were in her lap, and she stared right through the camera.

"Bec, Bec," he said. "What have I done? Oh God, Rebecca, I've screwed everything up. I've killed him. I know it, I know I've killed our little boy. That's what I thought you were going to do, and now I've done it. I got it all wrong." Tears gushed from his body. "Help me, Rebecca! Please!"

Exhausted suddenly, he sat down on the sofa with the photo still in his hands. Lights flickered around the picture but he only half noticed them. He closed his eyes and in seconds fell asleep.

He dreamt he was outside, behind the house, but it also was the lawn of Dr. Reina's Institute. He could see the huge building, just past the trees. And then he saw Simon. His son was running towards him, mouth open in terror. Behind Simon stood Dr. Reina, calm and sleek in a white suit. He held something gray and sparkly but Jack couldn't make out what it was.

Jack wanted to call out to Simon, tell him Daddy was coming, but Dr. Reina said "No, no, Mr. Wisdom, you must not interfere. Simon's treatment has begun." Jack wanted to shout him down but couldn't, for Reina's words had taken on solid form, a syrup that covered Jack's body and filled his mouth. He fell down and couldn't get up, could hardly breathe or see.

It was then that the squirrels appeared. With quick efficiency they gnawed away at the thick coating, first around his eyes and mouth, then his arms and legs—

He woke to see Rebecca standing in the living room.

Jack stared, afraid to move or speak. There were lights all around her. No, she *was* light. A thousand tiny lights, like butterflies, had taken the shape of his beloved Rebecca. "It's just another dream," he whispered.

"No," Rebecca said. "This is not my body but I am here. The Splendor have given me this gift so that I can talk to you."

"The Splendor?"

"The name for the lights you see. Jack, you must listen to me."

"Bec, I've killed him. I killed Simon."

"No! Simon is alive but he needs your help. He is trying to escape Reina right now, but he can't do it without you."

Jack jumped up. "What do I do?"

"He needs the cards and you're the only one who can get them to him."

"You mean the Tarot cards? Oh my God, Bec, I got rid of them."

She shook her head. "No, no, no. The Tarot of Perfection can never be destroyed. Please, Jack, you have to listen to me. Whatever you or I did doesn't matter. Only right now matters. Do you understand?"

"Yes."

"Then go around the back of the house. You will see the cards there, wrapped in blue cloth. As soon as you pick them up you will see Simon. You won't be able to hand him the cards but you can throw them to him. That is all you have to do. Do you understand?"

"Yes. Yes I do."

"Good. I love you, Jack Wisdom. I love you forever."

"I love you too," jack shouted. He was already running for the door.

Outside, it was evening but the sky was bright and red. Jack searched the back yard, and there it was, a small blue package lying in the grass. The squirrels stood on either side, like guards. For a moment Jack's old fears stopped him. Something in him tried to say "This is insane," or even "It's a trick, she's trying to hurt you." Out loud he said "No," and picked up the cards.

The sky caught fire.

Jack screamed and jumped back, for a wall of flame had appeared in front of him. He squinted into the blaze. He could see shapes on the other side... Simon was there! His precious boy was running right towards him. Though Simon seemed to run with all his might he didn't seem to get any closer. Behind Simon, Dr. Joseph Reina walked slowly forward, nearer with every step. Reina was smiling, and in his right hand he held a stone knife.

Through the fire Jack called "Simon!"

"Daddy," Simon cried, "help me!"

Jack didn't know what to do. He tried again to get through the fire but the heat pushed him back. If he tried to throw Simon the cards, would flames burn them up? Trust Rebecca, he told himself. He hurled the package towards his son.

Simon didn't know why his Dad wasn't coming to him. He could see Dad try but something pushed him back. And he didn't understand why he couldn't get away from Dr. Reina. He was running as hard as he could and Dr. Reina was walking so slowly, yet Simon remained as far away from his father as ever, and Dr. Reina kept getting closer.

Then Simon saw his Dad throw something. He couldn't see what it was but he knew it was important, his Dad wouldn't do it otherwise. It looked like it was about to fly right over his head, but he jumped up, just like when they played catch, and grabbed it.

Even before he looked at it he knew what it was. He could feel the blue cloth. The cards. His Dad had somehow gotten him the Tarot cards. On his knees now, he fumbled at the wrapper.

Only some twenty yards away, Dr. Reina laughed. "Simon, please," he said. "Tarot cards? What will you do? Tell my future?" Suddenly his voice shook the ground. "I *am* the future! I am Joseph of the Other Side. You have eaten me, body and blood. Three times, and now *my* mouth is open. I am the teeth of death, Simon Wisdom. You are my food. I will eat you and live forever."

Simon fell down in terror. At the same time he thought *He doesn't know. He thinks I ate the food.* He had a chance, but what should he do? What?

Run, he thought, then *No, the cards*. He fumbled through them, dropped half, fell over as he tried to pick them up. From just ten yards away, Dr. Reina laughed. "Simon, Simon," he chided. "Are you going to read your cards?"

Open-mouthed, Simon stared at him. *Simon, Simon.* He remembered now! What his mother had said that night in the living room.

Simon, Simon
Rhymin' Simon,
Take the time an'
Stop the crime an'
Set the children free.

He had to take the time. Not try to run. But what would that do? How would taking time stop the crime? Simon, Simon. What else did his mother say? "You're my perfect poem." A poem! He'd thought she was being nice but she was telling him he had to make up a poem. A magic poem could stop the crime.

Dr. Reina was only a few yards away now, his smile as sharp as his knife. Simon could hear his Dad yelling at him to get away but he couldn't listen. He closed his eyes and wished he could close his ears as well. "Tarot, Tarot," he whispered, then a little louder, "long and narrow."

Dr. Reina laughed—so close. He said "Verse? For your last breath? Do you hear your father? He wants you to say goodbye to him." Simon opened his eyes. Dr. Reina had stopped just a few feet away. Simon could see the bloodstains up and down the stone blade, he could hear the crying children, all the ones Dr. Reina had killed. Phillip was there, and a hundred more. "Set the children free," his mother had said.

As strong as he could make it, Simon called out
Tarot, tarot,
Long and narrow,
Be like knives
To save our lives.

Dr. Reina stepped back. He opened his mouth to speak, but nothing came out.

With all his terrified might, Simon Wisdom threw the cards at the monster.

The cards separated as they sliced through the air. Simon could see each one before it hit, and so could Dr. Reina, for he stared at them, unable to move, head shaking slightly, as if he tried to say "No, no, this is wrong." The first card to hit was the Fool. It cut right through his throat, setting forth a jet of blood so thick and dark it looked like oil. He held his hands up in front of his face, only to have the next group of cards cut off his fingers. More cards attacked his legs, his arms, his chest. Parts of him fell on the ground where they turned into black crystal, clothes and all, then broke into small sharp pieces that sank into the grass.

The very last card to hit him was the man hanging upside down by one foot, with light all around his face. It hit the eyes, and light exploded from it. For a moment Simon could see the faces of children, layer upon layer, neither happy nor sad but quiet, eyes closed, lips slightly open in a long collective sigh. And then they were gone.

Simon could never remember exactly when it all disappeared. One moment he was looking at the pieces on the scorched grass, and the cards scattered on the ground. Something must have hurt his eyes, for he squeezed them shut, and when he opened them again everything had vanished, the black crystals, the cards, even the Institute itself and the wide lawn. Instead, he saw his own back yard. There was Mr. Carlys' house, with the covered up swimming pool, and there were the two pine trees that Grandma called "the gateway to happiness." Amazed, Simon turned around. There was his father. Simon wasn't making it up. Daddy really was there.

On either side of his father stood the boy and girl, their gold and silver hair sparkly in the sun. Simon was happy to see them, and at the same time he thought *They're not supposed to be here.*

As if they could hear him—could read his mind—they smiled and nodded. They took a step back. At that moment, as if someone had hit the play button on the DVD, Simon's Dad called out "Simon? Are you really there? Oh God, Simon!"

They ran at each other so hard they bounced off and fell down. Daddy grabbed him, held him so long he couldn't breathe. "Oh, Simon," Daddy said, "My beautiful boy. My precious boy." Finally they stood up, and Daddy took his hand as they walked to the house.

In the living room Jack Wisdom picked up the picture of his wife. Faint lights sparkled around it. "It was your mother," he said to his son. "She told me what I had to do."

"Me too," Simon said. "She told me I had to make up a poem so that's what I did."

Jack smiled. "Your mother is a very smart woman, Simon. She loves us both very very much. And I love her. I love you more than anything in the world, but I love your mother too."

Simon said "I know, Daddy."

Jack looked startled a moment, then laughed. "Of course you do," he said. "Of course you do." He laughed again and hugged his son.

For Valerie Smith

The End

Master Matyas

There once was a boy named Matyas, who lived in his parents' inn, The Hungry Squirrel, a small dismal building on a dismal road that ran from the sea to the capital. Matyas cleaned the guests' rooms and carried firewood and swept the floors and brought the guests his father's watery beer and his mother's stringy food. He hated every moment. He was too good for this, too clever and talented. Sometimes he dreamed of himself as a great man, dressed in silk and gold, and standing in a tower while down below, the ordinary people would look up in fear and helplessness. Then morning would come and his father would kick him awake to begin his duties.

He was a thin gangly boy, this Matyas, with deep eyes and long lashes, and shiny black hair that always seemed to get in his face. He survived his work by mentally changing whatever he could. If he spilled food he imagined the stain as a treasure map. If some monk or educated traveler left behind a scrap of paper, he pretended it contained the secrets of kings, or even better, a magic spell to carry him away from the inn to a place with gardens and fountains and the tower he had seen in his dreams. Since he couldn't read it was easy to pretend.

At night, after his chores had finally ended, and he was so tired he knew he should just fall on his sleeping pallet by the pantry, he instead would wander the dusty hills and scrub flats and pretend he was on a sacred quest. He knew he would never find anything, for who would bring a holy relic to such a place, let alone leave it there. He simply could not stand the thought that he might live his entire life like his father, with no world beyond the streaked walls of the inn.

One night he was sitting on a bare hillock, putting off the moment he had to return, when he saw a large object move against the moonlit sky. At first he assumed it was a bird, but as he stared at it a shock like lightning jolted him, for he realized it was a man. In all Matyas's grand thoughts of what might exist in the world beyond the

Hungry Squirrel he had never even imagined a flying man. There were wizards, he knew, and sages, for travelers sometimes talked about their school far away in the capitol. None of those stories, however, had ever included the possibility that a man could fly.

As fast as he could follow on the lumpy earth, Matyas took off after the man. Several times he stumbled over rocks and bushes, only to get up and run faster. He could see the man clearly now, tall and thin with no shirt or shoes but only torn and filthy trousers. His hair was thick and dark and matted with dirt.

He descended to earth at the edge of a tangled stand of blackened trees. Matyas had seen this place but never entered it, for there was something disturbing about it. Though there were no leaves on the trees the branches entwined so tightly it was impossible to see into the center. Matyas had often thought that something terrible had happened there a long time ago. On the brightest summer day it was like a patch of darkness in the world of light.

The wizard—what else could he be?—squared his grimy shoulders and tilted back his head. "Come around me," he said. Matyas wondered if the wizard was talking to him. Did he know Matyas was spying on him? What terrible punishment would he enact? Change Matyas into some helpless little animal, a toad, or a snake? He was trying to decide if he should run away when a swarm of fireflies appeared all around the man's body.

"Open the way," the wizard said. The lights moved towards the trees. Where they touched them the black branches parted so that the wizard could enter.

Matyas knew this was his chance to escape and he should run home and hide behind the stove. Instead, he bent low and tiptoed forward, until he could see through the tunnel opened by the light.

After the sight of a flying man he thought nothing could amaze him, but now he had to stuff his fist in his mouth not to cry out. In the center of the trees there was a circular clearing, with the ground shiny and smooth like glass, and in the center of that circle there stood a black pole as smooth as ivory and inlaid with spirals of gold, and on *top* of that pole, perched like a bird, was a human head!

The face was strong, Matyas's idea of a warrior, with a sharp nose and high cheekbones, and yet it also appeared soft and gentle, almost like a girl. The eyes were closed, with long lashes. Thick golden curls set off delicate skin.

The man said something in a language Matyas had never heard from any of the guests. The words all flowed together like white water over sharp rocks. *Wizard talk*, Matyas thought, but when the head answered, everything that had sounded hard or sharp vanished, and Matyas knew it was in fact the language of the head itself. A language of angels. He could have listened to it forever, until he died of hunger without even noticing.

The head and the wizard spoke together for just a few moments and then the wizard turned to leave. Matyas barely had time to scurry around the curve of the trees and crouch down behind a rock. He looked up just in time to see the wizard rise back into the sky. Matyas stared and stared, and thought how he wanted nothing else in the world but *that*.

The trees had closed up again, dark and vicious. It made Matyas want to cry to think of that beautiful head trapped in those hateful trees. He stood at the edge of the wood for a long time, mouth opening and closing, until finally he called out, as firmly as he could "Come around me!" To his great surprise the fireflies appeared all around him, their flash so sharp they sent bursts of light up and down his skin. Before they could vanish he ordered "Open the way."

The trees parted like high grass blown in the wind, and there, at the end of the narrow tunnel, stood the head on its black and gold pole. Matyas moved forward in tiny steps. He wanted to say, "I want to fly," but he didn't know the words. Even if he knew how, he wouldn't have wanted to hurt that gentle language with his clumsy teeth.

He didn't have to. Before he could say a word, the eyes opened and stared straight at him, and the voice boomed, in Matyas's own language, "*Master Matyas flies in darkness!*"

Matyas cried out and fell back on the hard dirt. "What do you mean?" he said. "I'm going to fly? Me? Why did you call me master?" Gold-speckled eyelids came down as the head seemed to go to sleep. When Matyas looked around he realized the trees were starting to close in again. "Please" he said, "how do I do it? How do I fly?" Now the branches were scratching at him, and even while he tried to push them away he knew if he didn't leave now he would be trapped inside. He got himself up and ran out the narrow corridor, emerging onto the dull ground just as the trees locked back into place.

Over the next days Matyas thought of nothing but that moment of prophecy. Master Matyas flies in darkness. He was going to fly. And become a master. That must mean a wizard. A wizard! And fly! Over and over he would stop in the middle of sweeping, or piling up wood, or emptying a guest's chamber pot, and look up in the sky, or close his eyes, and smile,

If his parents caught him they would yell or hit him, call him a useless lazy fool. In such moments his body shook with anger, and his fingers twitched with the desire to cast some spell on them, burn them into lumps of ash and bone, turn them into miserable scurrying rats. How dare they hit him? He was a Master.

Or would be. First he had to get away from the Hungry Squirrel. He had always believed there was no life for him there, now he knew it for sure. His life would begin when he arrived at the college for wizards in the capitol. But how to get there? His parents would never send him, he knew that for sure. And it was much too far to walk. For two weeks he waited and waited for his chance, until finally it happened.

An elderly lady arrived one afternoon. She was thin and stooped, and dressed all in black except for a white shawl that she draped over her thin hair. Frown lines were so deeply etched in the sides of her mouth that if she ever smiled it probably would break her face. As she stood in the doorway and looked around with disgust she remarked how barren the road to the capitol was, and how grateful she would be to return there the following night. When Matyas's father (in between bows to the old creature) sent Matyas out to bring down her boxes of luggage from the top of the carriage, the master-in-training (as he already thought of himself) saw an unused iron grate on the back of the carriage. The next morning, after he and her driver had restored her boxes to their riding place, Matyas found his own place, squeezed into the narrow gap between the grate and the wooden back of the carriage.

For several minutes he held his breath and made himself as small as possible and wished he knew a spell to make himself invisible. Perhaps he did without knowing it, for his father, after bowing, and cupping his hands for the coins the woman dropped at him, called out "Boy. Where are you? Matyas! There's work to be done," but even though Matyas could hear him searching about the woodpile and around the building, it never seemed to occur to the man to look behind the old woman's carriage.

The ride was miserable. Metal wheels jolted on the rutted road, while dust, mud, and horse excrement flew up in Matyas's face. He was terrified the whole time that some rider, or a carriage with swifter horses, would pass them, and someone would yell up to their driver "Do you know you have a boy stuck in your back grate?" Every two or three hours they would stop and the driver would help the old woman step out to the side of the road where she relieved herself with loud grunts and sighs. Matyas shook with fear that the bored driver would wander to the back and spot him. He was sure what would happen. The driver would yank him out, beat him and kick him, and leave him battered on the side of the road. Luckily, the old woman seemed to demand that the driver stay in constant readiness to help her back to her seat, for he never discovered their secret passenger.

They rode until late into the evening. When darkness finally came Matyas felt a little safer, though he was hungry and all his muscles ached. Finally they arrived at the outskirts of the city, and the biggest house Matyas had ever seen, had ever imagined. Years later, he would revisit the place and laugh at how meager it was, but then he thought it a palace, with its white walls and gray shutters, its gables and turrets, its stone posts upholding a yellow balcony over the front door.

The driver jumped down and held open the carriage door. Matyas could hear the old woman complaining as she stepped out and took the driver's arm. He could hear her muttering and cursing the entire way up her mosaic tiled path until they slammed the door behind them. Quickly, Matyas tried to uncurl himself. Only—only, he was stuck. He couldn't seem to move any part of his body, jammed in so tightly for so long.

He heard the door again, heard the driver's heavy steps. In his mind, Matyas could see the man's thick shoulder, his large hands. He was whistling now, coming closer—

And then he was there, grinning down at Matyas, whose frozen body shook with fear. What would they do? He didn't mind a beating (as long as he survived), but what if they sent him back to his parents? The driver put his finger on his lips. Still smiling, he helped Matyas rise out of his iron tomb and step onto the cobblestones. "Better go quickly," he said, "before the witch sticks her head out the window and sees you." Like a duckling in his first steps, Matyas wobbled down the street.

He got over his stiffness soon enough, but not his amazement. The city was so huge! He had thought it would be very easy to find the wizards' school, it would be the biggest and grandest of all the buildings. Instead, there were so many mansions and palaces and churches he had no idea where to look. Maybe the school would shine with magical power. Maybe they kept whole cages full of those colored lights he'd seen in the woods. When he spotted a building with a silver stairway that spiraled up the back wall to a roof garden he slipped over the fence and scrambled to the top for a better view.

The city went on forever! How could there be so many buildings, so many people, all in once place? Sadly, nothing gave off so much as a shimmer. If he could fly, he could soar over the rooftops until he spotted the school. But of course—

"You!" someone shouted. "What are you doing there?" Matyas hurtled down the stairs as fast as he could.

Hours passed. He tried asking people but no one seemed to want to stop and talk with him, or if they did, they had no idea where the college of wizards might be. He was miserable and hungry and tired and feeling like a fool for having listened to a head on a stick when it struck him, didn't wizards study the stars? And if so, wouldn't they be on the highest hill? He found another house with outside steps to the roof. Instead of searching for magical glow he looked for hills, and buildings that rose above the rest. There! He saw a stone wall on top of a hill, and behind the wall copper rooftops that looked like moss-covered stones on a riverbank. In the middle of them a single tower rose into the sky. He recognized it immediately. He had seen it in his dreams.

He walked all the rest of that day and most of the night. He might have tried to sleep except that he had moved into such rich neighborhoods, with buildings that looked more carved than built, and streets that looked polished by hand, that he feared they would set dogs on him just for daring to walk there, let alone try to rest. So wizards like money, he thought, and was not surprised.

At least he didn't have to go hungry. Smells of roast meat led him to porcelain urns behind the houses. Garbage, he realized. The rich, it seemed, threw away more food than they ate.

At last he reached the wall. Could he be wrong? The buildings were made of ordinary stone and mortar, with iron gates, not gold, and no mysterious words or symbols, no explosions of multi-colored fire, no talking heads stuck on poles. No wizards soared overhead. And yet, there was that tower. He sat down by what he hoped was the main gate.

It was mid-morning before someone came out. The big doors swung open and four men stepped into the sun. They were young, at least younger than Matyas's father. They all wore striped robes over white trousers and plain sandals. No conical hats, no gold charms or spellstones hanging around their necks.

Matyas couldn't hear what they were saying, and didn't much care. It angered him that they didn't seem to notice him standing just a few feet away. "Please, sirs," he said.

They all turned towards him. The tallest, a man with a high forehead and sandy hair and thin lips, said "Who are you?"

"My name is Matyas. Sir."

"What do you want, Matyas-sir?"

To knock you down and walk on you. He said, "I want to go to your school."

A couple of them laughed but the tallest one said "Go inside our school? For what? Whatever you are selling we don't need."

"I want to become a wizard."

The man's mouth gaped, then he and his friends burst out laughing. One of the others said "Go home, boy We have enough wizards, I'm afraid." Another said "Did Johinnen send you? Fat man with a skinny beard? Told you to come here and say that to us?" The tall one added "We do not appreciate beggars making fun of us."

"I'm not making fun," Matyas said.

"Then leave."

"I want to learn how to fly." They burst out laughing once again. Matyas wanted to tear off their fancy robes and knock them down in the dirt. Instead he called out "Come around me! Right now."

Lights appeared in the air, a scattering of fireflies that hovered around Matyas then vanished within seconds. The tall man, who first looked startled when the lights appeared, now clapped his hands in a large sweeping gesture. "Bravo. A true display of power." And then, "I have no idea who sent you with whatever glamour to summon a flicker of the Splendor, but I suggest you run back and tell him his joke was not very funny."

Matyas didn't know what to do. Beg? See if he could get inside the gate and hide? Tell them about the head? They probably would just laugh again. He was pretty sure he could get the tall one on the ground and kick him senseless before the others could figure out how to pull him off. But suppose they conjured up a demon to eat him?

They had lost interest in him and were about to walk past— and Matyas was about to get down on his knees—when a dry precise voice called down from above, "I will take him."

In one motion the four all turned and stared up at the top of the tower. Matyas could make out a small figure in the single window. The tall man said "Veil?"

"Yes, Lukhanan. You have identified me. Your studies are progressing. Now if you can keep the boy entertained long enough for me to come get him he can begin to work for me."

"But Mistress," Lukhanan said, and he seemed genuinely confused, "He's filthy. He'll steal everything the moment you go to sleep."

"Then I will have to stay awake. I will think of you, Lukhanan, and laughter will drive away drowsiness. Now hold him for me."

Matyas's mind jammed with thoughts. *A woman. What could a woman teach him? He called her "mistress." That's like a master. Maybe she's a demon.* When the gate swung open again there was no demon or powerful sorceress, only a woman a little taller than Matyas himself. Her face was sharp and finely lined, with a wide mouth and narrow nose, eyes that looked very sharp inside wrinkles, and gray hair pulled tightly back and held with a silver clasp. She wore a long straight dress, as severe as a shroud, brown with gold and silver threads.

She looked at Matyas for what seemed a very long time, while he squirmed but managed not to look away. Finally, she turned to Lukhanan and said "There. You see?" as if she'd won some contest.

Lukhanan rolled his eyes. "Look at him. He can't even read."

Veil turned back to Matyas. "What is your name?"

"Matyas." He almost said "Master" but stopped himself.

"Can you read, Matyas?"

"No, ma'am. Mistress."

"Wonderful. Then you will not need to unlearn anything. Or at least not as much." She turned and walked back through the gate, with Matyas running after her.

When they started up the narrow stone steps Matyas said "I dreamed of this tower."

"Did you? And does it look the same?"

"Well, I only saw it from the outside."

"Oh, from outside all towers look the same."

Matyas soon found it hard to keep up with her. After only a flight he began to breathe heavily, after a second his shoulders sagged and he had to pull himself up by the plain wooden banister, after a third his legs wobbled and he didn't know if he could continue. Veil turned and looked at him, as if to say "Tired already? What use are you if you cannot even climb a few steps?" On the fourth flight he thought for sure he would faint, and almost begged her to stop so he could catch his breath. No. He would not give her any excuse to send him away. Or laugh at him. With all his might he managed to keep going. Finally they came to a low wooden door, unadorned, with a simple brass handle. Matyas almost wept when Veil opened it herself, for he had no strength left even to release a latch.

The moment they stepped inside, all Matyas's energy returned. He could stand again, and breathe easily. Curious now, he looked around. If he'd expected to see demons in cages, or angels trapped in circles of candles, or maybe eagle feathers as souvenirs from flights above mountains he had to settle for a simple room of wood walls, a plain unpainted chair, a rough wood table, a small fireplace, and books, books, books, some on shelves, some piled on the floor. There were a few other objects, such as a lumpy black stone in a corner, but no other furniture, and certainly no wondrous creatures. Two alcoves extended from the main room, one with a commode and a blue curtain for privacy, the other with a narrow bed. Without thinking, Matyas blurted "It's so ordinary."

Veil smiled. "Is it now? Then tell me, young Matyas, why you found it so difficult to climb the stairs."

Matyas stood up straight. "I didn't have any trouble."

"Oh? You looked in pain."

"I just told you, I was fine."

She laughed now. "Matyas, there was no shame in your weakness. I needed to test your talent and you have shown it. Remarkably so. Few practiced magicians could have made it even halfway up the stairs, let alone to the top."

Matyas squinted at her. Was she making fun of him? "It was just some stairs," he said.

"Look out the window."

He peered out. "It's just the courtyard."

"Look again."

Shaking his head as if at a madwoman, Matyas took a step closer to the window. He saw blackness, deep night, though a moment earlier it had been sunny. As if from a vast distance swirls of gray emerged, shot through with sharp jewels of color. It all turned, arms spilled out, grew then dissipated like puffs of smoke, replaced immediately by fresh spirals. Matyas stared and stared. He could dive in it, swim in it—

Veil yanked on his arm. He growled at her, tried to fight her off, but she only pulled her again. He turned to tell her to leave him alone when suddenly he realized how off balance he was, that if she had let him go he would have plummeted right out the window, down into— Now, when he looked again, there was only the courtyard.

Veil said "When I choose to reveal it this tower is the Ladder of Heaven. The first flight took you beyond the Moon, the second beyond Venus, third past Mercury, the fourth the Sun, and the fifth, well, the fifth flight, young Matyas, carried you past the birthplace of stars. Only the very wise or the very foolish can survive such a journey."

"Don't call me a fool," Matyas said.

Veil nodded. "I would not do that. But let me tell you a saying from an old friend of mine. It goes like this: The scholar hears of the gate and searches for it daily. The student hears of the gate and looks for it from time to time. The fool hears of the gate and laughs. Without laughter the gate would never open."

"I'm not a fool," Matyas said. He glanced nervously at the window.

"Oh, no need to worry," Veil said. "While you stay here it will remain a dull tower to an old woman's crowded retreat. As I said, I wanted to test your talent. I am satisfied."

"Then teach me to fly."

"Patience. We will begin your lessons soon. Now I am tired and I would like my hair brushed." She sat down facing away from him and held out a small brush of pig bristles set into polished horn. With her free hand she removed the clasp and her hair tumbled down her back.

"I'm not…" he started to say, then watched his hand take the brush. It felt warm and almost weightless. He ran it through her hair in long strokes, first jerky, with anger, but soon smooth and rhythmic. He had no idea how long he'd been doing it when Veil murmured "Thank you, Matyas. You may rest now." A finger pointed to the alcove with its small wooden bed with white pillows and a quilt of alternating squares of roses and squiggly signs. He was asleep as soon as he fell on the quilt.

He woke up excited to begin his studies. Instead of instructions, Veil gave him a list of chores to do. All day he cleaned, or ran up and down the stairs, or just put books away. In the evening he cooked a carrot stew then once more brushed her hair until she fell asleep. This went on for weeks. Every time Matyas protested that he had not run away from home just to do the same work, Veil simply said "When you are ready."

For awhile the regular students and even some of the teachers looked at him with respect, or maybe fear. He understood that Veil, who did not teach or attend councils, who was rumored to explore dark secrets in her tower, had not taken an apprentice in many years. Matyas practiced an aloof air as he moved through them on his errands. Over time, however, as the errands continued, the students began to snicker, then joke openly about such magical tasks as hauling wood.

One afternoon, Berias, one of Lukhanan's students, saw Matyas carrying two large water bags. "Aha," he said. "The sorceress's apprentice. Wouldn't it help to summon a demon to carry those for you?" His friends laughed.

Matyas wished he could call forth a demon to slap Berias's face. He pretended to ignore them and keep walking. Just a few steps. For all their brave talk they wouldn't dare to follow him into the tower.

Berias stepped in front of him to hold a sheet of parchment before his face. "Great wizard," Berias said, "Would you read this for us, please? We find it too subtle for our simple skills." Matyas rushed into the tower, but not before laughter rolled over him. He was shaking as he closed the door and set down the water bags. If he could have summoned a demon he would have ordered it to slash Berias's throat and scatter his blood across the courtyard.

He left the bags and ran up the stairs. Veil sat in her plain chair, her hands folded in her lap, her eyes open, staring at nothing. Matyas slammed the door. It took a few seconds before Veil slowly turned her head. "Where is the water?"

The Tarot of Perfection

Within the light were shapes—no, letters

"I don't care about that."

"You will when you get thirsty."

"Stop it. I want to know when you are going to teach me."

"When you are ready."

"You always say that! I'm ready right now. I have talent, you said so yourself. I want to start. Right now. At least teach me to read. How can I do anything with all your damn books if you won't even teach me to read."

She looked at him a long time, her face impassive. Finally, she said softly, "Matyas. Come brush my hair."

"No! I demand you teach me."

"My hair, Matyas. Now."

Should he leave? He could stamp out and show her he was not a slave. But then what? None of the other teachers would take him on, that was clear. If Veil turned him out for disobedience he would end up a beggar. And he would never learn to fly. With a great sigh he picked up the brush and began to run it through Veil's hair.

At first he jerked it down as hard as he could, hoping the bristles would pull out tufts of hair, one for every time she'd refused him. Soon, however, the motion calmed him, and he moved the brush in long smooth strokes.

Her hair became like water flowing all around him. He began to cry, he had no idea why, and his tears flowed into the sea of the old woman's hair. The water sparkled, lifted, became weightless waves of liquid light. It poured over him, lifted him, until he dropped his arm and closed his eyes and let light fill him and carry him.

Within the light were shapes—no, letters. They rolled over him, danced on his fingers, he tasted them in his mouth, some sharp or salty, others voluptuous or sweet. And numbers, and formulas, and gestures and words. He learned the language of demons, of the spirits of rocks and trees and places and objects he'd never known existed. He understood the constant whispers of angels, and knew now that the head in the woods was a Kallistocha, the saddest tribe who had ever lived. He learned, as if in memory, of the Great Change, when the early magicians took the universe away from arbitrary Powers and set up the laws of existence. He knew how to summon birds, and snakes, and lions. He could look behind the sky and under the night.

Finally the waves ended and Master Matyas fell to his knees. He opened his mouth to thank her but was shaking too hard to speak. "There," Veil said, "didn't I tell you you would be thirsty?"

From that day Matyas studied constantly. He still labored for Veil but every other moment he read and practiced. When the students laughed at him for chopping wood or carrying water he considered opening the earth beneath them, or causing their intestines to poke out from their bellies, but chose instead to ignore them. The jokes soon stopped. Maybe they were just good enough magicians to grasp that he was different now. Dangerous. He discovered that he didn't care.

Years passed. Learning so entranced him that he forgot other concerns. Then one night he woke two hours after midnight (she had taught him to tell time in his body, for there were magical operations that required precise knowledge of duration) to the sound of ravens. When he looked out the window there were two of them, black against the blue night. They circled and chased each other in a dance of delight. Matyas remembered the dirt-smeared man in the sky and he understood that all the wonders he had discovered were nothing if he could not fulfill the thing he had come to learn. He went over to his teacher, asleep in her chair. "Wake up, old woman," he said. "I want to fly."

Her eyes focused on him immediately. "Do you think that is mine to give?"

"Yes. If it can be done you can do it. And if you can do it you can teach it."

"How long have you been here, Matyas?"

"Twelve years."

"Have you ever seen me fly?"

"You know very well you have never revealed that to me. And I know very well that you only reveal what you choose. Do you think I don't know why the wizards call you Veil? You are a curtain of mysteries. You have lifted it more for me than for others, and I am grateful. Don't ever think I'm not. You taught me to speak to rivers and walk under the roots of mountains."

"Then what? You want me to lift my skirts all the way? I'm too old for that. You wouldn't like it."

"Save your jokes for Lukhanan. I saw a man fly, Veil. I told you that."

"Yes, many times. And I've told you that I do not know all the magicians in the world."

"It doesn't matter. You know all the magic."

"Oh, I doubt that."

"I want to fly. I was born for it."

"No one knows why he was born. Haven't I taught you that?"

"Enough. Teach me to fly."

She sighed. "Matyas, bring me that stone in the corner."

"What?" He looked around the room until he noticed the black rock, about twice the size of his foot, between the bookcase and the window. He remembered that he'd seen it when he first arrived, and probably hundreds of times since then, but he seemed to have forgotten it. He tried to remember the last time he'd looked at it, for ignoring knowledge was not only a kind of sickness, it could be dangerous. No. He could not recall it. He said, "If I bring it to you, will you teach me to fly?"

She shrugged. "Maybe."

In two steps he was there. When he tried to swoop it up it wouldn't move and he nearly pitched headfirst into the wall. He squinted at it. It was a trick, of course, like that climb up the stairway. He summoned all the spirits that hover at the ends of fingers to bring energy into his arms. He bent down and pulled so hard the veins in his neck threatened to break through his skin and send his blood flying in all directions. When it still wouldn't move he summoned the spirits who slept under the tower to wake up and push from below. Slowly he felt it stir, half an inch, an inch. Then he heard terrified shouts, from the courtyard, he thought, but when he listened he realized they came from people all over the world. He dropped the stone and sent away his helpers.

Exhausted, he had to lean against the bookcase to stand up. Veil said, "You see? How can you expect to perform miracles when you cannot pick up a single stone?"

Matyas said, "That was the night sky. You crazy old woman, you wanted me to bring you the sky. What would have happened if I had done it?"

When she smiled, flickers of light came through her skin. "Then maybe you wouldn't need to fly."

Matyas moved out of the tower that day. At first he thought he would ask for a simple room among the scholars but as he strode across the courtyard and saw how even the older wizards gave way to him, he decided he had let a selfish woman treat him like a child, and he deserved whatever he wanted. What he wanted was to study, and so he marched into the meeting hall of the council and said "I want rooms. Next to the library, with a good desk and a laboratory. Whoever is using them will have to leave."

There was a pause, during which two of the wizards glanced at Lukhanan who looked like he was trying to contain a spell of repulsion. Matyas almost laughed. Finally the head of the college nodded and said, "Of course, Master Matyas. Whatever you wish."

Matyas had thought he would miss her books most of all, the shelves that opened into chambers that opened into tunnels and caves, all of them crammed with books. The college library was no match for it, but if he lived alongside it he could roam its shelves whenever he wished. To his surprise and annoyance he missed not just her books but Veil herself.

The old woman became even more reclusive than before. Sometimes she would stand in her window (usually, people said, when Matyas was walking below). At rare moments she ventured out to dart across the courtyard on some unknown errand as quickly as possible, like some woods animal crossing a road. Once she even showed up at a council meeting where she sat in the back, as small and quiet as a child. Matyas wasn't there.

Matyas wondered how she lived without her slave to bring her water and food and lay a fire for the cold nights. There was no sign she'd found any new street boy. One afternoon he dared to ask one of the older wizards, a man named Malchior who, like Matyas, had never entered the inner circles. Malchior had come from overseas and still spoke with a thick accent, though Matyas suspected he did so deliberately, for the tones and sibilances seemed to get harsher as the years went by. Over a glass of marigold tea, in as casual a manner as he could, Matyas asked how Veil sustained herself. To his surprise Malchior laughed loudly. "Ah, Matyas," he said, "don't you know the three forbidden questions? What is the name of God's older brother? Where was your mother before the creation of the world? And most difficult of all, what does Veil eat?"

"But I have seen her eat. Ordinary food. I spent years cooking for her."

Malchior sipped his tea. "As inspired and well-taught as you are you remain, well, naïve. Do you really think she needed your rice and tomatoes?"

"Then why would she—"

"Perhaps she wanted you to feel comfortable. After all, *you* needed to eat."

Whether she needed food or not, Veil seemed to grow thinner. No, Matyas thought as he paused one day to stare up at her standing in the window. Not skinny so much as— He frowned. Her *substance* had gotten thinner. Light seemed to shine through her, as through a translucent painting of an old woman. Was it the light of day or some other world?

He stared up at her for a long time, hardly aware that the Sun had grown dark blotches, or that the ground trembled, or that people were yelling at him. Finally, when he thought she was about to turn away, he spun about so she would not be the first. Only then did he notice the fissures in the ground, or the people throwing up, or leaning against walls which themselves looked shaky. With a gesture Matyas steadied the buildings, with another he sealed the cracks in the earth. As for the people vomiting, they could clean themselves. He strode to his room in the library and slammed the door.

Three days later the council came to see him. He smiled as he noticed that they had left Lukhanan behind and brought Malchior in his place. Their demands were simple. Either Matyas stop his "duel" with Veil or leave. When Matyas asked 'What duel?" Malchior rolled his eyes.

Matyas said "Why don't you ask Veil to leave?"

Malchior sighed. "This is a serious matter. We have no time for verbal games."

Matyas considered. For several weeks he had thought of leaving the college. He was fairly certain he had exhausted all their resources and if he truly wanted to fly he would have to find some other kind of magic. Maybe all that kept him was his pride, or the hope that a stubborn old woman would give him the secret. He'd told her about the prophecy, and all she'd done was mutter "Never trust a Kallistocha." Maybe it was time to look elsewhere.

He set out the next day, packing only a sleep roll, a few clothes, a knife, a sheaf of papers and a pair of quills and a block of ink. At the gate, he looked back at the tower one last time, but she wasn't there. Goodbye then, he thought.

That night he made camp on a green and yellow hillside, by a soft stream. He found some sticks and set them on fire by writing a sacred name in dust on his finger and blowing it at the sticks. He closed his eyes and called a rabbit to come give its life to aid his quest, but when he opened them Veil stood before him. "Mistress," he said stiffly. "I am honored."

"There is something you must do," she said.

He rolled his eyes. "What? Drop the sun in a handcart? Suck up the oceans and spit them into water gourds?"

"You need to open the way to end a great evil."

He squinted at her. "What great evil? How am I supposed to end it?" She said nothing. "Tell me! Tell me what to do and I'll do it." Still nothing. "Damn it, the world is full of great evils. There are new ones every day. How can I end it if I don't know what it is?"

She was almost transparent now, her skin and muscles like rice paper, her veins like tubes carrying liquid light. For a moment he thought he saw images inside her body—a garden with two bright trees, a boy and girl holding hands. A man with a knife. Then everything inside her turned to light, blinding him. When he could see again she was gone.

He shook his head. Riddles. He realized suddenly that he was very glad he was leaving.

For months he traveled the world. There are ways to let the Earth carry you swiftly along its surface. It was not flying—it was nothing at all like flying—but it let him go very far in a short time. He visited centers of learning much grander than the college where he'd spent so much of his life. There were domes and cities all of glass, and some built entirely out of thoughts. Everywhere he went he asked the scholars for the secret of flight but none of them knew a thing.

There was one place he didn't go. Many times he thought to return to the Kallistocha, but could not bring himself to do it. What if he'd misunderstood? What if "fly" had meant something different than what he'd assumed? And something else—he could not bear to visit the wretched placed he'd lived in as a boy. He sent his parents money from time to time, and once, when he learned his mother was ill, he sent a healer with a potion Matyas himself had concocted. But see them?

Finished with all the grand and worthless schools and centers, he sought more secret places. He found hermits in desert shacks, child sorcerers who lived in trees. He traveled to libraries hidden in underwater caves. He learned nothing.

He became more and more angry, threatening the people he visited. He showed them he could burn the sides of mountains, dry up their rivers, vanish the letters from their books, the spells from their memories. "Tell me," he would demand. "I am Master Matyas."

Fed up with the wise and the great he began to trace his way through forests and rivers, following leads from one tribe to another, always in search of the oldest, the original, the truest. He watched ceremonies where people danced with masks and drums and strips of cloth to invite the gods to enter their bodies. When he stood up in the dance, however, and demanded that these prancing howling spirits teach him to fly they were as useless as the monks and librarians.

He came finally to a place he thought of as the end of the world, a giant rock on a flat red desert. There were paintings on the rock, circles and lines and spirals and dots, so old even Matyas couldn't decipher them. He closed his eyes to try to speak to the elementals in the rock. All he could hear was a rumble that might have been thunder. When he looked again he discovered himself surrounded by men and women.

They were naked, but covered in paintings and scars. Daubs of color, jagged lines, angular boxes and concentric circles formed some kind of code even Matyas could not begin to decipher.

They didn't look at him or speak to him, only sat on the rock and chanted, a low hum without melody. Matyas's head began to hurt, his skin tingled, and soon his bones were vibrating so intensely it felt like he was going to break apart. Savages, he thought. How dare they threaten him? It was some kind of trick. All that paint on their bodies, it didn't mean anything. There were no sacred names, no sigils, it was all just blotches and lines, the fantasies of ignorant children.

Damn them. His head hurt so much he nearly screamed. He called up wind demons to blow them off the rock. Nothing happened. He shouted for lightning. Nothing.

He stared at them, not at their faces but at the paint. Suddenly he understood. The lines and blotches were the history of the earth, their chant the song the world sang to itself when it first awoke. He tried to banish the pain and fear from his body, for if anyone could tell him the secret they could.

"Matyas!" He turned. One of the women had stood up. Short and lumpy, with drooping breasts and layered hips, she looked at him impassively, her face a mass of black rock painted in red and yellow ochre. None of the others took any notice.

"Who are you?" Matyas said. She didn't answer. Furious at women who refused to tell him what he needed to know, he stepped towards her, his hand raised. As he got closer the colors on her body began to shift, move together, flow into forms. Another step and he no longer saw the woman at all, but a garden, with bright flowers and a waterfall. One more step and he was staring at grass, surrounded by poppies and calla lilies. Sweet perfume ran through his body, mist from the waterfall moistened his face and arms which had become dry and cracked in desert winds. Matyas lost his balance and fell against a tree. There were two trees, he realized, very old and bent.

When he stood up again a naked boy and girl were looking at him. The boy had golden hair, the girl silver. "Who are you?" the boy said. "What are you doing here?"

Matyas ignored him. He looked around, sniffed the air so light and sweet, stared up at a sky that was layers of color and light. "I know what this is," he said. He looked at the two trees that looked like grand old dames at a manor house. "These trees," he said. "The Tree of Mystery and the Tree of Time. Yes?" The children said nothing. "And this place. It's the Garden of Origins."

The children backed away a step, and Matyas thrilled at the fear in their faces. "And you two," he said. "You're the Guardians. Day and Night. Sun and Moon."

The boy said "We don't know who you are but you don't belong here. You have to leave."

Matyas stood up straight, nearly twice as tall as the children. "I am Master Matyas. I have come to learn how to fly and I will not be refused."

"No," the girl said. "That isn't possible."

"Don't lie to me. I am sick of lies." He began to pace back and forth, like an impatient wolf. "You don't have any choice. I've penetrated your secrets and now you cannot refuse me."

The boy said "We cannot give you what we don't have."

"You're lying." Matyas pointed a quivering finger at him. "No more great powers and wonders telling me what they can't do for me. Do you have any idea what *I* can do?"

"Please," the girl said. "If you know what this place is, and who we are, then you must know that what we do is important. Please don't disrupt that."

He looked up and down her flat hairless body, smiled as she winced and turned her head. "Don't think you're so valuable. Or pure. Do you think no one knows what you really do with each other?

Do you think the world still needs you? I could kill you and the Sun would still get up and fall down, the Moon would still grow and wither. The magicians took the world away from you a long time ago. The Ancient Masters knew we couldn't trust you so they created laws. The world runs on geometry and numbers now, not games and stories. You're only good for one thing now. To teach me to fly."

"I'm sorry," the girl whispered. "We can't do that."

"Then you don't deserve to live."

The boy fell to his knees, held up his hands, palms forward. "Take me," he said. "Let my sister go."

Matyas laughed. "Aren't you afraid you'll unbalance the world? Make the Sun afraid to show his face? *Teach me to fly.*"

The girl said "We cannot give you what we cannot give you."

"Don't tell me that!" Matyas pointed the first and last fingers of each hand at the sky, with the other fingers and the thumb turned into the palm. Colored fire ran between the extended fingers.

The boy and girl hugged each other. They looked at each other and cried, and then their faces moved closer and they began to kiss. Light and dark shimmered up and down their bodies.

"Your true selves," Matyas said sarcastically. And yet, as he watched them he knew he couldn't kill them, though he couldn't say why. They deserved to die, arrogant powers who thought themselves so superior to a lowly human. But he couldn't do it.

His body shook with the energy built up in his hands. What should he do? A thought came to him. Of course! They weren't worth death, he should just do to them what village witches do to bratty children who steal a taste from the cauldron.

He lowered his hands. The fire leaped from his fingers to flood the boy and girl who cried out—and in their place a pair of green and black toads gulped the air. Matyas laughed, gestured again, and the frogs changed to swans frantically waving their wings. Again and again he changed them, goats, hedgehogs, foxes, until finally it all began to bore him. Something trivial, he thought, and with a final gesture turned them into squirrels. "Stay that way forever," he said, and walked away.

He found himself at the foot of a mountain. Confused, he looked up at dark tangled trees. Wasn't he just in a garden? A queasiness ran through him. He thought how he should go look for some food and a place to rest. In the distant valley he could see a town and he started to walk towards it, though he could not seem to gauge how far it was.

His legs hurt and he limped slightly. Wasn't there some way to move more quickly? He couldn't seem to remember. If only he could fly. He smiled at the thought. What would it be like to just open your arms and lift up into the air? A lot less painful than walking!

The sun went down and it was cold. The town lit up with hearth fires and torches, but it was too far away for him to reach it that night, so he piled up leaves against an old tree and hoped the animals would leave him alone.

He dreamed he was walking in a withered garden, past a pair of bent and broken trees, when he saw a great stone house. Closer, he saw a tall man in front of the black doorway. The man wore a white tunic and trousers, and red boots. His gray-brown hair was brushed back and his face was bright and strong, the eyes shiny, the teeth sharp and gleaming. His right hand held a stone knife pointed at the dirt and dripping blood.

Matyas stared at him, terrified. He had never seen this man but he knew who he was. Every magician and priestess knew of this man. *He was Joseph Reina, the Child Eater.*

'You can come closer," Reina said. "You can't do anything to me, and I won't hurt you."

Suddenly, Matyas remembered. He was supposed to end a great evil. Veil had told him that, and then he could fly. He raised his hands, fingers spread wide to gather power. Nothing. "I am Master Matyas," he said, with more confidence than he felt. "I've come to destroy you."

Reina laughed. "Why? You're just like me."

He woke up with a cry of pain, though he couldn't remember what caused it. The Sun shone without heat, as if the Sun itself couldn't get warm. He stood up all stiff and hungry, with no idea how to get food. He walked for hours, until he finally came to the city.

It was very large, with grand buildings of all sizes and colors, some with gold roofs, others made of glass and iron. In the center rose a steep hill, and on top of that stood some sort of castle with a stone wall and a tower whose top was lost in the bright Sun.

He walked up and down the cobbled streets, trying to remember how to get food. He was wearing some kind of robe, thick, with elaborate stitching, but when he reached in the pockets there was no money, just scraps of paper with odd markings, some leaves, and a couple of envelopes with foul-smelling powder. If they hadn't smelled so awful he might have tried to sell them but he couldn't imagine anyone would want them so he threw them away. A little of the powder got on the heel of his hand and it itched for most of the morning.

When he saw people with food he asked if he could have a little. Some laughed, as if he'd made a joke, others hurried away, still others looked angry, as if they wanted to say something nasty but didn't dare. Whatever the reaction, they all seemed to look first at his clothes, and it struck him that maybe he was someone rich or important, and people were afraid. Or maybe he'd stolen the clothes. He didn't feel like a thief but he really couldn't remember.

When he came to a street with vendors selling old clothes and broken tools from blankets on the ground he looked around until he spotted an old woman wearing a robe a little like his own. It was much thinner, with crude painted designs rather than embroidery, but there was a resemblance. "Please," he said, "would you like to buy this?" He fingered the front of his robe. The woman stared at him so long he thought she must not speak his language. Finally she held up a few tarnished coins. "Here," she said. She thought a moment, then reached over to her neighbor's blanket for a green tunic and trousers. "And this to change," she said.

He heard laughter as he walked away in his green clothes but at least he had money. He was very careful with it, buying only the simplest food and eating as little as possible. At night he slept in alleys or under stars. Vivid dreams troubled him but he could never remember them when he woke up.

His money ran out just as winter brought the first snows to the city. Now he needed warmth as well as food. He tried begging but never seemed to make enough in a day for even the most meagre meal. There was something about him that made people turn away. Oh, he knew he was dirty and smelled, but so did the other beggars. Something in him bothered people, they didn't realize it themselves, but they rushed away as soon as he approached them.

He would have to steal. He watched people walk by and wondered how he could knock them out and take their money. When he realized he could never do that he began to stare at shops closed for the evening, or darkened houses. This too he didn't dare. Finally, one evening, almost delirious with hunger, he attempted to pick someone's wallet from his pouch. The man was out with two friends and he stopped to buy a bottle of wine from a street vendor. When the would-be pickpocket saw the tan leather wallet full of coins bounce back into the open bag he could not help but follow them.

They caught him immediately. The intended victim did nothing, only smiled while the others beat and kicked him and threw him back and forth like a toy. When they left all he could do was stagger a few feet away, spitting blood, until he fell into a snow bank against the wall of a church.

He might have died there—he felt ready to die, and helpless to do anything else—except he heard a noise. Weeping. Somewhere, an old woman was crying. When he managed to raise himself up he spotted a woman with a splintered stick, stretched out in the road. Someone had broken her crutch and knocked her down, and now she couldn't get up.

He didn't think he could move but somehow he managed to pull himself along the church wall until he could launch himself over to her. Clumsily, he put his arms around her and lifted her to a sitting position. She didn't seem to mind his blood on her thin dress.

"Thank you, thank you," she whispered. "I'm so cold. God, I'm so cold."

As best as he could without letting her fall he took off his tunic and wrapped it around her shoulders. With the broken crutch in one hand, he managed to move her to the wall where she could lean back and rest. "Bless you," she said. "May God and all the guardians bless you forever." She closed her eyes and fell into a deep sleep.

Now he knew it would be a race for what would kill him first, blood loss, hunger, or the cold. He collapsed into a deep snow bank, hoping he could fall asleep and miss the actual slide into death.

If he'd been hoping for a soft bed he didn't find it. There was something hard in the snow. Something rectangular, with sharp corners. He lifted it up, stared at it. It looked like a package wrapped in blue cloth, about the length of his hand and not quite as wide.

He began to shake, and it was not from blood or hunger or cold. Memory was returning to him. He knew who he was and he knew what *this* was, even before he fumbled off the blue wrapping, before he saw the stack of painted cards, before he looked at the first picture, a joyous man hanging upside down by one foot over an abyss of light.

He knew who he was, Matyas, the most undeserving of men. And he knew what these cards were. A miracle.

For this was the Tarot of Perfection, the original, painted by Joachim the Blessed seven hundred years before Matyas's birth, and lost to the world for nearly as long.

Matyas clutched the cards against his chest and wept. He wept with all his might and all his heart and all his soul. His blood became tears, the snow became tears, the fires of the city became a river of tears. There was a saying about these cards, from Joachim himself. *Whoever touches the Tarot of Perfection, he shall be healed of all his crimes.*

Strength was returning to him now and he knew that no one would harm him and he should rest. It was what the cards wanted, he could feel it. He clutched them tightly against his chest and fell asleep.

He woke to sighs of sorrow. At first he thought it was the old woman, but when he looked around she was gone. He understood then that it was the Earth's pain he was hearing. This was what Veil heard, he realized. All those times she would sit in her chair, hands in her lap, eyes on nothing, she was listening to the world's sadness.

He reached into Perfection and pulled out a card. It showed a woman sitting up in bed weeping with her hands over her face. The night sky was behind her, black with pinpoints of stars. Suspended in the air behind her were nine swords, all horizontal and one above the other, like the steps of a ladder. The bottom sword was dark and heavy, a weapon of stone, and then each one became successively lighter, until the last was not a sword at all but a blaze of brightness stroked across the night.

Matyas stared and stared until the bed vanished, and the woman, and only the swords remained, huge before him, a ladder to the sky. He wrapped up the cards and put them in his waistband, then slowly he began to climb, clumsy at first, then with determination, even grace, until he stepped onto the final rung of light, and stepped off.

He was soaring over the city, wind in his face, trouser legs flapping like flags in a storm before he even realized he was doing it. Flying! After all these years. Down below, the lights and stones of the city ran together, and in the midst of the wind he could hear human voices, and the chatter of birds. He laughed and his body vaulted upwards, he inclined his head and tilted back toward the surface. When he closed his eyes the air swirled all about him, and he could almost believe that he himself did nothing and the world was simply turning beneath him. So this is it, he thought. It was never a trick, or a spell, or anything a teacher or a power could give you. It was simply a way of being.

Where should he go? Could he direct himself? He knew what he had to do, and as he thought about it he soared higher. Soon he was leaving the city, until all he could see of it was a stone tower, and soon that too was gone. Now he was flying over mountains, and the shadows that crouched between them. Time passed. He came to a place of very cold air and found himself drifting down to a small valley. As the ground became clearer he could see withered trees and dull flowers

The squirrels stood side by side, each with a glittering walnut in its front paws. One of the walnuts was silver, the other gold. Matyas spread himself face down in the dirt. "Forgive me," he said, "though I do not deserve it."

From somewhere inside him he heard the girl's voice. "It is not for us to forgive."

Matyas raised himself to his knees, bowed his head. "I understand. What I have done cannot be forgiven."

The boy said "No, Matyas, you understand nothing. You did what was necessary."

He lifted his head to squint at them. There was something he didn't understand, but it didn't matter. He said, "What is given cannot be taken back. I cannot break my own spell."

"Of course not," the girl said.

"But I can give you something new. A spell of alleviance." He tried to think but no magic came other than a statement that somehow seemed right. "Freedom will come with the one hundredth child."

The boy said "Thank you, Master Matyas," and the girl added "You have given and we have accepted. We release you and bless you."

"I don't understand," Matyas said. "All I do is cause pain."

The red one shook its head, and the gold walnut flashed with light. The boy's voice said "Your understanding is not necessary. If you wish, you may go to the One Who Knows." Then both squirrels ran off behind the trees.

"I don't understand," Matyas said. Maybe, he thought, the Tarot of Perfection would help him, and took the wrapped cards from his waistband. But when he tried to remove the blue cloth the cards gave off such intense light he could hardly bear to hold them, and wrapped them up again.

The One Who Knows. Of course. The one he'd avoided for so very long. He closed his eyes, moved his arms away from his sides, and let himself become lighter than dust. He flew for a long time now, empty of distractions, with only glances of the blurred earth below him. Only when he saw a low stubble of hills and a stand of dark trees did he let himself descend.

The trees were so entwined there was no way into them but he knew what to do. "Come around me," he said, and the Splendor appeared, a thousand dazzling lights. "Open the way." As soon as he'd said it the lights touched the trees and a path opened. He walked inside without hesitation, though he dreaded what he might hear.

The Kallistocha burned so brightly Matyas could not look at it but only stared at the ground, where pebbles of a hundred colors lay all about the black stick. "My lord," Matyas said, "help me. Once you called me Master and told me I would fly. I gave my life to that dream and all I have done is destroy what is good and necessary. You told me darkness and I thought you meant the color of the sky. Now my soul is black. Help me."

"You did what was necessary, Matyas. Accept your freedom."

"No! How can you say that? My mistress told me to end a great evil and instead I cursed the Guardians. I met the Child-eater and I did nothing."

"Remember Veil's words."

Matyas closed his eyes. Rocking back and forth slightly he let himself float in the river of memory until he caught that moment when Veil had stood by his campfire. She said "You must open the way to end a great evil."

"Open the way," Matyas said to the Kallistocha.

"Yes. The Child-eater is beyond you, but not beyond the Guardians. Your foolish spell has put them in a form where one day they will help the hundredth child destroy his power. Be grateful. Your anger has served the future."

"Thank you," Matyas whispered.

"Now go. Veil is calling you."

Veil. Matyas quickly left the grove, feeling the trees close behind him. As soon as he stood under the clear sky he opened his arms and left the ground. For a moment he was aware of a filthy boy who had hid behind a rock and now was trying to sound important as he did his best to summon the Splendor.

Matyas came down in the courtyard, with no idea what time it was except that it was night and no one was there. He ran up the narrow stairs, aware for the first time that every step was a story, whether of pain or joy, for the Tower of Heaven was built with human passions.

He found her in her wooden chair, back straight, hands on her knees as she stared out the window. Her hair flew about, tangled up in itself, while a yellow and blue dress hung loosely on her skeleton shoulders. She was nearly transparent now, as thin as air. A sweet smell filled the room.

Matyas knelt down and took her hand, so feathery he had to look to make sure he held it. "Mistress—" he began, but her free hand waved him to silence as gracefully as a silk stream.

"Please, child," she said. "No apologies. You did what I asked. You always did what I asked."

He smiled. "You haven't called me child in a long time."

Her laughter was dry and faint. "I didn't want to insult you."

"I brought you a gift."

"Ah. How nice. Old ladies like presents, you know."

He removed the blue package and held it out to her. "Oh good," she said. As she began to unravel the cloth Matyas averted his eyes, but no flash came out, and when he looked they were just painted cards spread out in her narrow lap. Softly, she said "Hello, Joachim. It's been a long time." She held up the card that showed a young man on the edge of a cliff with spirals of light behind him. A little louder, she said "Do you know, Matyas, that light travels? I suppose that's why it can be dark in one place and light in another. And here's the curious thing. Light always travels at the same speed. Time can slow down or speed up, people can get bigger or smaller, but light always remains the same. Isn't that wonderful? What do you suppose it tells us?" She put the card with the others and set the pack in her lap.

Matyas began to cry, for he knew very well what she was telling him. He didn't want to think about it, so he said "What will happen now? With the school?"

She shrugged, the gentlest movement. "No doubt Lukhanan will become undisputed master. It's all he's desired."

"Lukhanan is a fool."

"Of course, remember, the scholar hears of the Gate and searches for it daily."

Matyas responded "The student hears of the Gate and looks for it from time to time."

"The Fool hears of the Gate and laughs."

"Without laughter the Gate would never open."

Veil clapped her hands. "Lovely," she said. "I've missed you." She leaned back now and closed her eyes. "Brush my hair?" she said.

"I will be very happy to brush your hair." The old brush felt heavy and cold at first, but it warmed up as her ran it through the fine strands, careful to separate the tangles rather than pull at them. At first it was difficult, for no one had brushed it in a long time, but after a few minutes he could move the brush in long easy strokes, brushing it down her back like a waterfall.

Eyes closed, he began to sway in time with the strokes of the brush. Light streamed over him, light and images, as if the cards had lifted from her lap to get caught up in her hair. Sweet aromas filled him, bouquets of flowers mixed with a distant smell of the sea. Sounds drifted to him from very far away, voices, wind in mountains, a bell as pure and clear as the sky, a cry of delight.

He dropped the brush and opened his eyes. Veil was gone. The cards were gone. Only the chair remained, and the table, and the books, and the bed in the alcove where he'd slept for what now seemed like a few precious nights.

He bowed his head a moment, then went to the window. No spirals of dust appeared, only the tops of the buildings, faint in the first light of dawn. He stood there a long time, watching the stones change color with the sunrise. From below, in the courtyard, he heard voices, sounds of amusement, anger, pride. Finally, he stepped out onto the narrow window ledge, took a deep breath, and lifted into the sky.

For Callan Williams

The End

These stories were written with a series of antique fountain pens, in particular a 1920's Wahl pen inscribed with the name M. MATYAS.